Also by Nancy Bond

A String in the Harp
(*A Margaret K. McElderry Book*)
A NEWBERY HONOR BOOK

The Best
of Enemies

*For Alison
with best wishes
Nancy Bond*

The Best of Enemies

by NANCY BOND

A MARGARET K. MC ELDERRY BOOK

Atheneum   1978   New York

Map by Philip Bouwsma

Library of Congress Cataloging in Publication Data
Bond, Nancy.
The best of enemies.
"A Margaret K. McElderry book."
SUMMARY: Anticipating a lonely spring vacation
because her parents and grown brothers and sister are
preoccupied with their own pursuits, Charlotte becomes
involved in their town's annual Patriots' Day celebration.
[1. Family life—Fiction] I. Title.
PZ7.B63684Be   [Fic]   77-17363
ISBN 0-689-50108-0

Copyright © 1978 by Nancy Bond
All rights reserved
Published simultaneously in Canada by
McClelland & Stewart, Ltd.
Manufactured in the United States of America by
Fairfield Graphics, Fairfield, Pennsylvania
Designed by Marjorie Zaum
First Printing March 1978
Second Printing October 1978

For Sally

The town of Concord can be found on any map of Massachusetts, and although Patriots' Day has never been celebrated in quite the manner described here, it is celebrated in Concord each nineteenth of April. All of the characters in this book are purely fictional, however.

The Best
of Enemies

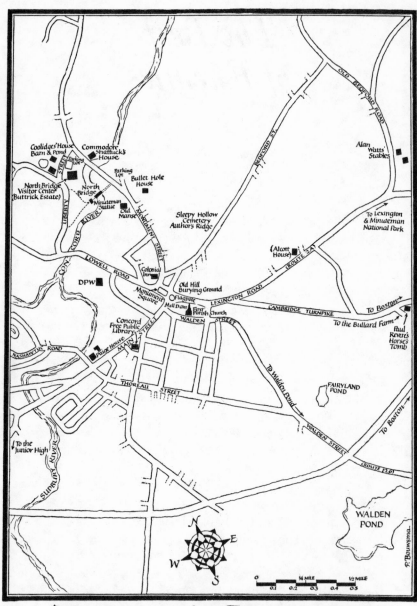

Town of Concord

Chapter One

AS THE FIRST WAVE OF STUDENTS BROKE ON THE JUNIOR HIGH cafeteria, the volume of sound expanded immediately to fill the hollow space between the scuffed floor and the steel-girdered roof. In the midst of it, Charlotte Paige stood aloof, a morose island of silence in a sea of cheerful pandemonium. She fancied she could see the huge plate glass windows bulge outwards under the deafening pressure.

On Fridays she was in the first lunch shift which began at 11:14. As she waited in line for her plate of macaroni and cheese, she occupied herself by considering the consequences if the noise actually got so intense that the windows buckled. Would they explode like cannon shot with deep, earth-shuddering booms, or would they break like ice on the river with a brittle, echoing crrrrackkkkk? Would the glass cascade in silver shards onto the floor, or hurl itself around the room in jagged spears?

How could they all bear it? How could they all make such an awful din without seeming to notice it? She forgot the windows and glanced irritably around. Here and there in line she could spot a few fellow sufferers, isolated like her in silence.

The rich, hot aroma of macaroni and cheese flooded through the kitchen door. It was one of Charlotte's favorite lunches and usually enough to make her mouth water, but as a measure of her depression this noon she scarcely noticed it. Ahead of her Ellen Hutchins and Marcia DiMeo compared

3

family plans, their faces keen with competition.

"—practically right on the beach—all the college kids go there. And we're spending two nights at Disney World on the way down. My cousin Annette says it's dynamite!"

"My mother thinks that New York City is the kind of cultural experience every girl my age ought to have. She went to college at Barnard so she knows all these neat people —artists and writers. She's taking me to museums and concerts and Radio City Music Hall—"

"Of course I'll have a super tan by the end of the week. Mom let me buy a new two-piece that's practically a bikini."

"I'll get a whole new summer wardrobe while I'm in New York. My mother says all the best stores are there, and Dad's paying for everything."

Drawing her mouth into a straight line, Charlotte tuned out and let their excited voices blur into the general uproar. She didn't envy either girl—New York and Florida were just places as far as she was concerned. She'd always looked forward to spending her vacations at home; there was plenty to do and her family was the best possible company. But this year without warning the comfortable pattern of her existence had begun to unravel. First Eliot left school, then her mother went back to work and Max got married. Her father plunged deeper and deeper into museum business, leaving himself little time for anything else, and even Deb had become increasingly withdrawn and preoccupied. There was nothing Charlotte could do to stop any of it; she could only watch with growing alarm as things fell apart. It made her feel small and helpless, which in turn made her resentful.

For the first time in her experience she didn't want a school day to end. When it did, she saw herself cut adrift for an empty week; left alone while the other members of her family went ahead with their lives. But time was against her. All around the junior high the clocks lurched forward, devouring the hours in jerky bites.

Inside the kitchen, a large, damp-looking cook thrust a plate of macaroni and wax beans across the counter to her and she accepted it without enthusiasm. Even the ice cream sandwich she treated herself to didn't raise her spirits much.

As she carried her tray out past the waiting line, she looked for a thin spot she could edge through to the empty tables by the windows. She found a gap between two-thirds of the baseball team, who were finding it uproariously funny to shove one another into a huddle of giggling girls, and Oliver Shattuck who stood carefully apart from them all. He was wearing a bilious green pullover that made his pale skin yellowy. It hung off his shoulders; worn by anyone else it would have looked a size too big, worn by Oliver it made him look a size too small. He paid no attention to Charlotte as she squeezed in front of him.

Seldom did anyone at lunch save her a seat, so she sat where she pleased—generally at a table made up of odds and ends. They knew each other pretty well by now, the odds and ends. Most of them had gone to school together for years. They talked if they wanted, but there was no compulsion among them to be social or to show off. The arrangement suited Charlotte well.

She chose her table and sat down facing one of the big windows. Beyond it an aggressive April sun glossed over the scum of winter: the dust streaks on the glass, the drifts of dirty sand where there had been drifts of snow not long ago, the threadbare mat of grass tinged with green, the gray trees faintly misted yellow. Spring was trickling into a world that had just been drained of winter.

Gradually the benches around her filled. To the casual observer the seating might have looked haphazard, but in fact there was a rigid pattern to it. Girls and boys seldom sat together, though they visited, and those who showed definite interest in one another made certain they sat at adjacent tables. The boys' tables were raucous with laughter and insults; the girls leaned together over theirs like conspirators. By flagrantly ignoring the boys, they made it plain they were acutely aware of them. This was a phenomenon Charlotte did not understand. When she ignored people it was because she didn't want to be bothered by them, and she wasn't.

She sat digging at her rapidly cooling macaroni in dissatisfaction, messing it into the beans, while conversation built around her.

5

"You going anywhere next week?" Her brooding was interrupted by Ruth Hyatt who clambered awkwardly over the bench next to her. Ruth was a friendly, nondescript girl, who talked instead of thinking.

Charlotte shook her head. "Nope."

"Neither am I." Ruth made a dreary face. "I'll probably spend the whole of vacation babysitting for my brothers. Gee, you're lucky being the youngest!"

"Mmmm."

"Wish I was going someplace neat for a change. I've never been *any*where special." She sighed. "You going to the parade Monday?"

Charlotte felt a flicker of comfort. "Of course. My brother Eliot'll be in it."

"I forgot," said Ruth apologetically. "He plays the flute, doesn't he?"

"Fife," corrected Charlotte.

"Of course I'll get stuck taking the kids again so I won't enjoy it much. Last year Tommy got lost and the police had to find him. You should have heard Mom yell! He got mixed up with the Chelmsford Minutemen. It was awful. Hi, Kath."

"Hi." Kath Schuyler slid in across the table, giving them each a direct, appraising glance.

"We were just talking about vacation. You doing anything special?"

It was a needless question, like many of Ruth's. That Kath spent every free minute she could scrape together at Alan Watts's riding stable was common knowledge. She declared that she would live there if her mother and the Massachusetts laws would allow it, and she was serious. Horses were her single passion—not in the usual dreamy, distant way, but in a grubby, hard-working, practical sense. She hung around the stables doing all the nasty little jobs nobody else wanted to, just so they would let her stay. In a mild way she fascinated Charlotte. Although Mrs. Schuyler sent her to school clean and neat every day, Kath was always surrounded by the faint tangy smell of horse. It clung to her the way cologne clung to Erica Fromme and the pungent smell of turpentine clung to Charlotte's sister Deb.

Kath's answer was predictable: "Working with the horses. I could get to ride Johnny in the parade Monday if his foreleg's healed. Alan's got a new hunter to school, and we're getting the outdoor ring ready for spring lessons."

"Oh, really," said Ruth, trying to sound interested. Charlotte wondered why she bothered. "Where's Andy?"

"Infected ear again. Been out since Tuesday. He wants to get his peas in this weekend, too." Kath dug into her lunch without fuss, chopping the stuff up and eating it efficiently. Charlotte could tell from the way she went at it that food was nothing special to her.

"Lucky Andy missing school," Ruth plowed on.

"He doesn't think so," said Kath around her beans. "When he misses school he has to stay in the house—Ma's rule. So he can't work in the garden either. It drives him crazy."

Andy was her twin, large and vigorous with red hair and a loud laugh—one of the boys Charlotte ignored. She had very little to do with Kath, either, except for incidentally at school.

"Eliot going to be in the parade?" Kath asked her.

"He leads the Fife and Drum Corps," said Charlotte with dignity. "And he's playing piano at the ball Saturday night."

"Oh," breathed Ruth, "are you going to *that*, too?"

"I don't know yet," replied Charlotte, although she had a pretty fair idea that she wasn't, but she hadn't finished discussing it with her mother.

"I would love to go," Ruth said, frankly envious. "I don't even know anybody who is, though."

"Not me," said Kath. "Waste of time getting dressed up in uncomfortable clothes to spend a whole evening *dancing*. It's stupid."

"Lots of people go and enjoy it," Charlotte was quick to point out.

"That's their problem."

"Your uncle's going to be in the parade, too, isn't he?" Ruth asked Kath. "I think he's cute."

"Skip?" Kath looked surprised. "He's in the Battery so he'll be there. That's what I'd join if they let girls. They use horses."

7

The Concord Independent Battery consisted of twenty-seven men and two brass cannons mounted on carriages which were pulled by teams of draft horses. Every year on the nineteenth of April, the cannons were ceremoniously hauled out of the brick Gun House, polished, taken to a hill overlooking the Concord River, and fired off at dawn. It was an honored tradition.

"I prefer the music myself," declared Charlotte.

"It's hard to choose," Ruth said with a little frown, as if she felt called upon to do so. "Look!" She lowered her voice and leaned forward. "There's that new boy, Oliver Shattuck. Do you know what I heard about him yesterday?"

Oliver had finally progressed through the line and was picking his way through the crowd to a deserted table-end nearby. He deliberately avoided everyone else and applied himself with great concentration to his lunch.

"He's awfully strange, isn't he? I don't think he talks to anyone."

"Why should he if he doesn't want to?" asked Charlotte. Kath looked disinterested.

"Well, everybody else talks to *some*one. Anne Levine said he's unbalanced."

"What does she know?" said Kath scornfully. "Anne Levine thinks everyone's unbalanced except her."

"She said that's why none of the private schools would take him," Ruth persisted. "He came here because they wouldn't have him and public schools have to take you, no matter what. He has violent fits."

"Has she ever seen him have a fit?" asked Charlotte, stirred by a faint breeze of curiosity. "He doesn't look violent."

"If he wasn't when he came to Concord, he probably is now," declared Kath. "And I wouldn't blame him. I'd have fits if I had to live with Commodore Shattuck."

No one, not even Charlotte, could disagree with her there Commodore Shattuck was notorious throughout the town as a "character." He had a well-earned reputation for being difficult and eccentric—even vaguely sinister. Eliot maintained that he was harmless and the stories about him were greatly exaggerated, but Charlotte, who usually accepted whateve

8

her brother told her as true, wasn't thoroughly convinced.

Ruth nodded. "I don't know how he can stand it. I couldn't, even if Commodore Shattuck was my great-uncle. I'd rather live in a home if I was an orphan."

"Who says Oliver's an orphan?" asked Charlotte. "I thought his parents were divorced."

"Depends who you talk to."

"What does it matter?" put in Kath. "Especially since he likes his own company better than anyone else's. It's almost time for the bell."

Charlotte discovered to her annoyance that she'd eaten her entire ice cream sandwich without noticing. There was nothing but the wrapper left on her tray; it was as good as wasted since she hadn't tasted it. Ruth hastily scraped up the last little blobs of Jello as the bell rang.

Like a huge pot coming to the boil, the cafeteria began to seethe as the lunch shifts changed. There was a great deal of half-eaten macaroni in the garbage bin beside the service hatch. Charlotte avoided looking at it as she added her scraps and passed her dishes through to the resigned, steamy kitchen crew.

Mr. Pianka had the dubious privilege of teaching Charlotte's American history class in the last period of the day. Many other teachers surrendered to the inevitable and either showed films or held vaguely structured study halls rather than attempting actual lessons, but not Mr. Pianka. This was his first year at the school and his students hadn't figured him out yet, though they kept trying. He was a formidable man, built like a football tackle, with tremendous shoulders, an immense neck, lots of curly black hair, and long arms and hands like catchers' mitts. Yet, for someone so large, he was amazingly quick and light on his feet.

And he was so full of history it came spilling out of him like floodwater over a dam, landing on his students with such force it knocked the breath out of them. He dragged them along in his wake willy-nilly, willing or not, and dunked anyone who caught a snag on the way. They were all rather afraid of Mr. Pianka, Charlotte as much as anyone else. He

created in them a nervousness that made them think, however, and Charlotte enjoyed that.

Today, appropriately, he spent the hour alternately firing
questions and chunks of information at his students like
grapeshot—all concerned with the beginnings of the Revolutionary War. Concord had played an important part in
1775, as they all knew intimately. It was impossible to grow
up in the town and be unaware of its individual place in
American history.

"At my last school," Mr. Pianka told them, "when I asked if
anyone could tell me what Patriots' Day was named for, the
only answer I got was 'a football team'."

There was a general snigger.

"I'm sure you know better, don't you?"

Nods and smug smiles. After all, it was their town he was
talking about. Patriots' Day, April 19, was an annual event in
Concord. It commemorated the Minutemen who had mustered
in 1775 to defend their property and rights from the British
Army. There were parades and ceremonies in most of the
towns in the county. Flags sprouted up and down Main Street,
Skip Bullard and the Battery shot off their cannons, and the
Concord Minutemen, reformed and revitalized after all the
years, marched through town to the music of Eliot's Fife and
Drum Corps.

Charlotte knew the ceremonies very well, connected to
them as she was by an older brother. Mr. Pianka knew them,
too; he was the most recent Minuteman in the Company.

As he bullied the class into actually using their last hour
and their heads a little, Charlotte paid particular attention and
couldn't help feeling a kinship with him. He had the same
contagious enthusiasm for local history that Eliot had; it was
limitless. During the countless hours she and Eliot had spent
together, Charlotte had absorbed a tremendous amount of information from her brother. She had to run to keep up with
him, but he was always willing to wait and lend her a steadying hand.

She listened now, critically, while Mr. Pianka reconstructed
the skirmish at Merriam's Corner where the British and
Americans had first encountered one another in the town; he

did it quite well, she decided generously. He painted a vivid picture of the scarlet column of soldiers marching along the muddy road, like an immense military centipede, while the local farmers watched apprehensively. It was a good story and he told it with appropriate drama.

The British reached the center of town, prepared to seize all American munitions, and found very little. Dr. Samuel Prescott had completed Paul Revere's furious ride through the countryside the night before to warn the citizens, and they had hidden most of their arms by the time the Redcoats arrived. Men had begun to muster, out of sight, ready for a fight if need be.

The confrontation finally came at the North Bridge, British on one side, Minutemen on the other. Shots were fired, men killed, and the Revolution had begun.

Charlotte was startled when the final bell rang. She'd forgotten to keep an eye on the clock and time had run out without her realizing. She landed abruptly in the present; vacation couldn't be postponed. The class which had reluctantly fallen under Mr. Pianka's spell, crumbled into twenty-six free seventh graders, wildly eager to pile into their school buses and leave the junior high utterly behind.

Over the scuffling, scraping confusion, Mr. Pianka made himself heard without actually shouting. "Those of you fortunate enough not to be taking exotic vacations outside of Concord will, of course, make every effort to attend all the ceremonies, won't you? Consider it an assignment. You can all read the chapter about the First Continental Congress, too. Got that? Those of you who aren't going to be here for the nineteenth can make reports on it a week from Monday."

There was the obligatory "A-w-w-w-w!" but it was very half-hearted. It was impossible to worry about reports so far in the future. Kids swept up papers, books, folders, and avalanched out of the room into the hall. Charlotte hung back, making a job out of collecting her things. She hated to be jostled and pushed in the middle of a crowd.

"You aren't anxious to leave us, Charlotte?" inquired Mr. Pianka. The room had cleared like magic. He was straightening his desk, which even after he'd straightened it looked as if it had been struck by lightning.

"Oh, yes," said Charlotte noncommitally.

Mr. Pianka glanced at his watch. "Wouldn't do to miss your bus today." He shoveled a heap of papers together and scooped it up. "Shall I see you at the drill this afternoon?"

She nodded. "I always go. Eliot expects me to."

"So he says. He claims he wouldn't feel properly dressed if you weren't there." Mr. Pianka grinned showing a lot of white teeth.

A little shyly Charlotte grinned back. By reminding her of her brother, the teacher's words took the worst of the chill off her bleakness. Suddenly anxious to get home, she picked up her books and headed for the door. Mr. Pianka was right, it was no day to miss her bus.

"See you later," he called after her.

Chapter Two

THE HOUSE WAS EMPTY. SHE KNEW IT AS SOON AS SHE LET herself in the back door with her key. The air was stale and undisturbed; even the cats were elsewhere on private business. Nothing breathed. She hated it.

There was the usual note from her mother, lying this time on top of a plate of brownies on the kitchen table. They were a sign Charlotte recognized only too well. Without even looking at the note she could guess what it said: that her mother was off at work somewhere this afternoon and wouldn't be home until suppertime. Whichever job it was— Charlotte didn't bother to keep them straight—it meant she had no mother to come home to. The brownies were to prove that she had not been forgotten, and they were never very successful.

Feeling ill-used, Charlotte bit into one and skimmed the blue memo paper that had KATHERINE DEWOLFFE PAIGE, DESIGN CONSULTANT printed in navy across the top. "In Lexington at the County Bank (862-8672)"—she was very careful about leaving telephone numbers—"Home by 5. Don't forget the rabbits." Then the round little face that meant "Love, Mother."

"Damn," said Charlotte out loud, defiantly breaking the roomful of silence. "Damn and blast!" She crumpled the note into a pale blue lump and left it, took three more brownies, and went up the back stairs to her bedroom, stomping for the comforting sound of it. The emptiness of the big Victorian house made her uneasy and depressed.

Her room was at the back, large enough to spread a variety of interests in with comfort. When she was ten she and her mother had repainted and decorated the room together in shades of green and blue and gold. It was no frilly little girl's room—Charlotte was no frilly little girl. It was welcoming and attractive, but recently she had begun to feel a niggling, formless dissatisfaction with it, she wasn't sure why.

The room looked the same as always, perhaps fuller of clutter, but not basically different. There were art supplies that Deb had either lost or cast off: sketch pads and a practically brand-new set of colored pencils, bottles of India ink, squares of art gum, and a T-square that Deb had borrowed long ago from Max. Two of her watercolors hung on the walls: *Spring on the River* and *Farm Stand*, done in what Deb called her "Naive Period." She had gone into abstractions now and deplored these, but Charlotte liked them. Her father had had them framed for her, along with several museum exhibition posters and a copy of Dürer's rabbit.

Off and on Eliot was teaching her to play the recorder. The battered music stand he'd loaned her stood awash in a sea of sheet music, the mouthpiece of an alto recorder in its trough. Laid out on the floor beneath one window was a matchstick model of Old Salem Village which Max had painstakingly constructed for a high school civics project; his MIT sweatshirt hung prominently over a chair.

There were books everywhere. They had a way of drifting into Charlotte's room and accumulating in haphazard piles in the corners, on chairs and windowsills, beside the bed. They seemed to come by themselves from all over the house, but they had to be forcibly removed, usually by their annoyed owners, because they never drifted out again on their own.

Pieces of her family lay scattered all around; Charlotte had a little trouble finding herself among them now and then lately, especially when she came home from school to an empty house. The clutter in her room made her feel even lonelier on days like today. She was reminded yet again of the people who weren't there.

Abruptly she uncoupled this depressing train of thought and went over to gaze out her windows. From the two on the back of the house she could see over the mucky, thawing garden to the river, and beyond it. Through the bare trees on the far bank rose the sudden round bulk of Nashawtuc Hill, a hazy amber in the sunlight. In another month the roofs showing through the basketwork of branches would be hidden in great fountains of new green leaves. The cold, metallic river would have sunk between its banks. The button bushes would be vivid with spring and loud with birds.

But a chilly shadow still lay across Concord this mid-April, thin but persistent. Winter clung to the air with cold, sharp-nailed fingers and wept bitter gray rain.

There had been much warmer days in March, when summer seemed deceptively close and the sun coaxed bulbs out of the stiff earth around south-facing house foundations. Eliot had brought great whips of dead-looking forsythia into the house to force into yellow explosion, and he took Charlotte to cut pussy willows in a West Concord swamp where skunk cabbages were starting to unfurl their green elephant ears, and peepers sang.

But Charlotte knew from experience that New England springs were notoriously unreliable. Some were long, drawn-out and gentle; others came and went overnight—in one warm, wet evening the bare woods burst full-blown into leaf and by morning it was summer; still others played irritating hide-and-seek games with winter, as this one was doing.

Eliot felt the wind change this year and drafted Charlotte to help mound soggy leaves gently over the rash little crocuses and the blunt green daffodil, tulip, and hyacinth blades. The front hall closet stayed full of mittens, boots, parkas, and wool coats. And the storm windows were pulled down again.

As she changed, Charlotte considered the afternoon. Without Eliot and the parade practice at four, it would have been as empty as the house. She made a rude face at herself in the mirror as she scrambled into jeans, jersey, and a sweater, scattering her school clothes on the bed. If she didn't hang them up, her mother would. She dug wool socks out of the bureau knowing it would be cold on the Buttrick hillside and hunted her boots. Only the left was anywhere to be found;

its mate wasn't under the bed with the other things, or stuck in the back of the closet. She was about to curse when she remembered that Deb had put a patch on it for her two days ago, so she stumped unevenly down the front stairs to find it put tidily away in the coat closet.

Deb had done her usual efficient mending job. She was handy about fixing things, from plumbing to electric mixers to rubber boots. It offended her to have to throw anything out because it was broken. Extraordinarily practical for an artist, Mr. Paige was fond of saying, with the fatherly indulgence that he knew would make his elder daughter bridle.

Charlotte dawdled over the funny papers with a couple of brownies until she couldn't stand the silence any longer. Cold feet or not, she finally pulled on her parka and set off for the park.

On her way out the back door, she noticed one of Deb's bandannas draped across a kitchen chair—it was the blue one with OSH KOSH B'GOSH printed on it in large white letters. It seemed a handy thing to wrap the remaining brownies in to keep the crumbs out of her pocket, so Charlotte borrowed it, making a careful mental note to replace it, preferably before her sister saw it was gone. Deb had gotten odd and difficult lately; her temper had a very short fuse and was easily ignited.

As she pedaled her bike slowly up Main Street past the neat Colonial symmetry of the houses, the wind bowled along behind her, pushing her toward the center of town with rude force. To save time, and because it was daylight, she turned left through the municipal parking lot and took the shortcut past the Department of Public Works. The back road crossed a patch of tangled swampland behind a supermarket, then swung by the cinder-block office and garage of the DPW. Conical piles of wet sand and coarse gray road salt stood around it like prehistoric mounds, abandoned and decaying. The yard was a desolation of stiff, rutted mud. In the daylight it looked bleak; at dusk, dimly lit, it was sinister. Charlotte never came home this way in the evening. But it joined Lowell Road near the river and saved her having to thread through the snarl of cars in the middle of town, so she used it when it felt comfortable.

Up on the hillside, overlooking a gliding gray-blue coil of the Concord River, sat the Buttrick Estate. It had once been an elegant private residence with terraced gardens climbing down to the river-meadow and a fine view of the Old North Bridge, but almost twenty years ago the Buttricks sold their property to the United States Government. It had become the headquarters for the National Park. Maintenance and grounds-keeping were basic rather than painstaking these days, and Eliot still regretted the loss of the glorious iris gardens.

Thousands of tourists each year tracked through the house and over the lawns. Huge copper beeches shaded concerts and pageants, demonstrations of colonial militia, afternoon naps, and picnics, grandmothers, affectionate couples, tiny children and dogs in the summer. It was a favorite place for school field trips during the rest of the year.

In spite of the chill this afternoon, the sunshine had lured quite a few people out of doors. They marched briskly about, trying to ignore the sting in the air, pretending they didn't see the smoke their breaths made and didn't feel the cold seeping into their shoes like ice water.

Charlotte left her bike against one of the trees near the parking lot. The Minutemen hadn't begun to arrive for practice yet; the cars were a mixed lot with mainly out-of-state license plates. Rather than stand still and freeze, she went off on a tour of the grounds to see who was around. She passed a group of stout, sensibly dressed women puffing up the dirt track from the Old North Bridge.

". . . to cover them in the winter, Mildred. But now look at those rhododendrons, and it's as cold here as in Michigan."

"*I* didn't think it was all that good, personally. The soufflé had fallen and my soup . . ."

Their voices dwindled behind them. Tourists, Charlotte thought smugly. They always gave her a satisfied sense of belonging. Last year for her birthday, Eliot had presented her with a T-shirt that said NATIVE across the back in large green letters. He understood the feeling—they shared it.

By the bronze battle map at the end of the terrace a sharp-faced woman shook a lone blue mitten at a small boy. "Well, where do you *think* you left it?" He wiped his nose with the back of his hand and shook his head. Charlotte detoured around them and took the flagstone steps to the garden two at a time.

Overhead the sky was a brittle blue, scoured by the wind with such vigor that there were worn white patches in the color. The trees rattled their stiff branches in protest at being tossed into life. But there were great fat buds swelling along their limbs and color rising with the sap into their twigs and shoots. The willows shook their yellow streamers into the cold dancing air and shadows leaped and swung across the earth. Shadows at four in the afternoon. Bright, hard sun. Color. Red-winged blackbirds clacking and shouting across the sky, song sparrows singing among the bare river bushes. The rock-solid winter ground dissolving into rich, wet-smelling mud, and spring creeping up the hillside through the dead grass like green flame.

Charlotte stood on the brick terrace above the river, watched it race between its banks, and saw the wind cast nets of tiny ripples over its smooth, sliding surface. A mallard drake paddled in the shallows hunting food and talking to it-self loud enough so she could hear. There were tiny ice islands still caught around last summer's sodden reeds, but the deep spring odor of river water came reeking up the hillside to her, pungent and familiar.

On the south-facing slope which fell away from Charlotte's feet, flakes of yellow sun shone up out of the coarse field grass: hundreds of daffodils rocketing into bloom. Tiny blue squills dusted the ground beneath the trees.

In spite of the boisterous, tossing air and the coldness in the wind and river, life was stretching under the sun, under the surface.

Charlotte lost her boundaries and merged with the spring world, felt its electricity pour through her as if she were a conductor in a circuit. She was swept with a pure, elemental satisfaction at being a part of life.

It didn't last very long, it never did. It lasted only as long as she didn't think about it, as long as she could keep her mind blank and simply feel. When she became conscious of the sensation it was gone.

The spell was broken from outside this time, by a couple coming toward her around the house: a man and a woman, short and very dark, dressed in thin city clothes, arguing in a violent foreign language. The woman kept giving the man little shoves with the tips of her fingers and saying, "Enh? Enh?" while pointing down at the Old North Bridge with her other hand. He responded by shaking his head vigorously and flaring his nostrils at her. They ignored Charlotte as if she weren't there at all, and for her part, she gave them a horrified glance, then resolutely faced away and drew herself together. What a spectacle some people made of themselves in public! How could they bear to?

She concentrated on the view below her. To the left, where the river bent in a sharp elbow, cars flashing in the sunlight crossed the Monument Street Bridge. And beyond the bridge a neat dark red house was just visible, settled securely into the riverbank close to the road. Willows swung over it; it looked well-cared-for and ordinary. It was Commodore Shattuck's house. From it he kept a sharp eye on the National Park and its affairs. In the normal course of events, Charlotte would hardly have thought twice about him or his house, but Ruth Hyatt's comments about his great-nephew were fresh in her mind.

All the old stories about the Commodore and several new ones had been passed around the junior high since Oliver joined Charlotte's class three months earlier. He neither confirmed nor denied any of them, but his odd detached behavior made him a target for gossip. Whatever the house actually looked like inside, and whatever the Commodore was like to live with, Oliver never let on a word.

The Commodore had been in the navy in World War II. According to one source, his house was decorated like the inside of a ship with hanging lanterns, bunks and hammocks, and tables with rims around them to keep the china from sliding off. There were supposed to be rope ladders instead of regular stairs and a ship's wheel in the front window of the attic. It was a wonder the windows weren't round and screwed down, but perhaps they would have cost too much to remodel.

A more ominous rumor had it that there was no furniture at all in the house anywhere. Just a few crates and cardboard boxes for tables, mattresses on the floor, rooms full of empty bottles and mounds of old newspapers and magazines. The rumor, if you chose to believe that one, went on to say that no one had cleaned the house in decades, that it lay quietly mouldering, inches deep in dust and far worse. But if that were true, Charlotte's common sense asserted, why were there clean, pressed curtains at the windows and pieces of green lawn furniture on the tidy little patio beside the river? Besides, she couldn't imagine anyone—not even Commodore Shattuck—voluntarily living that way.

A third story ran that the Commodore was a hoarder. He lived in only two or three rooms of the house and kept his valuables stored in all the others under lock: silver, antiques, paintings, jewels, gold in various forms. There were vault doors on the rooms with combination locks and the windows at the back of the house were barred. He collected and he stored and he gloated. No one Charlotte knew had ever been inside the house, but many swore they'd seen lights in the attic at all hours of the night.

Those were the most interesting stories. They were beginning to die a little now; there was no fresh fuel to add. Oliver was certainly the right great-nephew to keep any secrets the Commodore might have. Strange man, strange boy, strange stories. Charlotte frowned at the inoffensive little house. Perhaps even her own empty one was preferable to what Oliver had to return to every day.

By the time she got back to the parking lot, the Militia had begun to arrive. Cars trickled steadily in: sedans, hatchbacks, and station wagons nosed into the parking spaces. Out of each climbed colonial minutemen in full rig: knee breeches, homespun shirts, fawn waistcoats, clay pipes, pewter flasks, powder horns, leather pouches—the lot. They settled their tricorn hats, blew their noses, stuffed their car keys into hidden pockets, and pulled out their weapons—long, dangerous-looking flintlock muskets, some with bayonets. The men gathered in untidy, jovial knots, chatting and smoking and adjusting one another's straps and buckles.

Over at the flagpole, the Fife and Drum Corps was collecting. Eliot's battered blue VW buzzed through the gate and squealed to a halt. Charlotte detached herself from the spectators who were gathering instinctively in the right place, even though this was an unscheduled practice. Now that Eliot had come she felt sne belonged with the Minutemen.

He unfolded himself from behind the wheel, tall and thin, jointed like an extendable yardstick, and immediately found and grinned at his youngest sister. He waved his tricorn at her before cramming it down over wild, wiry hair and fished under his seat for his fife.

Charlotte's enthusiasm cooled slightly at the appearance of Skip Bullard from the other side of the car. Skip might be Eliot's best friend, but he was neither family nor a Minuteman, so there was no reason for him to be here now. He belonged to the Concord Independent Battery, but they weren't rehearsing this afternoon.

"Hey, Charlie," he called across to her pleasantly, leaning his chin on the roof of the car.

"Hi."

He smiled a little at the lack of warmth in her voice, as if he were enjoying a secret joke. Charlotte didn't understand Skip; without doing anything in particular he made her feel very young. Eliot, on the other hand, always made her feel like one of the group.

Round-faced Johnny Hawsbrook with his fine fair hair standing on end like a ragged halo was sorting through a dog-eared pile of music. There were twenty in the Corps: Johnny was librarian and Eliot the leader, and they were all extremely good. Eliot and Johnny between them had unearthed a tremendous amount of Colonial music, then adapted it—with flourishes—to suit their purpose. The Corps was often asked to do special concerts.

"Who ripped the last five bars off my copy of 'The York Fusiliers?' " demanded Eliot. "How can you use a piece of music that ends like this?" He demonstrated.

"Catchy. Leaves 'em guessing," Ray Simms, another fifer, advised.

Eliot made threatening noises in Johnny's direction.

"Seems to me," said Skip blandly, "that you ought to know all the music from memory by now. If you were *really* good—"

"There's much too much music to learn it all," said Charlotte, quick to her brother's defense.

Eliot grinned. "Someone appreciates the difficulties of my position at least! Your trouble, Walter, is that you do not have an artistic soul."

Skip was unrepentant. "You don't need an artistic soul to learn music off by heart—don't give me that, my boy."

"None of this is getting us the least bit forrarder!" cried Ray, brandishing his instrument. "They're starting to form up, O Leader. Come on, you great ugly—"

Eliot blew a deafening blast on his fife. "Expletive deleted, ladies present."

"I'm not really," said Charlotte. "I know quite well what he was going to say."

Eliot scowled at her fiercely. "Horrible child!"

"You just said I was a lady."

"You just said you weren't."

"Shut up and get in line. Atten-*hup!* Inspection!" roared Skip. "Paige, get that hat on straight."

"It's my hair, sir. I can't do a thing with it," said Eliot.

Skip reached over and mashed the tricorn down around Eliot's ears. "Much better."

"You'll ruin the hat," protested Charlotte.

"Have to teach it who's boss," Skip told her.

Still laughing and talking, the Minutemen arranged themselves in orderly rows. Charlotte spotted Mr. Pianka, massive and cheerful in his uniform. He saluted her with his musket.

"He's a shrewd one, that teacher," observed Eliot. "You're lucky to have him, Charlie. Oop, we're off. This is it, men."

The Fife and Drum Corps took its place at the head of the column behind the Color Guard.

"Eliot," called Charlotte before he was completely lost, "can I have a ride home after?"

"If you want to hang around till we're through, Chuck. It'll be a cold couple of hours, but I do like a sympathetic audience."

Skip snorted. "An understatement if ever I've heard one. I frequently wonder if you'd exist without an audience, Eliot Paige."

Charlotte tried to think of something quick and rude to fire back at Skip, but before she could, Eliot gave a laugh and marched out of range. Charlotte was left standing with her brother's friend. She glanced at him to find he was watching her with his amused expression. Her mouth flattened into the straight line known in her family as Charlotte's Revenge.

"Where'll you watch from, Charlie?" he inquired amiably.

"I'm not sure." She was evasive.

"Oh well." Skip shrugged. "I think I'll go out by the spruces. Want to come? We can keep each other warm by huddling."

"No thank you," she replied with careful politeness. "I guess I'll go sit on the wall."

Skip nodded sagely and limped off after the Minutemen. His stiff knee gave him a peculiar rolling stride that ought to have looked more awkward than it did.

Chapter Three

ONCE HE WAS GONE, CHARLOTTE NO LONGER BOTHERED TO HIDE her disappointment; she knew that if Skip intended to stay and watch Eliot, they'd end up taking him home afterwards. She would hardly have Eliot to herself at all this afternoon. By the time they got back to their own house, the rest of the family would be there—not that Charlotte disliked her family, on the contrary, but she was increasingly jealous of the time she had with Eliot by herself.

When he took the Department of Public Works job in Concord last fall, she was sure she would see more of him than when he went to school at the Boston Conservatory every day. She'd been wrong. Eliot spent long days out working and was often called on weekends to plow or sand roads and fill potholes—it had been an extremely hard winter with violent storms and lots of snow. And of course, Skip was around.

Charlotte didn't like being jealous—it made her feel mean and small, but she couldn't seem to help it. She didn't want to share Eliot with anyone, least of all Skip. Eliot was her best friend as well as her brother.

The company captain put two fingers in his mouth and gave a piercing whistle. At once the Minutemen came to order, ready to get down to business. Eliot signaled the drummers who began to thump out a basic rhythm, and the Militia fell into step.

In the windy afternoon they looked splendid. Their banners snapped overhead and the drum beat changed. The fifers brought their instruments up and Eliot launched them into an up-tempo version of "The White Cockade." They put in all the twists and flourishes he'd worked out—the music was brave and exuberant. Gathered under the trees, the spectators raised a respectable cheer and Charlotte warmed with pride.

There was no point in staying where she was, however: the Minutemen would soon be out of sight around the big evergreens. So she picked up her bike and rode slowly out the "In" gate of the parking lot, back on the road to where it ran along the crest of the hill. At the highest point, she dismounted and scrambled up to sit on the chest-high stone wall with her legs dangling and the sloping meadow spread below her.

The Company hadn't gotten far; it had halted at the edge of the field, and the Captain was gesturing to them, explaining this year's parade details. Seldom were two Patriots' Day parades exactly alike: someone always came up with a better way of doing things. Once in a while, as Eliot remarked cynically, it actually *did* turn out to be an improvement. Although she knew he was shouting, Charlotte couldn't hear Captain Sutton from where she sat. His words were caught by the wind as they left his mouth and blown into the swirling air over the river.

She examined the spectators with a critical eye: a fairly large group for a cold afternoon, and all feeling they were getting something free because they had happened on the rehearsal by accident. She spotted Skip, leaning against a tree trunk at the edge of the field, his hands in his trouser pockets. He seemed to be staring at the ground, but when he put his head back suddenly, she noticed that he wasn't alone. There was a short, stocky figure beside him wearing a black greatcoat and a knitted navy blue cap. With a start Charlotte recognized Commodore Samuel P. Shattuck.

Skip took a hand out of his pocket and made a wide sweep down the hill. When he shifted she could see the Commodore more clearly. He stood straight as a tent peg driven into the frosty ground, his fine white hair escaping in a fringe around the cap, his chin tucked into his collar. He and Skip were intent on their conversation.

The Minutemen were on the move again. Charlotte turned her attention to them. Tatters of "Yankee Doodle" blew up to her; a handful of notes scattered on the afternoon. The Militia marched briskly down the dirt track and disappeared into the yellowing willows that lined the approach to the Old North Bridge. The music stopped abruptly and the men reappeared to try another formation.

Drifts of solid-looking cloud were piling in the sky above town. They caught the light and glowed like blown embers. It was cold sitting on the stones and Charlotte's feet were unpleasantly damp in their rubber boots. After a while, she swung her legs around and slid awkwardly down to stand behind the wall, on the shoulder of the road, where there was a little protection from the wind that swept up the hill. Her bicycle, as if bored with inaction, had fallen on its side and lay ignored on the ground.

No bigger than toy soldiers now, the Minutemen marched through the trees and across the hump-backed Bridge. The clouds rolled closer, draining the colors out of the afternoon, and the wind turned mean-tempered. Charlotte propped her chin on her hands atop the stone wall and brooded about the week ahead.

She only half-watched the activity below; the music was thin and far away. Up here by herself she was disconnected and melancholy, but she hadn't the energy to leave her hilltop to join the people by the river, nor the inclination to join Skip. The promise of the afternoon faded with the light.

She was much too sunk in gloom to notice the tall, angular figure that approached her warily. It was a man who had come out of the orchard on the far side of the road with a furtive backward glance. His gait was a peculiar cross between a creep and a lope, as if his legs weren't quite in gear, or were unused to meeting solid ground when they came down.

The first Charlotte knew of him was when he fell over her bicycle and landed hard on the ground at her feet.

"Oooommffff!" he grunted as the breath abruptly left him.

Charlotte jumped violently and looked down with startled eyes as the man rolled back and forth, clutching his ankle where it had caught a pedal. "Oioioioi," he moaned softly in what seemed to be considerable agony, his eyes screwed tight shut. His long bony face was creased in lines of misery. To Charlotte he seemed to be making a great deal of fuss over a relatively minor accident. She didn't think he could possibly have broken anything, only bruised himself.

"I'm sorry," she began, not really sorry at all and wondering if he'd blame her because it was her bicycle. "But you couldn't have been looking where you were going. It wasn't my fault."

"Frib it!" he exclaimed.

"Pardon?" He made her uneasy. She hoped he wasn't foreign—there were quite a few foreign tourists in Concord at this time of year, and most of them were very hard to communicate with. She studied him carefully through her glasses in the dwindling light. He was wearing some odd kind of costume—a uniform perhaps—that was creased, not very clean, and didn't fit: a red jacket with several gold buttons missing, grubby white knee breeches, wrinkled stockings, and cracked black workman's shoes which looked uncomfortably small for the rest of him. He had longish dark hair that was going thin on top, and a struggling beard.

He was, Charlotte thought suddenly, exactly the sort of unsavory person she had been told over and over never to have anything to do with. Suppose he was only pretending to be hurt? It happened. It had happened to a girl at her school last year and she'd moved away. No one had seen her since.

"Aw gor," said the stranger. "Gor and drabbit!" The force had gone from his voice and he sounded alarmingly close to tears. Gingerly, he began to work his ankle back and forth.

"Well, it can't be broken then." Charlotte was relieved. "Walk on it," she advised. She wished he'd pick himself up off the ground; by now she was anxious to get away, but she felt she couldn't as long as he was down. Which of course was ridiculous—he'd be far more dangerous on his feet.

The sound of fifes and drums, though distant, blew reassuringly over the wall. The Minutemen had apparently finished their drilling at the Bridge and started back to the parking lot. Charlotte glanced down the hill and saw them making all haste through the twilight. At the flagpole Captain Sutton would give them final instructions for Monday, then they'd disband, eager to get home to their suppers. If she wasn't careful, Eliot and Skip might assume she'd gone ahead on her bike and she'd be stranded with this suspicious person. Absently she chewed a lock of hair.

"Gor!" breathed the man, bringing her back with a thump. He'd hauled himself cautiously up on the wall beside her, just enough so he could peer over the top. His eyes were round and white with alarm. He took a deep breath, blew out his hollow cheeks, and said something completely unintelligible with a question mark at the end.

Charlotte groaned. He was indeed a foreigner. She bent and made a half-hearted lunge for her bike, but the man let go of the wall and shot out a hand to catch her wrist. She froze.

He squinted at her intently, his hand clamped viselike on hers. There was a long, cold-looking expanse of forearm below his cuff, a red knobby wrist, then calloused, black-edged fingers. That's probably the last thing I'll notice in my life, she thought a little wildly. But nothing else happened. In some rational compartment of her mind, she reflected that screaming would not do any good—it might just make him violent—so she swallowed the noise in her throat.

"Pardon?" she said, furious at the quaver in her voice.

He repeated his question with a kind of desperation, but it was no better. "English," said Charlotte loudly, "I speak English."

"Aye, an' me!" he shouted back furiously.

"Then you don't need to yell and you can let go of me," she declared firmly.

The man looked at his hand as if it weren't part of him, scowled and unclasped the fingers. Charlotte was unutterably relieved. She could always leave her bike and run if she had to.

After a moment of silence, while they regarded one another, he tried again, this time with a shorter question. "They gaffers," he said, " 'oo be they?"

"Down there?" said Charlotte, puzzled. "The Concord Minutemen, of course."

"Gaw!" Awkwardly he straightened to his full height and looked again. "Gaw." A spasm of pain crossed his homely face. "I bin right smikered, 'aven't I just. Lookit all them sojers!" He spoke to himself as if he'd forgotten she was standing there. "E niver sez there'd be all them. 'E sez, Beaky lad, it'll be a piece o' scram. A razzle. Them's 'is very words."

Charlotte frowned. If it was English he spoke, it was a queer, unfamiliar kind. "Who are you?" she asked bluntly. "And what are you doing here? You look as if you're supposed to be a British soldier, are you?"

He jumped as if he'd been stung and glanced apprehensively over his shoulder. " 'Ow'd you twig that? I niver rucked."

It took her a moment to translate. "Well, you are wearing a red coat and it looks like part of a uniform to me."

"Aw fadge it! I 'ates these duds," he said bitterly. "I 'ates this 'ole narky twank, is what. Wisht I'd niver come."

"Are you by yourself, or are there more of you?" If he had friends around she thought it would be prudent to leave, and in that case, too, they could take care of him. She'd had enough of this strange person. It was getting quite dark now and she didn't want to miss Eliot. "If you don't mind I think I'll take my bike and go home."

The man uttered a low moan at this and bent to fondle his bruised shin. It sounded as if he were muttering, " 'Ome, 'ome, 'ome," but suddenly, "Blood!" he cried in horror. "Blood! I'm muller'd!"

There was indeed a dark, blotchy stain on his left stocking. He raised accusing eyes to Charlotte who shifted uncomfortably.

"There's not very much," she said defensively. "And it was your own fault for not looking where you were going. *You* crashed into *my* bicycle. You may have wrecked my bike."

"Muller'd! Muller'd!"

She stared at him in bafflement. She had met lots of peculiar people in her life—the various members of her family were in the habit of bringing them home whenever they wanted. But she hadn't met a character like this before. Here was a hulking great adult wandering around a bone-chilling hilltop in the April dusk wearing a soldier's costume and swearing in a foreign language, almost on the verge of tears because he'd barked his shin on a girl's bicycle. Put straight in her mind like that, Charlotte could have no doubts at all about the wisdom of standing there talking to him. She ought to have left before this.

But the wretched desolation of this miserable man struck a responsive chord somewhere inside her. Common sense to the contrary, she recognized genuine unhappiness and realized that the ankle was only a part of it. Her conscience pointed out that he was behaving the way she had often wanted to lately. She reminded her conscience with asperity however that she was only a twelve-year-old child, and the stranger was a grown man. But in an odd way he comforted her.

"Stop fussing," she ordered briskly, feeling in her pockets. Yes, there it was: the remains of her brownie supply, still wrapped in Deb's bandanna. She pulled it out. The one brownie left was crumbling. With a pang of regret, she offered it to the man and folded the square of cloth into a long strip. "Eat that while I tie this around your ankle. And hold still."

He examined the brownie suspiciously, his mouth still open but the moan temporarily silenced. "Eh?" he said finally.

"Eat it," she repeated. "Bandage. Ankle."

He understood. He snatched the brownie, stuffed it into his mouth, leaned back against the stone wall, and rolled his stocking down from the knee. Underneath was a hairy white leg with a superficial but unpleasant-looking gash on top of the ankle bone. Blood had begun to dry around it, but more started when he unstuck the stocking. Wrinkling her nose in distaste, Charlotte squatted down and wrapped the impromptu bandage around his shin. She knotted it tightly and as quickly as possible; pressure was supposed to stop bleeding, if she remembered her sixth grade first aid. She had never liked playing doctor games.

The man whimpered shamelessly. He was a dreadful baby; she was starting to be sorry she'd felt sorry for him.

Overhead the clouds had welded into one great steel-colored mass. Caught beneath it, the wind prowled up and down the exposed hillside, poking restlessly into holes and corners, rattling the bare trees like bones. Walls, bushes, buildings merged in banks of darkness.

Charlotte stood up abruptly. "I have to go. My family will come looking for me if I don't." Couldn't hurt to let him know she was expected somewhere.

The man said nothing. Charlotte righted her bicycle. "I expect you can find your own way back to town, or wherever you're staying."

If he made a reply, it was lost in the welcome buzz of a VW engine. A single blinding headlight cut a hole in the dusk straight toward them and behind it Charlotte could see the lights of other cars; the Minutemen were dispersing. The one-eyed VW swerved toward the side of the road and stopped beside her.

Chapter Four

"HEY, CHUCK!" CRIED ELIOT, LEANING OUT. "THERE YOU are!"

The familiar sound of his voice made Charlotte suddenly aware of how uneasy she'd been feeling. "It's about time you got here," she returned.

With a scrunch, Eliot pulled on the parking brake and climbed out to help her lift the bike onto the rack at the rear of his car. Charlotte wondered how she was going to explain her strange companion to him, but when she looked around, she discovered the man had gone. Vanished like smoke.

"Almost missed you, Charlie. I expected to find you in the parking lot after practice. Good thing Skip knew which direction you'd gone or I'd have driven out the other way."

"I thought I'd wait for you here." Charlotte was puzzling over how such an awkward person had been able to disappear so completely and soundlessly. She crawled into the back seat behind Eliot. Skip's left knee didn't bend much, so he always sat in front. She cleared enough room to sit among the clutter of music, work boots, bits of uniform, old apples, and ragged sweaters. "One of your headlights is out," she reported.

"Damn," said Eliot mildly. He settled his tricorn on the back of his head and let out the clutch. "How would you describe the music this afternooon, friends? Splendid? Breathtaking? Polished and professional?" He was in very good spirits.

"You aren't fishing for praise, are you?" inquired Skip politely.

"Good Lord, no! Only an honest assessment of our performance. What d'you think, Charlie? Magnificent may be a little strong, but it does come to mind, what?"

"Eliot, were you the only soldiers around today?" asked Charlotte.

"Hmmm? Not quite the spontaneous reaction I'd hoped for! Why?"

"I just wondered if there were any Redcoats practicing with you."

Eliot shook his head. "Not unless we scared 'em off early with our unsurpassed musical ability, Chuck. Were there supposed to be?"

"Odd you should ask," put in Skip. "Commodore Shattuck mentioned British soldiers this afternoon."

Eliot grinned. "I saw him reviewing the troops as usual."

"About the soldiers," Charlotte said. She didn't like being sidetracked, especially by Skip.

"No one's told us about any," Eliot replied. "Sutton would've said. But this isn't a special year like the Blazing Bicentennial—just a good old-fashioned local celebration. Give Concord back to the Concordians. Natives, and friends by invitation only. Hey, what did you think of that new bit we did with 'The White Cockade'? Jazzes it up a little, don't you think?" He hummed a bar or two.

"Oh, you did it on purpose then," said Skip." "I wondered if it was actually supposed to sound like that or if you had a finger caught in one of your holes."

"You are a great disappointment to me, Walter," Eliot said sadly. "Your tin ear is still nothing but tin in spite of the years I've dedicated to your education."

"It sounded great," said Charlotte from the back seat. "It really did."

"*You* appreciate fine music, Chuck."

"You know—" Skip began after a minute. He broke off to grab the door handle as Eliot shot expertly into a solid line of commuter traffic inching toward Concord center. "You know, it's odd that the Commodore should be muttering about peculiar people this afternoon, Charlie."

"Why? They're all over the place these days," said Eliot amiably. "They're allowed everywhere."

"Shut up and drive," said Skip. "That's what we pay you for. He didn't mean your average peculiar person. He was asking if I'd seen any noticeable groups traveling about together, behaving strangely, sounding foreign. He was oddly secretive about it—asked all his questions in a sort of casual, roundabout manner, but he really wanted answers."

"What did you say?" Curiosity overcame Charlotte's distrust of Skip.

He shrugged. "I said no. I haven't."

It was a terrible temptation to tell them about the man she'd met on the hillside, but as she was about to, Eliot said, "I suppose we'll get the same half-hearted Redcoats from Merrimac, Connecticut, this year, done up in red jackets and periwigs."

"Not from what the Commodore said—or what he *didn't* say." Skip shook his head. "He expects something."

"Do you believe Commodore Shattuck?" asked Charlotte.

"Why not?"

"He's so *peculiar*," she objected. "There are all kinds of weird stories about him."

"You can't always believe what you hear," Eliot intoned piously.

"Nothing wrong with being peculiar so long as you don't hurt anyone," said Skip. "Most of the better people are odd. Your whole family, for example."

"We are not!" protested Charlotte, scandalized. She waited for Eliot to agree with her, but he didn't.

Instead, he gave a muffled snort, then a hoot of laughter. "I'm sorry, Chuck, but Uncle Skip's right. So's his family odd, come to that!"

"No argument," agreed Skip.

"How can you say that about us?" Charlotte demanded of her brother.

"It's indisputable. We're all very practical about being impractical with our lives, Charlie. There's Max sinking time and money into a degree in architectural engineering, when he doesn't even know there'll be a job for him when he's done,

34

married to a children's librarian with an M.A. in archaeology. Deb's busy teaching over-privileged toddlers to finger paint during the day so she can afford to weld mobile constructions in the garage at night. I gave up a perfectly good career in classical music so I can dig ditches for the Town of Concord. And if they don't enthusiastically encourage us, our parents don't *dis*courage us, either. Why should they? They're doing what *they* want. Even if you wanted to grow up straight, Chuck, which God forbid, you haven't a chance."

"You make us sound like a joke," Charlotte declared, deeply wounded. "What's wrong with trying to be normal?"

"First you have to decide what 'normal' is," Skip advised her.

"And what's normal for one person may not be for another," Eliot said. "It's more important to fit your own pattern, not force yourself into someone else's." His eyes met hers briefly in the rearview mirror. "Don't worry about it, Charlie, you don't know enough to worry yet. Wait and see. It's a mistake to set your mind in concrete before you grow up."

"Even after," added Skip.

Eliot nodded.

His words were meant to comfort her; she realized that, but they stung in her eyes like soap. There they were, the two of them in the front seat, telling her that they were grown up and understood, and she wasn't and didn't. They had age and experience in common; there was a gulf between the two of them and her. And, she thought despairingly, it would always be there. She would always be twelve years younger than her youngest brother.

"Cats' whiskers, what traffic!" exclaimed Eliot.

"I didn't think you'd noticed," said Skip. "I was sure you had us on automatic pilot."

Monument Square was choked with slowly moving cars. They streamed in from all directions, mixed round, and streamed out again. Eliot drove the VW right into the thick of them, hunched over the wheel, his eyes straight ahead. The trick, he had explained many times to his apprehensive family, was never to let another driver know you saw him. Eliot had developed excellent peripheral vision during the three years he'd commuted to the Conservatory in Boston.

At the far end of the Square, the clock in the First Parish Church tower glowed like a low yellow moon. Six twenty-three. Once past it, the car gathered speed. Charlotte wished they didn't have to take Skip home, they would be very late themselves as a result, but there was nothing to be done except get Eliot away as soon as possible.

"Well, Eliot?" said Skip as they neared the Bullard farmhouse. "Have you told them yet?"

Eliot hissed softly. "I'm waiting for the right moment, with my usual flair for the dramatic."

"Hmmm."

In the darkness Charlotte frowned. She wanted to ask, "Told who what?" but didn't want to admit in front of Skip she didn't know, so she kept quiet. Her heart sank when Eliot pulled up in front of Skip's house and switched off the lights and engine.

"Don't we have to get home?" she hinted broadly.

"In a minute," her brother said, opening his door. "Skip's got some stuff for me in the house."

Skip climbed out and pulled the seat forward for her. "Come on in, Charlie. No point in freezing out here."

"That's all right, I can wait." She'd rather stay where she was to remind Eliot that they had to hurry. She was also afraid that if she went in with them she'd meet Skip's niece and nephew, Kath and Andy Schuyler, which would be uncomfortable.

"Suit yourself," said Eliot. "I'll only be a few minutes."

No matter that she'd made the choice herself, she felt abandoned sitting alone in the dark car. Above, in the house, were lights and warmth and people. She allowed herself to drift on self-pity.

After about ten minutes Eliot emerged from the house with Skip and a third person—Mrs. Schuyler.

"—hot but the fishing'll be good," Skip was saying as they approached. "I'm itching to see those mountains! Here I am twenty-five and never been further west than Springfield, Massachusetts."

"Hayseed," exclaimed Mrs. Schuyler affectionately. She and Skip were brother and sister. They had been born and had grown up in this house, on this piece of land which had been a working farm until a few years ago. Now Pat Schuyler and her husband were raising their six children here, with Skip as resident uncle. "Hi, Charlie," she said, bending to the window.

"Hi," said Charlotte. Mrs. Schuyler did not fit her image of a mother; she seemed very young and persisted in wearing clothes that made her look like a high school student: jeans and T-shirts, or corduroy skirts and jerseys. She even wore her hair in braids sometimes.

"I came out to ask if you and Eliot want to stay for supper. There's mounds of spaghetti and salad. George isn't home yet and the kids are getting cranky, so I thought we'd go ahead and eat."

"Thanks," said Eliot hopefully.

"What about Mother? She'll have supper ready for us," objected Charlotte, horrified at the prospect of eating with Andy and Kath and the other four Schuyler children in their own house.

"You can call her," suggested Skip.

"It's too late, she'll have it made by now."

Reluctantly, Eliot said, "Charlie's right, it is late. We'd better go. Thanks anyway, Pat."

"You're always welcome," Mrs. Schuyler said with a smile. "I don't suppose you know what time I can expect George home, do you?"

Eliot shook his head. "I don't know where he got sent this afternoon. I left the DPW early because of the practice."

"He'll turn up just as we're finishing," said Skip. "He always does. You ought to have married a banker, Paddy."

She snorted.

The smell in the Paige kitchen was more complicated than spaghetti. It was dinner rather than supper.

"Mmmm." Eliot sniffed appreciatively. "Lamb curry?"

Mrs. Paige stood at the kitchen sink slicing mushrooms into quick neat pieces, one eye on a pot of water just coming to the boil, the other on a cookbook in a plexiglass holder. She neither paused with her knife, nor shifted her attention. "Lamb curry," she confirmed.

"Canniest nose on the Eastern seaboard." He scooped up a handful of lamb scraps.

"It will not, of course, taste the same without the lamb," his mother remarked. "You didn't happen to bring Charlotte with you, did you?"

"Yes," said Charlotte, coming in and beginning to shed her jacket and mittens on the kitchen table. "Had to put my bike away."

"Good, darling. Eliot, I hope you didn't leave your car in the driveway. Your father's late this evening with a trustees' meeting and he will not be happy if he can't get into the garage."

"No fear. I need a drink after all that marching about in the bitter cold."

"Hang up your jacket, Charlotte, will you? And see if Deb needs help with the table."

Charlotte made a face at her mother's neat back. She knew she was being scolded for being late—it was her job to set the table in the evenings.

"Two tablespoons of butter and a pinch of thyme," Mrs. Paige read aloud through her half-glasses.

"Come on, Chuck," said Eliot out of the side of his mouth. "Better leave the kitchen to Julia Child."

Together they went through to the front hall. The coats in the closet were packed tight enough so that Eliot could shove theirs in among them without bothering about hangers. Cautiously, Charlotte put her head around the dining room door and saw with relief that Deb had finished the table and gone.

In the living room, Eliot had flung himself down on the couch with his shoes off and his heel coming through one sock. Camomile was already curled smugly on his stomach, purring. They looked as if they'd been settled for hours instead of barely sixty seconds. Eliot was immersed in the *Sierra Club Bulletin* and was keeping time to some internal rhythm with his feet. A glassful of pale amber liquid and ice stood on the floor beside him.

Charlotte dropped into one of the green wing chairs beside the fireplace and waited for her brother to notice her. The room lay heavy with silence; Cam's purr was the only sound. She glared at Eliot with fierce concentration, forcing her presence toward him until he must feel her staring. He ought to look up and talk to her. But he didn't, he just went on reading, absently scratching Cam's orange ears. To Charlotte, hunched in her chair, he suddenly looked very large and unfamiliar. He looked like an adult. He drank cocktails, he went places and had secrets she no longer knew anything about. The feeling she'd had in the car earlier, when he and Skip had been talking, rose through her like an ice-cold flood. Panic, that's what it was. I'm being outgrown like an old suit, she thought with sudden desperation, and there's nothing I can do! I don't understand.

Deb appeared just then with a glass of V-8 in one hand and a plate of cheese and crackers in the other. "*There* you are. Missed the table again, didn't you? Honestly, Charlotte, I don't know how you manage it. When I was your age I didn't get away with that kind of thing, I can tell you."

"I was with Eliot," Charlotte defended herself. "I couldn't come home until he did. It was too dark to ride my bike." She reached gratefully for a Triscuit and the chance to forget the icewater in her stomach.

"You've always got an excuse, haven't you? What's your excuse for the rabbits? I fed them again this afternoon. Their water was simply disgusting, poor brutes. And you"—without waiting for an answer, Deb went to stand over Eliot—"you can sit up and let someone else have a piece of couch, if you don't mind. Dad'll be in in a minute, I heard his car."

Eliot glanced up and smiled benignly at her. "Had a good day, have you, Deborah?"

"Don't push your luck, Eliot," she warned. "I've been doing papier maché half the day and cleaning it out of little girls' hair the other half. You'll rot your stomach drinking that stuff."

"Ah, but it's *my* stomach," he pointed out and swung his long legs over the edge of the couch. Cam opened her eyes wide and extended her claws so she wouldn't fall off. "Ow! Vicious beast!" Eliot unhooked her with care. "She's much harder on my stomach than bourbon, if you want to know."

Deb ran a hand through her short black hair, shook it into place, and sat down.

"—last of the dragons," said Mr. Paige jubilantly over his shoulder as he came into the room. "I now have the delightful task of replacing her!"

"Mrs. Prescott's resigned," said Deb.

Mr. Paige's craggy face broke into a cheerful grin. "Free at last, hallelujah, I'm free at last! For a genteel, cultured, middle-aged woman, that woman has the skin of a rhinoceros. I thought I'd never do anything bad enough to offend her. But at last I seem to have done the trick, and we can really begin to get the museum in shape."

"What did you do?" asked Charlotte with interest. "Was it really awful?"

"Do you know, Charlie, I haven't any idea what it was. Since I took over as director she's weathered the modern art and the auction—even the arts and crafts fair last summer. She protested loudly, but she hung on. When she called this afternoon to tell me she'd resigned she refused to say why. It's rather gratifying to know I still have the knack of alienating people—I was afraid I'd lost it in Cambridge. Makes me feel positively young again instead of ancient and doddery."

"Rubbish," said Deb. "You're busier now than you were at Harvard."

"Alienating people?" asked Eliot innocently.

Deb ignored him. "What about arranging a field trip for my third-grade classes, Dad? I'm getting desperate for something different to do with them."

"You must be if you're willing to organize the mothers into transporting them," Eliot said. "But why have a serviceable parent if you don't use him?"

Deb shot her brother a venomous look and he grinned.

"I suppose we can withstand an attack of third grade," agreed Mr. Paige. "Give me some dates. How old does that make them? Ten?"

"Only eight," corrected Charlotte. "Ten's fifth grade."

"Don't wither me, Charlie, I'm an antique," said her father with a laugh. "Well, Eliot, what do you think of the Red Sox this season, hey?"

The lamb curry was excellent as usual. Mrs. Paige served it with fresh apple and pineapple, hard-boiled egg, coconut and almonds, mounds of rice, and a raw vegetable salad. Candlelight polished the cherry table and softened the corners of the dining room. It obscured Deb's, Eliot's, and Charlotte's old clothes and set Mr. and Mrs. Paige in their element. Dinners were something of a ritual; they brought the Paiges together, close enough to touch, for a brief period each day. Charlotte was just beginning to understand her mother's quiet insistence that dinner be a family meal.

She stirred her curry into her rice, took a double helping of pineapple, and spread it out across her plate. She didn't really like curry. For just an instant she thought with longing of spaghetti and thick, gloppy tomato sauce, then glanced guiltily around as if she expected someone to have noticed her slip. Of course no one had—how could anyone see what she was thinking? All the same she concentrated on her curry while she opened her ears to the conversation, even though it didn't particularly interest her.

They were discussing the new vacancy on the Pierce-Courtland's Board of Trustees and suggesting ways to fill it.

"A flaming radical," advised Eliot, "like Franklin Haynes, Jr. He'd stir things up for you."

"No flaming radicals." Mr. Paige was firm. "I want someone young, attractive and well-respected to encourage young members."

"What about an artist?" suggested Deb. "Maura Polsky's got lots of energy and tremendously creative ideas."

"Isn't that the woman who makes things out of bed springs?" inquired Mrs. Paige.

"Not just bed springs, Mother, all kinds of utilitarian objects. She believes art can be created out of *any* material."

"We have all the ideas we can cope with right now. I need people who can carry them out. I want to turn that museum into an arts center for the whole region, and I can do it if I have the right people to work with." Enthusiasm radiated from Mr. Paige like a field of electricity. He loved complicated projects—challenges of all kinds, work that made unreasonable demands on his time. Turning a staid little private art museum into an arts center was right in his line. The Paige family hadn't had a regular vacation in the two years since he'd taken on the job.

"Did you know," he said to Deb over his vegetables, "your *Silence in a Crowd* is starting to rust? It's making yellow streaks on the concrete base."

"Good. It's supposed to. That's why I made it of scrap iron. I told you it wouldn't be finished until it had weathered."

"That's doubtless why Mrs. Prescott left," said Eliot, shoveling a mound of salad onto his spotless plate. "Couldn't take the rust."

"Then she's got even less artistic taste than I thought," replied his sister with asperity. "That sculpture won first place at the New England Art Association Show."

"And it's caused a great deal of comment among our members," put in Mr. Paige.

"For or against?" asked Charlotte rashly, earning a wink from Eliot.

Deb glared at her. "People who don't know what they're talking about shouldn't—"

"I think I may have left the rice on, Deb. Would you check the stove for me?" asked Mrs. Paige.

Without another word Deb got up and went out to the kitchen.

Her mother sighed. "I wish I knew what's the matter with her lately. She hasn't smiled in days, and she's always on the defensive."

"It's a phase," suggested Eliot helpfully. "We all go through them. Charlie, pass the curry."

"Please," said Charlotte.

"Hmm?"

"Is it her job, do you think?" asked Mr. Paige. "I thought it was going pretty well."

"She doesn't talk about it much except to complain, and she hasn't even done that recently. I suppose it isn't terribly rewarding to teach art to babies when you really only want to practice it yourself."

"I don't think it's the school," said Eliot around a mouthful of rice, "I think it's Geoff."

"Oh, Lord, I hadn't even thought of him. He seems like

such a nice, steady young man."

"He is, but my sister Deborah is not what I'd call a nice, steady young woman."

"Why would it be Geoff all of a sudden?" Charlotte asked. "She's been going out with him for ages. I just wish she'd stop being cross all the time. It's a bore."

"Can't be much fun for her either, Charlotte," Mrs. Paige pointed out. "I don't think she wants to be cross."

"Well—"

Mrs. Paige gave her head a little shake and Deb reentered with a bowl of fruit. She looked round as if daring anyone to say anything about her temper. No one did.

"Charlotte, you can clear since you missed setting the table tonight," said Mrs. Paige.

Charlotte made a face.

"Come on, Chuck!" Eliot sprang to his feet. "You need the help of an expert."

"Expert!" said Deb sarcastically. "You haven't cleared a table more than twice in your entire life."

"Some of us have to practice, others of us are born with the gift." He gave her a pat on the head and she made a half-hearted swipe at him. "I have been waiting in vain for just one of my loving family to inquire how parade practice went today so I can tell you how marvelous we were."

"You always are," said Mr. Paige. "We knew if we waited long enough you'd volunteer the details."

"We were inspired. Weren't we, Charlie?"

She answered his grin with a smile. "Perfect," she agreed.

"It's gonna be a crackerjack parade this year, I promise you. Now that we're rid of all that Bicentennial nonsense we can get back to business."

"The Bicentennial was a good, authentic American cele-bration," declared Deb. "Eliot, are you just going to stand there holding that dish of rice?"

"I must agree with Eliot," confessed Mr. Paige. "The Bi-centennial was an awful lot of trouble at the museum. Have you any idea what a small percentage of contemporary art goes harmoniously with red, white and blue bunting?"

"I thought you didn't like it either," Charlotte challenged

her sister. "You said it was a cheap excuse to sell junk."

"Oh, who cares now anyway? It's over," she exclaimed. "I'm going out to my studio. If anyone calls, say I'm unavailable."

"Even Geoff?" Charlotte asked.

"I don't care *who* it is!" And she was gone.

Eliot raised his eyebrows significantly and Mrs. Paige sighed again. "I just hope she doesn't get careless when she's in a mood like this. She could conceivably set the garage on fire with her welding torch."

"She's much too practical," said Mr. Paige. "You could always go out and sit with her if you're worried."

"Oh, Gordon, don't be silly. I'd probably worry much more if I actually saw what it is she does with that thing!"

"You mean she's reached the age where you still worry but can't do anything about it," said Mr. Paige slyly.

Charlotte, poised in the doorway with a load of plates, said, "*Do* you worry about us?"

"That's what mothers are for," observed Eliot.

"You can't worry much about me."

"Whyever do you say that, darling?" Her mother looked surprised.

"You're never here when I'm home anymore," Charlotte burst out. "I'm only twelve and you don't know what I do, so how can you worry?"

"Charlie, that's nonsense," said Mr. Paige. "Your mother's got a great deal of confidence in you. She thinks you're old enough to look after yourself while she's working and I think you are, too."

"She didn't work when *they* were my age."

"Of course not, darling, you were a baby then; it was you I was looking after more than Max or Deb or Eliot."

"But you don't have to work now, does she, Daddy?" Charlotte appealed to him, carried away by her own explosion. "It isn't money, is it? Other people's mothers don't work." Even as she said it she realized she'd made a mistake and blown her case to bits. One thing neither of her parents tolerated from any of their children was an argument that began "Other people . . ." Mr. and Mrs. Paige required their children to think, act, and respect themselves as individuals.

That meant not doing or saying what other people did for want of a better reason.

"Charlotte," said Mrs. Paige calmly, "I have spent twenty-eight years raising children and I've loved it. But now you're old enough to take some responsibility for yourself and I'm ready to give it to you. You aren't old enough perhaps to understand that I *do* have to work, not for the money, but because my job is important to me. One day I think you will. You know you can always get hold of me if you need me. I'm never very far away. I love you very much, my darling, but there are other things in my life."

Charlotte compressed her lips into that thin, straight line and backed rebelliously through the swinging door. Why should she struggle to understand them if they wouldn't understand her? How can they, asked a little voice in her head, when you don't understand yourself? Ruthlessly she silenced the voice. Beyond the door she could hear the low, reasonable hum of her parents' voices. She imagined it wasn't Deb they were discussing now. Where had Eliot gone? He'd dumped his token load of dishes and bolted. If he wasn't going to do any more than that, neither was she.

Deb, in a baggy brown cast-off sweater of Max's, came down the back stairs and paused to fix Charlotte with an accusing eye. "You're just going to leave those, aren't you, and let Mother clean up again."

"It's none of your business!"

"God defend me from children!"

As Charlotte worked on an appropriate retort, Deb changed direction. "Have you seen my bandanna?"

Charlotte was caught short, "Oh, umm—" She saw it instantly as she had last seen it, knotted around a bony white ankle. It would be blood-stained and wrinkled by now. She grimaced inwardly, or thought she did, but something must have shown on her face because Deb's eyes narrowed.

"You have seen it, haven't you? Did you take it, Charlotte? You know it belongs to me."

"Well, I did see it in the kitchen—" began Charlotte.

"And what did you do with it?" Deb pursued her relentlessly.

A half-truth might be better than a lie and was certainly

better than the whole truth. "I wrapped some brownies in it to take with me this afternoon," she confessed. "But it got messy so I thought I'd wash it before I put it back."

"You had no business taking it in the first place," said Deb crossly. "You've got to learn to respect other people's property. It wasn't yours to use and you didn't even ask."

"You weren't here."

"That's even worse! I want it back tomorrow washed *and* ironed. Clear?"

"It's just a bandanna," grumbled Charlotte.

"But it's *mine*." Deb stalked out and slammed the back door.

Charlotte wondered how she was going to get through this vacation without coming to pieces. Why should people care so much about a crummy bandanna and so little about her?

Chapter Five

WHEN CHARLOTTE FIRST WOKE SATURDAY MORNING, HER ROOM
was full of lemony spring sunlight. It felt very early; she lay
with her nose buried in the pillow, absolutely still, and concentrated. There were no getting-up noises being made anywhere on the second floor that she could hear. One of the cats,
Lapsang Souchong, lay stretched in the trough made by her
body on the mattress. He was wedged in tight: very large,
very heavy, very comfortable. When Charlotte wriggled over
to look out the window, he opened his cold blue eyes a slit
and gave her a look of frozen reproach.

It really wasn't worth getting out of bed yet, she decided.
Much better to withdraw under the blankets and leave someone else to start the day. At least the sun was shining.

But when she opened her eyes again, it wasn't. A formidable layer of iron-gray clouds had clogged the sky and the
trees along the river tossed back and forth as if in dismay. The
promise of a good day was wiped clean off the face of the
morning and Charlotte wondered if she'd dreamed it.

Lap had vanished, gone about cat business, leaving a de-
posit of gray-black hair on the gold blanket. There were
breakfast smells oozing up the back stairs, and someone—
doubtless Eliot— had a Mozart horn concerto turned up loud
on the kitchen radio. It wrapped itself cheerfully around the
bacon, toast, and coffee.

This time there was no going back to sleep, Charlotte was

47

too thoroughly awake. If she lay in bed there would be nothing to distract her from feeling bored and unhappy. Besides, she reflected hopefully, if she turned up dressed for breakfast with the rest of her family, she might get herself included in something.

With that in mind, she dressed hastily, raced through the bathroom, smoothed her hair down with her hands, and ran down to the kitchen. She wasn't quite quick enough to catch everyone, however. As she arrived, she could hear her father's car reversing in the driveway, and her mother was nowhere in sight.

"Good morning to you! Good morning to you!" sang Eliot exuberantly, scraping a charred corn muffin into the sink. The counter was filmed with a fine layer of black crumbs. He was scraping in time to Mozart which gave the music an interesting percussive effect. "A burned muffin if you can tell me which concerto!"

"Seventh," said Deb without looking up from the sketching pencils she was sharpening. Neat blond wood shaving cascaded over her penknife into the wastebasket.

"There are only four," said Charlotte smugly. "Third?" she hazarded.

"Give that lady a charcoal-broiled corn muffin! You are a prodigy, Charlie, a genuine prodigy. Naturally, as your mentor and guide, I must take some credit for molding your raw talent."

"Third, seventh, what's the difference?" said Deb with a shrug. "They all sound the same, especially at top volume."

"And what, pray tell, is the difference between a number two lead pencil and a number seventeen?" responded Eliot as he sent a perfect hail of crumbs into the sink. "Muffin, muffin, who's got the muffin?" There wasn't much of it left in his hand.

"You have made a mess, haven't you? There is no comparison between lead pencils and concertos. Among other things, lead pencils do not deafen you."

"Concerti," corrected Charlotte.

"Who *asked* you?" demanded Deb. "What is this, *Name That Tune?* I don't need it first thing in the morning."

"It's good for you," declared Eliot. "Gets the juices cir-culating, stirs up the gray cells."

"Nuts."

"Are you going sketching?" Charlotte asked her sister.

"Good guess," said Deb. "What gave me away?"

"Anyplace special?" she hinted broadly. Deb had often taken her along for company, had in fact taught her a great deal about drawing, but that was before she had begun to teach art for a living.

"Don't know yet. I haven't made up my mind. I'm just go-ing *away*." Her tone told Charlotte that she did not intend to ask for or agree to company. These days she was mostly in what Eliot called a not-very-coming-on humor.

Earl Grey, in a playful mood, lay on his back and batted the string on Deb's open portfolio with his velveteen paws.

"Eliot, if you don't keep your cat out of my art supplies, I'll tan his hide for a brush wiper."

Cramming the end of his muffin into his mouth, Eliot swept the gray tom cat up and set him on his shoulder where Grey settled like an immense fur collar, a pair of feet on either side of Eliot's neck.

"And you," Deb continued relentlessly, turning on her younger sister who was heaping Grapenuts in a bowl, "where's that bandanna? You promised me, and I need it to keep my ears warm. I can't concentrate with cold ears."

"Um, not dry." Charlotte tried to sound innocent and sin-cere. "Still damp. You'll have it this afternoon."

Deb shot her a meaningful look, more effective than a threat.

"Use my earmuffs," offered Eliot helpfully.

"Darling, I hope you're going to have more of a breakfast than a bowl of cold cereal," said Mrs. Paige. She appeared from the dining room, dressed to go out in a tailored rust wool suit.

"I'll put fruit on it."

Mrs. Paige's mouth quirked slightly, but she made no com-ment. Instead she held out a desperately-ill-looking African violet in a blue porcelain bowl. "Help. Does anyone have any suggestions? I have watered this plant and fed it African violet food, put it in the sun, then moved it to the shade, kept it cool, tried warmth—it's had all the advantages I could give it. And look what it's done, the ungrateful object." Its leaves hung down limply all around the pot. They were the color of ripe bananas.

"Did you talk to it?" inquired Eliot. "Did you make it feel truly welcome? Perhaps I could play it some recorder music."

"Eliot, dear, I really don't have time for this now. I'm looking for practical suggestions, not humor."

"You have come to the wrong place then, Mother," warned Deb.

"Don't be hasty." Eliot pulled his face into serious shape. "I expect you've overwatered it, Ma." He scrutinized the violet with care. "It looks terminal, I'm afraid. Root rot has a solid hold on the victim."

"In words of one syllable, pitch it," translated Deb.

Mrs. Paige gave a disgusted sigh. "What a shame. I did hope I could keep it alive long enough to show Jean this weekend. It seems so horrid to have to tell her I've killed my birthday present in less than a month. I don't suppose I could dry it out?"

"Like an alcoholic!" Eliot grinned.

"Put it in the oven," suggested Charlotte.

Ignoring them both, Deb said briskly, "Jean simply has to learn like everyone else not to give you houseplants, Mother." She sorted her pencils into their case.

"Well, I haven't time to fuss. I'm due in Lexington at nine fifteen to meet with the bank manager and the architect. I'll do the shopping on my way home—perhaps I could buy another violet that that looks like this one. There's a thought."

"How underhanded," exclaimed Eliot.

"I don't want to offend my daughter-in-law. Ham for dinner tomorrow?"

"With scalloped potatoes," Eliot suggested.

"The kind with lots of cheese," said Charlotte.

"And calories," put in Deb ominously.

"Jean's bringing the dessert—I haven't any idea what."

Deb shook her head. "Very rich and fattening," she predicted. "Why are you letting her?"

"She offered, darling; I couldn't very well say no."

"It's not as hard as you might think."

"Where'd Dad go?" asked Charlotte, although she was sure she knew the answer.

"To the Museum. They're putting up the new show this weekend and he wants to be sure they do it right this time. There was such an awful fuss over the picture that got hung upside down at the last exhibit."

"And so there damn well should have been!" declared Deb. "Whoever hung it was an absolute—"

"Deb, would you get rid of the corpse for me, dear?" interrupted her mother smoothly. "Just dump it out in the shrubs."

"You are in a rare mood, aren't you?" Eliot observed pleasantly to his sister.

Mrs. Paige glanced thoughtfully at her three children and chose not to comment on the atmosphere among them. It was her belief that they were old enough to sort themselves out without parental intervention in all but the most drastic situations. "The show opens Thursday evening with wine and cheese and the Junction Jazz Band. Gordon wants us all there if possible."

"He's signed me up to play Scott Joplin on the piano," said Eliot. "Sounds like quite an event—good thing Mrs. Prescott got out when she did."

"Charlotte, you can wear your new green print." Mrs. Paige was thinking aloud. "And you'd better get your suit cleaned, Eliot. If you take it today, I'll pick it up Thursday morning."

"Not *the* suit," said Deb in exaggerated horror. "Mightn't cleaning cause it to disintegrate?"

"Then I would buy a new one," Eliot replied, unruffled by her sarcasm. "Why should I have more than one suit at a time anyway? I can't *wear* more than one, can I? What business has a ditchdigger with a Brooks Brothers' wardrobe? That would be pretentious."

"You aren't really a ditchdigger, darling," Mrs. Paige protested mildly.

"Roughly translated, that means, 'I wish you were still taking music at the Conservatory, Eliot,' " he said with a grin.

"You said it, *I* didn't," she replied. "Deb you can bring Geoff, of course."

"Thanks," said Deb curtly. "I won't."

Eliot raised his eyebrows until they disappeared under his curly forelock. "Oh-ho?"

"It hasn't a thing to do with you," she snapped. "Any of you. I don't know when I'll be home." She swept up her sketching equipment and exited.

"What was that about, do you suppose?" asked Mrs. Paige.

"Root rot," said Eliot cryptically. "Charlie, don't turn into an emotional female, will you?"

It's too late, I already have, thought Charlotte with despair.

Mrs. Paige followed her elder daughter to the back door. "Suit, Eliot," she reminded him.

He made a face, wiped the cat expertly off his neck, and dashed up the back stairs.

Charlotte looked up from her cereal to find her mother's eyes resting on her. She waited, leaving it to Mrs. Paige to say something first. "You will be all right on your own today, darling? You could come to Lexington with me if you like, but I'm not sure what you'd find to do. I expect you'll be happier here and I promise to be home for lunch."

She wanted Charlotte to tell her she needn't feel guilty about leaving her alone. "When's Max coming?" asked Charlotte noncommitally.

"Not till this evening, I'm afraid. Jean has to work today. Look, here's your allowance." Mrs. Paige fished in her wallet. "And if you want scalloped potatoes, will you buy half a pound of Gruyère from the Cheese Shop? I really must go—I can't keep Jonathan waiting. Have a good morning, and change the rabbits, will you?"

Blast those rabbits! Charlotte glared at the door as it closed behind her mother.

"I'm late, I'm late, I'm late!" chanted Eliot, pounding down the stairs.

"For what?" wailed Charlotte as she saw her last hope vanish.

He held out his arms and pirouetted: sweatshirt, tattered

jeans, work boots. "Gotta build a reviewing stand the moderator won't put his foot through this year; gotta paint markers on the parade route." He gave his sister a calculating look. "Charlie, would you mind awfully dropping this off at O'Brien's for me? I don't know when I'll do it today."

"Wel-l-l—"

"Aha! you could leave it on your way to pick up my hat, how's that?"

"What hat?" He caught her off guard.

"My tricorn. I have to wear it tonight and I must have left it at Skip's yesterday. Can't find it anywhere."

"But—"

"I really appreciate it, Chuck. Thanks!" He dropped a limp navy blue bundle in the chair beside her, grinned a Cheshire Cat grin—all teeth and no eyes—and was gone like everyone else. The door slammed, the VW gave a startled roar, and that was it.

Charlotte was left with a bowl of sodden Grapenuts, a disgruntled cat still setting its whiskers in order, and a dying African violet. The silence of the house closed around her like a fist, hard and oppressive. She pushed the Grapenuts into a heap, then smashed it.

The stupid suit! The very sight of it made tears burn her throat. She'd do it for him—*and* she'd get the hat. It was useless to pretend she wouldn't. She couldn't refuse Eliot, but more and more, lately, she found herself wishing that he weren't able to slide around her so easily. She couldn't imagine refusing Eliot anything.

His desertion hurt the most, but they'd all of them gone—they were all leaving her. So, the hell with the whole lot of them! She soothed her hurt feelings with rebellion and felt a little better. Deliberately, she left her breakfast dishes unrinsed and didn't bother to make her bed. She was tempted to ignore the rabbits as well, but reconsidered as she put on her jacket. That might mean more trouble than it was worth.

The rabbits, a pair of them, lived in one of Max's more durable architectural models in the backyard. In a fit of enthusiasm he had built them a scale reproduction of the Boston State House, complete with gold dome, now weather-worn

The rabbits represented one of Max's many schemes for making money. He had bought a pair to breed, after reading how easily they had babies, on the theory that he could sell their offspring for pets. The theory had never been proven or disproven: the rabbits had never produced anything other than quantities of hard round pellets. They just sat in their State House, ate, and got fatter. Several half-hearted attempts had been made to get rid of them, but Max resisted.

And now that he wasn't here any more, they had somehow become Charlotte's responsibility. Why did people always assume that children liked animals? Of course, some animals weren't bad: Eliot's cats, for instance, were at least interesting and quite clever. They were independent and undemanding. Max's rabbits were worse than useless. They were smug. No one ever asked Charlotte if she wanted them; all of a sudden Max had Jean, and Charlotte had a pair of dumb bunnies.

This morning they were very grudging about shifting over for her as she raked out the soiled chips and dumped in fresh ones. She was once again tempted to go off and leave the back of the State House unlatched in the hope that they would escape and disappear forever. But as she looked at them, so well-fed and self-satisfied, she knew they wouldn't; they'd stay right where they were and she'd be scolded for carelessness when someone—most likely Deb—discovered the door wasn't properly shut. She would probably always have those rabbits. They looked perfectly capable of lasting longer than she did.

Chapter Six

THE WIND HAD HAMMERED THE CLOUDS INTO ONE THIN, UN-
broken sheet across the sky. Behind it the sun lay like a tar-
nished quarter, giving no warmth, casting no shadows, a ghost
of itself. The air was cold and raw, but in spite of it the streets
of town were busy with Saturday traffic.

Charlotte hauled out her bike and cycled moodily up Main
Street. On either side the lawns had been raked and the gardens dug over; winter debris cleared carefully away in anticipation of spring and summer. The first hint of warmth
threw people into a frenzy of activity after a long, barren
winter.

The Porters and the Everetts had hung huge American
flags over their dignified Colonial housefronts in honor of the
nineteenth. Mr. Swann was standing on his porch roof wash-
ing the upstairs windows, wearing his battered felt hat, his
pipe clamped between his teeth. He lifted his sponge to Charlotte in solemn salute.

Outside the library, members of the Garden Club were
busy raking out shrubs and turning over flowerbeds. Among
them Charlotte recognized several neighbors and friends of
her mother. A team of three was deftly plugging huge pots
of red and white tulips into planters beside the steps. The
flowers looked very bright and brave, but frequently one
of the women would glance upward and frown. Charlotte
passed them by on the other side of the street, concentrating
on the cars ahead.

It was becoming less and less easy, she discovered, to talk politely to adults. She wasn't overcome by a sudden desire to be rude to her parents' friends, nor was she overwhelmed by shyness. It was rather that they made her uncomfortable—quite unintentionally, she realized, but uncomfortable nevertheless. Without meaning to, they made her depressingly aware that she was still a child. The interested questions about school and her friends and hobbies, the comments on how grown up she was getting only emphasized the gulf between her and them. When trapped into conversation because she hadn't been quick enough to avoid it, with horror she heard herself mumbling awkwardly, self-conscious and confused.

From the lampposts up and down Main Street, small American flags snapped in the wind. The pillars of the savings bank had been wrapped in great festoons of red, white and blue bunting.

In the old graveyard by the parking lot an active troop of Cub Scouts was collecting litter in plastic trashbags, directed by a pair of determined leaders. It certainly didn't look like an efficient operation, but they seemed to be enjoying themselves. Charlotte looked at the rowdy free-for-all and felt a twinge. Willfully she misidentified it as relief at not being part of such a scene.

The store windows were full of patriotic displays: red, white, and blue clothing; maps and old photographs; imitation antique pewter, commemorative plates and dishtowels. Mr. Gurney had filled his pharmacy windows with strange and unpleasant-looking colonial apothecary equipment: small mallets and forceps, tins of louse powder and ancient bottles, mortars, little hooked knives and scalpels, whose uses Eliot said it was better not to contemplate, and medical books in Latin.

In the middle of town a policeman directed traffic like a dance band, cueing cars and pedestrians by turn. Boys hung about the street corners and in front of Woolworth's where they could watch one another and catcall back and forth. Charlotte recognized a lot of them, but she didn't know any well enough to stop and talk to, so she pedaled by, up Main Street and out Lexington Road. It was going to be an unsatisfactory morning all the way along, so she decided she might as well make her trip to the Bullard Farm and get the worst over with.

Why couldn't Eliot ever take care of his belongings? If he lived forever he would probably never stop leaving them behind him. He shed them the way his cats shed fur—indiscriminately, anywhere he happened to go. Charlotte couldn't begin to remember the number of times she'd backtracked for him to collect hats or gloves or books or music—any of hundreds of portable objects. Each time Eliot apologized and was grateful, contrite, and instantly forgivable. But he never reformed, and she always obliged, even when she grumbled.

Revolutionary Ridge marched beside her out Lexington Road, raggedly fringed with trees behind the solid old houses. Overhead, elms and maples laced their fingers under the gray weight of sky. On the right lay a wild-grown field, tangled with burst milkweed, cattails, sedges, and grasses, at the edge of which stood the Gun House, a building the size of a small garage, that housed the two cannons. Its doors were kept securely locked as a rule. They were shut tight today—nothing odd about that—but there was someone leaning against one of them, a man Charlotte didn't recognize. She knew she didn't recognize him because she looked him over with great care. He was wearing a somewhat faded red uniform jacket, and she thought for a moment that he might be the foreigner from the hillside, with Deb's bandanna tied around his shin. But the face was wrong—this man had thick dark hair and a moustache. His hands were cupped casually around a cigarette; over them, however, his eyes watched her closely. When they met hers, he dropped his hands and gave her a cheeky grin and a wink. Charlotte's face went warm with embarrassment and she pushed on quickly. Out of the corner of her eye she saw him give a half-shrug. He lingered in a back corner of her mind for quite a long time.

The road out of town was empty of life. It led through a gray maple swamp, still stark and wintry. A handful of snowflakes blew around Charlotte, no more than a quick, cold promise that burned her cheeks and was gone, but it added to her depression. She was mad with impatience to be done

57

with winter. December and January belonged hip-deep in snow; by February blizzards were growing tiresome, and by March snow was absolutely unwelcome. There wasn't anything spring snow was good for: it seldom came hard enough or lasted long enough to close school, and it turned black and slushy overnight. It invited colds and bad tempers and wet feet.

The Bullard farm road was marked by an ugly little cement house that had a door but no windows. Until she was nine, Charlotte had believed Skip Bullard's authoritative claim that it was Paul Revere's horse's tomb, as had countless gullible tourists specially directed to the spot. He was so straight-faced with the story. She knew by this time that it had been built at the corner by the electric company for some mysterious purpose, but even she had to grudgingly admit that Skip's story was far nicer. Now, as she passed it, she thought of Eliot and Skip and sighed. There was a knot she couldn't undo.

Ahead, the Bullard farmhouse showed red among the trees. The sight of it gave her something immediate and solid to grapple with, oddly reassuring. Skip was unlikely to be there; he usually spent his Saturday mornings coaching a boys' swimming team in Bedford. Until his hockey accident in college he'd been very athletic, now swimming was the only sport he could keep up. Eliot, who hated water like one of his cats, had spent hours and hours exercising with him in swimming pools until Skip's injured leg grew strong again.

Mr. Schuyler'd be out somewhere hard at work with Eliot on the DPW crew, painting lines on the street or nailing up "No Parking" signs, but Mrs. Schuyler's huge blue Dodge was parked by the house. Skip teased her unmercifully about that car, claiming there were parts of it no one had ever explored. He called it Big Mamie. But his sister imperturbably pointed out that she could pack all the kids and both dogs into it. There were six noisy, tearing-around kids, including Andy and Kath, which sounded like a mob to Charlotte. But whenever she made one of her infrequent visits to the house with Eliot, there always seemed to be many more than six children racing in and out, fighting, playing games on the stairs, drinking grape juice and eating cookies in the kitchen, or curled up on the battered furniture. She didn't see how anyone could bear the clutter, the confusion, the shouting and demands.

She left her bike next to the car and walked up to the front door. Where the doorbell button should have been there was a round hole crisscrossed with Band-Aids to prevent anyone from sticking a finger in it. She tried thumping on the door, but got no response, not even a bellow from one of the dogs.

Chewing a strand of hair, Charlotte picked her way around to the kitchen, noticing with guarded interest the extraordinary number of abandoned vehicles lying about the yard: a wheelbarrow, two tricycles locked in combat, a large plastic truck, several skateboards, a single rollerskate, and a scooter without a back wheel. Scattered among them were tennis balls, plastic Indians, toy cars, a one-armed baby doll, and tooth-marked dog bones.

Mrs. Schuyler evidently saw her coming from a kitchen window, because she opened the back door before Charlotte reached it.

"Hi, Charlie," she said as if Charlotte dropped by every day. "Come on in if you can get through the door!" The same kind of litter lay about on the floor inside. Mrs. Schuyler swept some of it aside with one sneaker. "I'm always afraid someone's going to break a leg on one of these damn Lincoln Logs," she remarked cheerfully.

"Um," began Charlotte.

"Cold out there, isn't it? Feels like snow, God help us!"

"It has a little," volunteered Charlotte.

"Ick. The town's run out of snow removal money for the year, George says. Seems ridiculous to spend thousands of dollars clearing away stuff that will melt by itself eventually. Money down the drain!" She grinned. "I suppose you were too young to remember the Patriots' Day storm of 1967. Want a mug of cocoa, Charlie? I just made the kids some."

"Well actually, I just came—"

"Warm you up." She had somehow already gotten back to the stove with a milk carton in one hand and a saucepan in the other. "Marshmallow?"

"I just came for Eliot's hat, really," Charlotte continued with determination. "He thinks he left it here last night."

"Hat?" Mrs. Schuyler finished pouring and spooned in a great deal of cocoa powder.

"Tricorn. Part of his uniform."

"Haven't seen it. But that doesn't mean it isn't here—I haven't got as far in as the living room all morning. We've been fingerpainting." Which accounted for the smudge of blue on her left cheek. It seemed an odd thing for a grown woman to spend her time doing.

"Somewhere"—she inspected an army of mugs and cups on the drainboard by the sink—"there must be a clean one. It's an unwritten law around here that you never drink out of the same cup twice. Carl, stay out of the pan cupboard until you've washed your hands." A little boy with bright red fingers let go of the cupboard knob, leaving his mark on it. "I wanna pan for green. Cindy's took it all."

"Charlie, watch that milk for a minute, will you?"

Mrs. Schuyler disappeared into the dining room leaving Charlotte by the stove with a spoon in her hand. Through the doorway she heard, "Cindy, you don't need *all* the green paint. Carl can have some too."

A smaller voice lifted in indistinct argument.

"Absolutely not. You won't either of you have it much longer if you don't share. Understand? Clean-up in fifteen minutes anyway."

Charlotte glared at the milk which was starting to froth around the edges. She was incapable of moving. The warm kitchen was making her damp inside her parka; she didn't understand how she had come to be standing where she was, or how she could have accepted a cup of cocoa when all she wanted was to retrieve Eliot's tricorn and beat it. The milk bubbles rose dangerously against the side of the pan, and still she stood frozen in place, watching.

Mrs. Schuyler was back, wiping green paint onto the seat of her jeans, and she whisked the pan off the burner seconds before it boiled over. She poured it into a mug, which Charlotte hoped not very optimistically was clean, and gave it a brisk stir with the spoon, which she removed from Charlotte's limp grasp. "There you are. Why don't you take off your jacket and go talk to Andy while you're drinking it? He's been shut in the house almost a week and he's getting stir-crazy."

"Andy?" Charlotte glanced at her in alarm.

"Uhum. Ear infection again. He can count on two a year, poor kid." She added reassuringly, "It's not contagious. Change of face'll do him a world of good. Go on, you can look for Eliot's hat in there at the same time—Andy may have seen it. I've got to run the twins through the bathtub so they look presentable for a birthday party."

Powerless to refuse, Charlotte allowed herself to be prodded gently but firmly through the narrow passage into the living room. She was doomed, particularly since Andy seemed to be where the hat was and the hat was what she had come for. She couldn't leave without it after getting this far.

"And find out what Paddy's up to, will you? He's been ominously quiet for the last half-hour."

Who, or what, was Paddy? Charlotte suspected he was a child, but she had no idea what she was expected to do if Paddy was misbehaving, nor even what constituted misbehaving around this house.

The living room was every bit as cluttered and untidy as the kitchen. There were dog hairs on the scattered rugs and stuffed chairs and dust kitties under a table by the front window on which stood a jungle of green plants. There was a copper pitcher by the wide fireplace filled with a dusty dried arrangement of cattails and grasses and pressed leaf-sprays and a great mound of ashes between the black andirons. There were books and coloring books and bits of train, limp stuffed animals, dog toys, and building blocks in drifts around the edges of the room like flotsam at the high-tide mark. In the middle of the floor lay Skip's bad-tempered yellow mon-grel, Alice, flat on her side. A very small tow-headed child in grubby overalls and a red jersey was sound asleep, using her ribs as a pillow. Alice lifted her head to glare at Charlotte and gave a muffled "whurp." Charlotte glared back as bravely as she could. She was not fond of dogs.

"For Pete's sake, don't wake him up," begged Andy from

the couch. "I'm sick of playing gas station."

"Is that Paddy?" asked Charlotte. The four younger Schuylers were not normally part of her world, so she had no reason to know their names. She knew Andy and Kath only because they were in her class at school.

"Yup."

"Your mother says you've got an infected ear," she said, groping for something to say, and thought how dumb that sounded. If anyone would know about the infected ear it would be Andy.

But he nodded with a wry smile. "All week. I'd really even rather go to school than have to stay indoors for a whole week. I'm getting so far behind."

"With school?" She was surprised that he would care. Andy Schuyler was not a particularly willing student.

He unhunched from his corner and sat up, scruffing his hair into rusty peaks with his hands. Although he and Charlotte had only a passing acquaintance based on several classes at school and Eliot's friendship with Skip and Mr. Schuyler, he didn't seem to find it strange that she should suddenly have taken a notion to visit him by herself. He hadn't even asked why she'd come; he simply welcomed the intrusion. His eyes came into focus at her question and a spark of interest kindled in their brown depths. "Not school. Plowing for potatoes, planting peas, digging parsnips," he answered promptly.

"Oh." All of that meant little to Charlotte. She had unzipped her parka but wouldn't commit herself as far as taking it off. She sat on the edge of one of the shabby chairs opposite Andy and noticed with disgust that her cocoa had a dark brown skin on it.

"Dan's doing some of it, and Skip when he has time, but there's so *much* in the spring."

"Isn't it awfully early to plant anything? It's so cold and there were snowflakes this morning." Surreptitiously she glanced about the room, hunting Eliot's hat, and wondered how soon she could depart without giving offense. What could she do with the cocoa?

"Peas should be in by mid-April or they won't be ready for the Fourth of July. Everybody wants 'em then—you miss the best market if you don't have any. A little snow right now helps. My granddad used to call it poor man's fertilizer. I've got cold frames to see to. Beets, carrots . . ." He rattled off a list of vegetables.

With her finger, Charlotte pushed the skin back to the edge of her mug and took a long swig. The cocoa drained hot down her throat, making her splutter a little. It wasn't unpleasant. "You haven't missed much at school," she interrupted when she got her breath back.

"Never do. After I learned to read and multiply and divide, I figured it was all kind of a waste for me."

"What do you mean?" Charlotte was struck by the idea.

He shrugged. "It isn't doing me any good. I'm not learning anything *useful*."

"Useful how? Would you rather plant vegetables all day?"

"Yeah." Andy grinned.

He's serious, she thought, shocked. "You want to spend your whole life digging holes in the ground?"

"Mmm. Why not?" His pleasant face became instantly intent. "It's a good life being a farmer. Hard maybe, but it's honest and valuable. I *like* digging holes in the ground. All I need is the right equipment and enough time and I can make this farm go again, I know I can. I can learn everything I need to know myself from now on, if only they'd understand that and let me get to it."

"Your father gave it up," Charlotte pointed out. "Eliot says farming doesn't earn enough to live on around here."

Andy pulled himself back down into the corner and frowned. "You can do it if you know how. Other people do. There's good land in Concord—look at all the farm stands. Someone has to grow all the vegetables you eat, why not me? Once I'm through with school I'll have the time to cultivate a lot more of the fields than the patches Dan and me've got under so far."

From his tone of voice, Charlotte could tell Andy had had this argument before with someone a number of times. "You aren't old enough to run a farm," she objected.

"Yes, I am," he replied confidently, not at all affronted by her bluntness. "I *want* to and that's what makes the difference."

Why should she argue with him? What was it to her what

Andy Schuyler did? She set her empty mug on the floor, a little surprised to find the cocoa gone, skin and all. "Have you seen my brother's hat?" she asked abruptly.

"What?"

"Hat. Black, felt—a tricorn hat. He left it here."

"Is that what you've come for?" he asked with interest.

She nodded.

"I think I saw one on the dining room table. Might be Eliot's."

Charlotte stood up and Alice whurped again. Her ribs heaved; the child's head bounced gently up and down. Carefully, Charlotte edged around the dog and up the two steps into the oldest part of the house. It had been built by the Bullard family over several hundred years in distinct stages and grown from a symmetrical little farmhouse into a big rambling one. Pat and Skip had actually been born in one of the upstairs rooms. The floorboards were wide and worn and creaked arthritically as Charlotte walked across them to the dining room.

On the long oil-cloth-covered table at the far end lay the remains of the finger painting: bowls of jellylike paint beginning to crust around the edges, drifts of paper towels, paintings in all stages of completion, puddles of tinted water. The rest of the table was strewn with Golden Books, a sock on knitting needles, a half-finished jigsaw, a pipe and tobacco pouch, and Eliot's tricorn lying upside down full of someone's shell collection.

Indignant, Charlotte dumped the scallops, snails, and clams out in a heap and shook the residue of sand onto the floor. She inspected the hat closely for damage, but couldn't honestly find any.

Tumbling down the stairs came the sounds of a noisy bath: shrieks and splashes. No point in trying to find Mrs. Schuyler to tell her the hat was found, Charlotte decided. She went back to Andy. "Someone put shells in it," she said accusingly and zipped her parka.

"I thought it was in there. I suppose you're going?"

She nodded. "I have lots of errands."

"Well," said Andy, "see you." He looked discouraged.

"Bye."

It was unlikely, Charlotte thought, that their paths would cross again before school started. She felt rather sorry for him, forced to sit there all day being bored, but it was good to get away and cycle back to town, and she soon forgot him. On the road she ran into another flurry of snowflakes, this one longer and quite vigorous. It whirled around her in a billowing curtain, temporarily isolating her from the rest of the world.

Chapter Seven

IT WAS NEARLY LUNCHTIME. CHARLOTTE'S STOMACH, WHICH had been lulled into complacency by the cocoa, began to sound the alarm. By the time she reached home she felt quite hollow and was relieved to see her mother's car in the driveway.

Mrs. Paige had the kitchen table laid out in squares of fabric samples and was consulting paint charts as she made notes on a yellow pad.

"There you are, love," she said with a welcoming smile. "I was just beginning to wonder. Come and tell me which you like best— the persimmon with this tweedy stuff, or the bittersweet? Of course the colors will look completely different under those ghastly fluorescent lights, but Jonathan wants the order in this afternoon, so he'll have to take what he gets. There. What do you think?"

Charlotte studied the little circles and squares carefully, first in one combination, then another. "That one," she said finally.

"Bittersweet. Hmm. I think I do, too. Bittersweet it is then. And clam chowder. How's that?"

"Good." Warmth crept up from Charlotte's feet inside and out. "Does that finish the bank?"

"Lord, I just wish it did. There's some kind of confusion over the tellers' counters and the manager has just decided he wants chrome chairs instead of walnut, even though I told him they're wrong for the desks. Then I've still got to do something about the washrooms." Mrs. Paige stacked her samples and put them back in her leather satchel, then got up and turned the heat on under the chowder. "Have you had a good morning, darling?"

Charlotte shrugged. "Not very."

"Get some spoons, will you? What was wrong with it."

"When's Max coming?"

"In time to change clothes and have supper with us to-night."

"Why do I have to stay home by myself this year?" Gloom wrapped Charlotte like a damp towel. "I don't see why I should when everyone else gets to go."

"Charlotte dear, I know it doesn't seem fair that you should get left behind, but honestly what would you do at the Patriots' Ball?" asked her mother with brisk sympathy. "There won't be anyone else there your age—it'll be all couples. You wouldn't really have much fun, would you?"

They had had a discussion about the ball last year, too—Charlotte just testing the water and quite willing to pull her toe back when she found it cold. But Max had been home then. Jean couldn't get away from the library for the evening, so Max and Charlotte had passed the time playing Monopoly, drinking ginger ale and beer, and eating quantities of buttered popcorn. At quarter to twelve they had gone, arms linked and singing, up to the square to hear the bells and see Dr. Prescott and cheer the Minutemen as they marched up the Milldam to the flagpole.

Last year that had satisfied her utterly—to bundle up and join the milling, festive crowd on a velvet black midnight, to watch the big man in a riding cape and tricorn gallop into Concord on a snorting, prancing horse, shouting, "The Regulars are coming!" even though she knew it was really Geoff Reynolds in a costume on Alan Watts's favorite mare. Lights blossomed suddenly all along Main Street and the church bells hurled brittle showers of sound out of the steeples over everyone gathered below. Then out of the confusion of noise came the fifes and drums. Exuberant and proud, Charlotte and Max and everyone else shouted and clapped.

But this year Max had Jean, and Charlotte was to be left home alone. "Eliot could take me as well as Deb," she pointed out obstinately.

"He's in the orchestra, Charlotte, you know that. He won't have time to look out for you."

"I don't need looking out for. I could just sit and watch and not be in the way or anything."

"Darling—" began Mrs. Paige, exasperation creeping into her voice.

"Damnation!" cried Deb banging into the kitchen, her black hair wind-touseled, her cheeks becomingly pink, her eyes blazing fury. "You wouldn't *believe* it! In the middle of Concord, in the middle of the day, in the middle of crowds of people. The *nerve* of him!"

Charlotte and her mother exchanged a startled glance, quite forgetting the argument underway.

"What happened?" and "What is it?" they asked simultaneously.

"I can't even talk about it properly, I'm so mad!" Deb stormed through the room and out into the front hall. They could hear her slamming around in the closet, then she stomped upstairs to her room. There were several bangs of various sizes, the sound of footsteps along the upstairs hall, then she rampaged down the back stairs into the kitchen again. In the meantime, Mrs. Paige got out another bowl and plate and put another French roll in the toaster-oven.

"Well?" demanded Charlotte, consumed with curiosity.

"Don't devil your sister," reproved Mrs. Paige unconvincingly.

Deb looked a little calmer, but her expression was thunderous. "I have been openly harrassed, accosted, propositioned, and followed all around the Town of Concord this morning. I couldn't believe it at first, but he wouldn't leave me alone. It was like a bad movie!"

"You weren't actually harmed in any way, were you?" asked Mrs. Paige carefully.

"Oh, of course not, Mother," said Deb crossly. "But my personal freedom has been seriously infringed upon. I wasn't planning to come home this noon—I intended to stay out and get some work done, but I couldn't. I have never experienced anything like it."

"*What?*" cried Charlotte with impatience. "Who was it?"

"How should I know? I've never seen the man before in my life—and I hope I never do again, but he followed me all the way home. He may still be outside lying in wait."

"Sit down and have some hot lunch," advised Mrs. Paige sensibly. "You'll feel better."

Deb took a deep, exasperated breath and swung herself onto one of the chairs. She addressed herself to the bowl of chowder set in front of her until it was half gone. Then she put down her spoon and looked at her mother and sister. The fury had left her, but not the resentment. "I was inoffensively going about my own business. I went up into the Burying Ground at the head of Main Street—the one overlooking the Square. I got myself set up to do some peaceful sketching; there wasn't anyone around to distract me and I started to work really well. I must have been there about an hour and my feet were getting cold, so I stopped to jump around a little, get the circulation back. Perfectly normal. Then I noticed this man standing there, leaning against one of the tombs, watching me. I don't know how long he'd been there—I'd been quite absorbed in my work." She paused, tearing her roll into tiny furious fragments.

"And then," prodded Charlotte.

Her mother forgot to frown at her this time.

"He just stood there, staring. When he saw me look at him he grinned and winked at me. A total stranger! Then damn me if he didn't try to pick me up. Oh, the lines he used! I've never heard anything like it. I didn't know people actually said things like that!"

"Did he say anything obscene?" Mrs. Paige asked matter-of-factly.

Deb scowled. "Nothing like that, Mother. It was just so—so *juvenile.*"

"What did you do?" Charlotte wanted to know.

"I ignored him at first, of course. Then when he didn't stop, I told him I didn't want any part of him and if he didn't shut up and go away, I would leave. He just went on grinning as if he didn't believe me, and he went on talking. So I packed up my stuff—and damned annoying, too, because I'd blocked out another view I really wanted to finish—and left. I thought I'd go somewhere else for a bit, then come back when he was gone. But he *followed* me. He wasn't even covert about it, he just walked along whistling. *Whistling!*"

"What did he whistle?" asked Charlotte.

"How should I know?" Deb exclaimed irritably. "I didn't want anything to do with him so I didn't listen. We went all over town together. He even followed me into Brigham's when I got a cup of coffee. Anyway, I finally gave up and came home. I couldn't do any work with him around."

"Of course not, darling. But did you report him to the police? He was certainly bothering you and they probably could have stopped him."

"No," said Deb. "I didn't report him. Bloody male chauvinist! Thinks all he has to do is smile at a woman and she'll rush for him with open arms. Oh, how I *hate* the type! Charlotte, don't get mixed up with men. Ever."

"What about Max and Eliot and Dad?"

"Don't be thick," snapped Deb. "You know what I mean."

"I don't either," muttered Charlotte, slathering her roll with butter.

"Can you describe him?" Mrs. Paige was being practical.

"You bet I can—no fear. One of those tall, smooth-looking types. Superior. Knows exactly how good he is. Sandy hair, lots of white even teeth, strong chin, blue eyes—nothing behind them except conceit."

"Sounds rather nice," commented her mother dryly.

"Oh, for—"

"I didn't say anything. I'm sorry!" Mrs. Paige held up her hands.

"He's foreign to boot. British. With one of those posh upper-crust accents."

Charlotte squinted thoughtfully at a piece of roll.

"Then he's probably only a tourist passing through and you'll never see him again, darling," soothed Mrs. Paige.

"I hope you're right, because if I do I'll flatten him with my self-defense "

"You only ever went to two of those classes," objected Charlotte with her mouth full.

"Swallow first, love. But she is right, Deb. Don't for heaven's sake do anything dumb. We support a perfectly good police force."

"I can take care of myself," stated Deb firmly. "I am perfectly capable of handling my own life, Mother."

"Of course you are, but you don't have to do it single-handed all the time."

"Yes, I do. Until I've convinced certain people that I'm independent."

"Your family's convinced already."

"That's not who I had in mind."

Charlotte had lost interest in the conversation. She didn't understand why Deb had suddenly become so argumentative and wrapped up in herself. She wasn't much fun to be around. But when Charlotte had rashly confronted her sister with this fact not very long ago, she had been treated to a long and vehement lecture on sensitivity to other people and consideration, and how she ought not to talk about things she didn't understand. Charlotte had retired in injured silence and left Deb pretty much alone since then.

She finished her chowder, then finished what was left in the pot, and was about to go up to her room, when she heard her mother say, "Then why don't you take Charlotte with you this afternoon if you go out sketching? It would be nice for both of you to have company, and that might take care of any problem. I've got to go into Belmont to order the curtain fabric for the bank, but I expect I'll be home before Max and Jean."

"I have errands to do," said Charlotte quickly. "Lots of them." She'd lost her appetite for Deb's company during lunch; she knew Deb wouldn't pay any attention to her if she went along and it would only be a long, cold afternoon.

Deb shrugged. "I am not going to ruin my entire day because one subnormal male gets a charge out of bothering women. I think I'll go up to school later and straighten out the supply closets." She looked challengingly at her mother and sister. "And that's because they're in a hopeless mess and have to be done, and the light's gone, and it's gotten cold.

Not because I've been intimidated."

A flicker of something, quickly suppressed, crossed Mrs. Paige's face, but she didn't say anything. Charlotte judged the time had come to clear out of the way if she wasn't going to be pushed into doing something against her will. "I'm just going up to get my library books," she said, making for the stairs.

"You could come along with me if you want, Charlotte," began her mother.

But Charlotte shook her head vigorously. "I'd be bored. And the fabric store makes my eyes sting."

"All right, darling, but do be home before dark. We'll have to have an early supper."

Once her mother was gone and Deb had disappeared into her studio, Charlotte wrapped herself up in outdoor clothes again and set out to complete her errands. As she left the house, she took a good look around for the man who had followed her sister home. Her curiosity was thoroughly aroused: she wanted to see the person who could be attracted to Deb in one of her vile tempers.

There was no problem spotting him. He was, as Deb said, quite open about what he was doing. At the moment he was walking in brisk circles on the opposite corner, still whistling, his hands thrust deep in his trouser pockets. He paused and gave Charlotte a thorough inspection as she wheeled her bike down the drive. Unabashed, she stared back at him.

She had half-expected to find him wearing a red jacket, but he wasn't. He was dressed with casual care for a cold afternoon in slacks and a fisherman's knit pullover, a long black scarf with two yellow stripes thrown dashingly over his shoulder. His warm breath escaped in a white thread. Even Charlotte had to acknowledge that he was good-looking. In fact, in view of Deb's past interest in men, she couldn't understand why her sister was so indignant at being approached by this one. Just to spite Deb she gave the man an encouraging wave and he made a little bow in return. He continued his circles as she cycled down the street.

The sun was still visible through a veil of cloud, but all the colors of the day had bled together into shades of gray and a mean-minded little wind kicked up miniature whirlwinds in the street. Most of the kids had gone from the drugstore corners, driven indoors by the cold.

Finding the coast clear, Charlotte detoured through Gurney's for a Mars Bar to sustain her until supper. When she was by herself, she noticed, she got far hungrier far more often than when she was with other people.

A couple of junior high boys were huddled over the magazine rack by the door, leafing through *Sports Illustrated*. Mrs. Gurney in her blue nylon smock stood behind the counter discussing the comparative merits of hand creams with a woman Charlotte recognized as her father's newly resigned trustee, Mrs. Winthrop Prescott. Every now and then Mrs. Gurney aimed a black look at the boys, who were not supposed to be reading the merchandise.

There were two other customers in the drugstore. One was a large, red-faced young man in an enormous frayed duffel jacket and trousers several inches too short, who was scrutinizing the postcard selection with tremendous care. The other was Oliver Shattuck, who, if appearances could be believed, was reading word for word the labels on all the bottles of cough syrup.

Charlotte viewed these two suspiciously, but neither took any notice of her, so she took her candy bar to the counter, eager to pay and be off, but Mrs. Gurney's attention was fully occupied with Mrs. Prescott.

The man at the postcards hummed to himself, the two boys snickered self-consciously, Oliver read on, and Mrs. Prescott tried another hand cream. Charlotte shuffled from foot to foot.

Finally Mrs. Prescott made a decision, paid, and left. With the cash register still ringing, Mrs. Gurney called severely, "You boys there, do you intend to buy that magazine now that you've handled it? We can hardly sell it as *new*—" She shook her head crossly as the boys shoved *Sports Illustrated* back into place and jostled each other through the door.

"Can I—" began Charlotte.

"Lovely cards, these," remarked the strange man. "I've

73

'arf a doz 'ere, luv. D'you want to count 'em, or d'you trust me?" He grinned roguishly at Mrs. Gurney, whose complete attention he had caught with the word "luv." His accent was unmistakably British.

"I'll count them, thank you," said Mrs. Gurney primly.

"Suit yourself, luv. I think me mum'll fancy the one of the church, don't you? And this green bloke 'ere's for me Uncle Sid. Mebbe you can tell me where to find 'im when 'e's at 'ome? Wouldn't want to miss seein' 'im."

"Who? Your Uncle Sid?" Mrs. Gurney sounded confused and suspicious.

"I think he means the statue," volunteered Charlotte who was looking on with interest. "It's the Minuteman at the Old North Bridge. Out Monument Street."

"Ta very much," said the man politely. "Not far? Walk there, can I?"

Charlotte nodded, suddenly shy.

"Now this one"—he handed Mrs. Gurney a picture of the Old Manse—"is for me sister. She's dead keen for 'istorical 'ouses."

"Yes, yes," interrupted Mrs. Gurney. "I can see you do have just six cards there. That's sixty-three cents with the tax."

He nodded and pulled a fistful of change out of his jacket pocket. "Give us a 'and, will you? I 'aven't got the 'ang of these little bits of money yet." Mixed in among the quarters, dimes, and pennies in his palm were bigger, foreign-looking coins.

Mrs. Gurney drew a loud disapproving breath and delicately picked out the right change.

"You wouldn't sell stamps then, would you?"

"No."

"Pity. But as me Uncle Sid would say, what can't be 'elped must be endured. Tira, then!" He pocketed the cards and strode out.

"Charlotte Paige," said Mrs. Gurney reprovingly, "haven't you been told not to speak to strange men? It isn't proper."

Charlotte was on the verge of arguing, when she changed her mind. Buying her Mars Bar had already taken far too

74

long, so she merely said, "Yes," took her change and escaped. At the door she glanced back. Oliver Shattuck had disappeared.

One of the problems of living in a relatively small town is that a tremendous number of people know who you are, she reflected with irritation. They did business with your parents and they nailed you every time you went near them.

It happened again, as she knew it would, when she went into the dry cleaners. Mr. O'Brien, the proprietor, greeted her with a wide smile that displayed all the gold caps on his teeth. When she was little, these used to fascinate Charlotte, but now she was old enough to find them embarrassing.

However, the smile vanished as soon as Mr. O'Brien identified the screwed-up ball of navy flannel under her arm. With real pain he took Eliot's suit out of her hands and spread it on the spotless counter. "You must never, never treat a good piece of worsted that way. The wrinkles! It won't wear! The shape—gone."

"It's not my fault," said Charlotte defensively. "He gave it to me that way." So don't give a lecture, she added silently.

Mr. O'Brien shook his head sadly and smoothed the suit. "It'll never last this way."

"Mother says she'll pick it up Thursday morning."

"We will do our best, of course," he said resignedly, then brightened. "And how is your mother, Charlie? I haven't seen her lately."

"Fine," answered Charlotte abruptly. Why on earth should she have to have a polite conversation with the dry cleaner? Why should it matter to him how her mother was?

"Good." The smile was back. "And you? How's school going? I looked for you all winter at the basketball games. You know my boy Danny's a forward. Got real talent for sports. Now it's baseball season already! Where does the time go?"

"I don't really like that sort of thing," Charlotte said. "It's too organized."

"How can you play basketball without being organized? You ought to try, Charlie. You could be a cheerleader. You'd look good in the uniform—I should know, I clean them."

She stifled a shudder. "I don't think so, Mr. O'Brien. It's just not my kind of thing."

"I thought all girls wanted to be cheerleaders. With the pompons? No? Maybe next year. You never know how you'll feel in a year."

She had a pretty good idea that however she felt in a year it would not be like a cheerleader. The conversation had gone far enough, she decided, and pulled on her mittens.

"I'll tell Danny you were in," promised Mr. O'Brien with a conspiratorial look.

Charlotte could imagine Danny's reaction to that. He was one of the loud-voiced, energetic boys at school she habitually avoided.

"Thank you," she said insincerely.

At the door she was almost knocked flat by a large, well-muffled figure, draped in a miscellaneous collection of sweaters and scarves. He was wearing at least two of each.

"Whoop! Beg pardon, kiddo!" he exclaimed in a round, deep voice. He unwound several feet of red and white muffler and peered at her. "Didn't even see you!"

Instead of continuing on her way, Charlotte stopped dead, her hand on the doorknob. She waited to hear what the newcomer would say next; he was British.

"Tell me what you can do with that, mate," he said dropping his bundle in front of Mr. O'Brien. "Sorry lookin', innit? Been through the wars, it has—even been slept in."

From Mr. Brien's voice, Charlotte could tell he was deeply distressed. "What . . . is . . . it? Or should I say, 'was'?"

"'S a uniform, mate. White trousers, red jacket—see? Mind you, they don't exactly match and there's a button or two gone missing, but beggers can't be choosers, hey? And Beaky's a rum size to fit. Flipping hard to find anything at all for him, I can tell you."

"Oh," said Mr. O'Brien sadly. "A uniform. I honestly don't know if I can save it, it looks pretty far gone."

"'Well, anything you do's bound to make it look better. It can't look worse, now can it? We've got a problem with time, though. It's sommat of a rush."

"How much of a rush?" There was an edge to Mr. O'Brien's voice.

"We've got to have it late this afternoon, mate."

"*Today?*" He momentarily lost control.

"That's it. We're in a bit of a hole, see, and there'll be a proper row if we turn up one uniform short. The old man has a narky temper. He's been waiting years for this, he has. Don't want to disappoint him."

"Well, I—"

"Name's Hardcastle, with an haitch. One of us'll be round to collect it at half-past four sharp. Right? Cheer-o, then!"

Charlotte scooted through the door before Mr. Hardcastle had a second chance to collide with her. He swept past with a hearty "Tira!" rewinding his muffler, and strode off down the street.

Thoughtfully Charlotte watched him go. She was remembering what Skip had said the night before about Commodore Shattuck talking as if he *expected* a group of foreigners in Concord. When she counted up the men she'd noticed so far, she certainly had what amounted to a group; small, to be sure, but brought together by more than coincidence she had a strong suspicion.

After buying her mother's cheese for the potatoes, she went into Woolworth's where she hunted in vain for a blue bandanna to match the one she'd borrowed—it seemed permanently—from Deb. None was exactly right, which meant she'd have to admit she'd lost the real one. With reluctance she bought a replacement out of her own allowance; then, to cheer herself up, went over to the snack counter and ordered a vanilla Coke.

As she sat brooding down her straw, she became aware of two men sitting together at the end of the counter. One of them was Commodore Shattuck himself. The other was someone she didn't recognize: a small, thin man with a stiff brush of grizzled hair and a brown face, lined like a dried apple. He sat bolt upright on his stool, while the Commodore hunched over his hamburger and cup of coffee. They were deep in conversation, quite oblivious to everyone else. The Commodore said something that caused his friend to give a sudden, explosive bark. Charlotte blew out instead of drinking in, and spluttered, but the Commodore's face creased in a fierce smile, and she realized that the other man had been laughing. Commodore Shattuck clapped him genially on the back, said something else, and the man stood up as if he were coming to attention.

"And you found the key with no trouble, did you?" inquired the Commodore, raising his voice.

"Och aye. Richt whaur ye said."

"All they asked, Jimmy, is that you go easy with the furniture, it's valuable stuff, and have a care about fires."

The short man gave an indignant snort. "Yer no dealin' wi' a half-wit, ye ken! An' ye've promised we'll no hae the bobbies round oor ears for bein' there."

"*You* aren't dealing with a half-wit either," replied the Commodore dryly. "I've taken care of that."

"Richt then. I'm off."

Commodore Shattuck stood up, too, they shook hands—a brief, firm up-and-down—then the stranger left and the Commodore returned to his lunch.

Slowly Charlotte finished her Coke, twisting her stool back and forth as she meditated on the curious fragment of conversation she'd just overheard.

Chapter Eight

THE GARDEN CLUB WOMEN HAD FINISHED THEIR WORK OUTSIDE the library and gone; its grounds were neat and empty, waiting for spring to flood them. Inside the building business was brisk; the library offered free asylum from the dismal afternoon and many people were taking advantage of it.

Charlotte slid by the main desk unnoticed, returned her books and paid her fine to an aide in the children's room. She was just congratulating herself on her inconspicuousness when Mrs. Wilson spotted her, and escape was out of the question.

"Hello, Charlotte, I haven't seen you in a long time. Can I do anything special for you?"

"Just returning books," said Charlotte, adding, "Thanks."

"Let me know—I've got a couple of biographies you might like. That was a nice article in the paper last week about the Museum. Tell your father I'd be interested to know how he gets his publicity, we could use a little more for our programs. I don't think—"

Mercifully she was cut short just then by a mother doing her son's history report on Passamaquoddy Indians. "We can't use an encyclopedia," she informed Mrs. Wilson, "it has to be three *real* books."

The children's librarian sized her up expertly with only the barest shadow of irritation on her pleasant face. "You want the section over here, 970.1. I'll show you. Excuse me, Charlotte." As she led the woman off, Mrs. Wilson called over her shoulder, "Say hello to Max and Eliot for me, will you? They haven't been in for months and I miss them." Charlotte nodded.

Max and Eliot together had put in years of service as library pages and were fondly remembered by most of the staff, who always sent messages to them by Charlotte. That was true practically wherever she went in Concord; Max and Eliot, and Deb and her parents were widely known. For years it had been a source of pride to Charlotte that she should be associated with such an illustrious and well-liked family, but lately she felt traitorously resentful at being no more than a conductor of greetings—someone's sister or daughter, instead of an individual herself.

Sparing a wistful thought for the biographies she might have liked, Charlotte wandered back into the main library and smack into Miss Beaman, the head reference librarian, who looked at her blindly and said, "Excuse me," which meant she was in the midst of tracking down information for someone. When she wasn't, she tended to be quite brusque. In high school first Max, then Deb, then Eliot, had attempted time after time to stump Miss Beaman with obscure reference questions. They had a bet among them which had never been collected.

Collision with Miss Beaman jolted Charlotte back to consciousness; she paid attention to the people milling around her. Two in particular made her pause. They were standing by the bust of Louisa May Alcott, locked in a furious whispered discussion, and she noticed several things about them simultaneously: the taller of the two men was wearing a used-looking ski jacket, meant for someone with much shorter arms—a good two inches of red cuff showed below the sleeves; the smaller was the man Commodore Shattuck had been talking to in Woolworth's. And they both had foreign accents. Charlotte froze, as if playing Statues, and strained to hear what they said.

"Well, it ain't my fault, Cap'n, and I ain't takin' no blame f'r'it," the one in the parka said petulantly. "Tweren't me got the orders fouled up. I could've told you it'd happen, though."

"Bluddie lot o' incompetents, the pack o' ye! Damnation! If it wasna for Boutwell-Scott we'd no hae a brass farthing amang us. And whaur's oor gear gone tae, I ask ye? Minneapolis! Wha the de'il kens whaur Minneapolis is onyway? A braw wee paraffin stove and a' those bonnie tents, tae say nocht o' oor clothes."

"Gar, if I'd've known what a muddle this would be, I'd've resigned me commission sooner'n get involved, I can tell you." The man in the parka looked bleak. "Me new suit, gone to Minneapolis. Me mum'll fair skin me, she will."

"Whinnin' an' snivellin' and ye ca' yersel' regular navy, do ye, Leftenant! I dinna ken how I thoucht I wad mak' a troop o' soldiers out o' you lot. The Commodore'll skelp us single-handed. Wheesht!" He suddenly became aware of Charlotte.

"Gerroff," the Leftenant said to her rudely.

Charlotte opened her mouth to deliver a stinging retort, but all she managed was "Ouch!" for someone chose that precise moment to kick her hard in the left shin. Through a grimace, she saw a figure in a blue knitted cap disappear hastily into the reading room. She was outraged by what she recognized as a deliberate, unprovoked attack; the kick had been too well-placed to have been an accident. Indecisive for a moment, she hesitated, then set off after her assailant.

The air in the long book-lined room was thick with the pursuit of knowledge. It was not a place that welcomed frivolity, and Charlotte had never liked it much. It was too formidable and full of information she didn't know and didn't particularly want to. This afternoon the reading tables were occupied mainly by industrious college students, home for spring vacation and feverishly researching term papers. Books, papers, notebooks littered the tabletops like mounds of rubble thrown up on a construction site.

Methodically Charlotte inspected the room from end to end. No blue wool hat, but her eyes came to rest on an irritatingly familiar figure hunched over a huge book. Oliver Shattuck. She stared at him in vexation. Although he appeared deeply absorbed in his volume, he still had on his jacket and gloves, and she knew with absolute certainty that it was his foot that had dented her ankle.

She walked belligerently across to his table and sat down in an empty chair facing him. He didn't stir, but the girl beside Charlotte sighed and shifted her debris over. Charlotte ignored her. Oliver continued to read with absorption. Charlotte propped her chin on her hands and concentrated on him fiercely. The book open in front of him was Volume III of *The Oxford English Dictionary*. Charlotte settled her bottom and continued to stare.

At last, with great reluctance, as if he couldn't help himself even though he didn't want to do it, Oliver raised his head and looked at her. Wordlessly they struggled, eye to eye, locked in the weighty silence of the room, until Charlotte thought her head would burst with the effort and she had to blink. She saw a flash of triumph in Oliver's green eyes.

Reaching deliberately between the reading lamps, she pulled his blue knitted cap out from under the dictionary and dangled it in front of him. He snatched it back and stuffed it in his pocket, no expression on his face.

"Why?" demanded Charlotte in a furious undertone. "Why did you kick me out there? What have I ever done to you?"

"It was an accident," Oliver declared a little too loudly.

The girl beside Charlotte hissed.

"How'd you know it was me anyway?" he added.

"I know."

Several heads turned toward them in annoyance.

"No proof," said Oliver. "I'm busy. You're interrupting my work."

"Phoo!" said Charlotte and slammed the book shut, only just missing his fingers.

"Why'd you do that?" His eyes blazed like an angry cat's.

"Because. I want to know why you kicked me."

"You were in my way. You've lost my place." His thin face was drawn thinner with dislike.

Charlotte's mouth was a straight line.

"If you two want to fight, go somewhere else and do it properly, why don't you," suggested the girl next to Charlotte.

"This is a *public* library," returned Oliver coolly.

"This is a public *library*," retorted the girl. "You are creating a nuisance."

"She's creating the nuisance." He nodded at Charlotte. "I was reading until she came."

"People don't read dictionaries," stated Charlotte.

"Shows how much you know."

"Out!" exclaimed the girl. "Get out, get out, or I'll call the wrath of Beaman down on both of you and have your cards revoked!"

She meant it, Charlotte decided. It was time for retreat. But before she left she warned Oliver, "If you *ever* do anything to me again, you'll be sorry!"

He looked brazenly up at her. "Then stay out of my business," he replied cryptically.

"*Your* business? I wouldn't dream of getting into it. I wouldn't—" She stopped abruptly as something clicked in her mind. "You know those two men, don't you?"

"Which two men? Where? I don't know what you mean."

"Oh yes, you do. I heard one of them mention the Commodore and I only know of one Commodore. You didn't want me to talk to them, did you?"

The girl half-rose threateningly. "This conversation is not entirely without interest, but as it has nothing to do with the Industrial Revolution and the economy of northern England—"

Oliver slid down in his seat and looked immovable. Charlotte glared at him. "All right. I'll go. But I'll remember, and just you watch it, Oliver Shattuck." She felt that this was rather inadequate under the circumstances, but she was unable to think of anything else to say.

If it hadn't been for Oliver, she would have simply left the library and gone home. But his curious and objectionable behavior had fired Charlotte's determination. She knew she was right: he had some connection with the two strangers she had overheard and she made up her mind to find out what it was. The men were still there, huddled with one of the librarians who seemed to be drawing them a map. She kept nodding and pointing, then making new squiggles on the piece of paper that lay between the three of them.

Charlotte resolved to do some investigating. Deliberately she pulled up her parka collar and loitered in the front hall, examining an exotic collection of beaded flowers in the exhibit cases. They had been made over the course of seven years by the Misses Viola and Ophelia Wardlaw of Barrett's Bridge Road, she was informed by a white typed card. "Painstaking attention has been paid to botanical detail. All the specimens represent Concord flora . . ."

The two men were on the move. Out of the corner of her eye she saw them and shrank into her collar like a turtle, bending so close to the glass case her breath fogged it. All those microscopic beads! Thousands and thousands of them! How on earth would you pick them up, much less string them on wires . . .

'Noo a' we've tae do is find tithers. Scattered to kingdom come, I shouldna wonder. How am I tae rin a decent invasion wi' an army like this one? Leftenant!"

"Yessir?" The Leftenant's voice was heavy with foreboding.

"I gie ye three-quarters o' an hour tae find the rest and bring them back tae HQ. 'Tis an order. Now jump tae it!"

"Aw fegs!" whined the Leftenant. "It's me that gets the worst bits. Why do I always get the worst bits?"

"Cut yer blatherin' and buckle to," snapped the Captain. "I want ye a' present an' accounted for, or there'll be richt trouble, d'ye ken?"

The Leftenant raised a sigh that rustled the papers on the bulletin board and stalked out the front door.

"Ach, Sammy, Sammy, how the de'il did I get intae this?" muttered the Captain sadly. "Micht as weel send a horse for a ladder, as pull this lot intae shape."

He toggled himself into his greatcoat and followed the Leftenant out. And Charlotte followed him. And a tense figure followed her, pulling his blue knitted cap down around his ears.

In order to shadow the men properly, Charlotte was forced to leave her bike at the library and pursue them on foot. Although she carefully refrained from turning to look back, she knew she wasn't the last person in the little procession that made its way up Main Street. She imagined she could feel waves of animosity striking her from the rear and it gave her a perverse pleasure. A thin shower of snowflakes eddied around the afternoon. They skittered like talcum powder on the cold road and frosted the rough, raw earth.

Charlotte regretted having kept her parka on in the library; under it she was chilly and damp. She hugged herself and thought for a minute about being curled up on the sofa at home with a cup of cocoa beside her and a warm cat against her stomach. It was an appealing idea and if it weren't for Oliver Shattuck she might have turned it into fact, but he kept her moving forward.

There was no need to pretend she wasn't following the man ahead; he was too absorbed in his own thoughts to notice. In the middle of town both he and the Leftenant disappeared briefly into Gifford's Market. Charlotte studied the piles of fresh fruit in front of the store and allowed herself a glance over her shoulder. She encountered a look of pure hostility from Oliver who was lurking beneath the overhang of the old bank next door. If looks could kill, she and Oliver would certainly make the next Police Blotter in the *Concord Journal*.

The door swung open and the Leftenant stumbled onto the sidewalk as if he'd been given a good push from behind. "Awa' wi' ye!" cried the Captain, as a great warm draft of barbecued chicken smell exploded on the cold air. Charlotte sucked it in hungrily. The Leftenant gave her a suspicious squint and she forced her face blank and shifted up to peer into the Christian Science Reading Room. The Captain quick-marched past her with a brown paper bag clutched to his chest, muttering something unintelligible, and the Leftenant struck off across the street.

After a minute's indecision, Charlotte elected to follow the Captain. Wherever he was going, the "others" he had spoken of would also end up, and she saw merit in taking the most direct route instead of traipsing all over town first. That Oliver chose the Captain, too, clinched it.

Up through the empty square they went, one after the

other. In front of the Town House, the Captain stopped to reconnoiter and Charlotte slid behind the War Memorial, her heart thudding pleasantly. Oliver managed to disappear completely, but he was back again as soon as the Captain stepped off.

Although he didn't look like the usual overnight guest, Charlotte had thought the Captain might be heading for the Colonial Inn, but he walked right by it without slackening pace. For someone as short and slight as he, he made surprising speed. The gray afternoon was closing overhead. The ghostly sun had been totally exorcised, and although the snow didn't amount to anything, it kept spitting down the wind.

There were no people on the sidewalks along Monument Street, so Charlotte let herself slip back from the Captain a yard at a time. There was no danger of losing him: the street was broad and relatively straight. The quick walking made her steamy inside the layers of nylon and her nose was running; she had no idea who the man ahead of her was and where he was going, or how he'd react if he knew she was tailing him. The emptiness of this part of town impressed her—there were houses on both sides of the street, but no one out walking and she felt vaguely apprehensive. But there was Oliver, hard on her heels, glowering with ill-suppressed rage.

When he reached the entrance to the North Bridge Park, the Captain turned left into it and marched down the wide path between the regimental rows of trees. His boots thudded on the hard-packed dirt. Feeling even less sure of herself, Charlotte stuck with him, but kept close to the tree trunks. The park, too, was deserted except for the three of them, and it occurred to Charlotte for the first time that she was right in the middle and vulnerable from both sides. She hardly knew Oliver but had reason to find him unsympathetic, and she didn't know the Captain at all. She had no idea what either was capable of, and whoever the "others" were, they were bound to be along soon. The air under the trees was brooding and thick, ominous. Charlotte kept on, but it was becoming more and more of an effort.

At the river, the trees drew back against tumbled stone

walls to make an open semi-circle. In its center stood the monument which marked the battle at the Bridge in 1775: a tall granite column holding up the gray sky like a tent pole. Beyond it the ground sloped down to the cold, dark river where the timber bridge arched across it.

On the far side of the Bridge stood the bronze Minuteman, with his musket and plow. The sight of him reminded Charlotte of the man in Gurney's drugstore who had asked how to find the statue. With a shiver she glanced around; she was sure he was one of the Captain's "others"—perhaps somewhere nearby at this very moment. Although he hadn't seemed very sinister earlier, she didn't much want to meet him now. But there was no sign of him.

The Captain's steps rang hollow on the boards of the bridge; they slowed, then stopped. At the highest point he paused and gazed downstream toward the Buttrick House. Charlotte hung back at the edge of the trees. Something bright on the ground against the gray stones of the wall caught her eye. It was a wreath of red and white carnations with a blue rosette, and it rested against the flat stone memorial to the British soldiers who had been killed near the spot. Each Patriots' Day the grave was decorated; that wasn't unusual. The violent, revolutionary disagreement between England and America was history, the enemies had long since become friends again, though on different terms.

But the odd thing about this particular wreath was the gold lettering on the ribbon. It read TO THE MEMORY OF GEORGE III. Charlotte frowned curiously.

"Hey!" A loud whisper practically in her ear made her jump.

"What did you do that for?" she demanded angrily, turning on Oliver. Her hands clenched in fists inside her mittens.

"What do you think you're doing here?"

"Same as you," she responded shrewdly. Then trying for the upper hand, "I know you've been following me. I figured if I ignored you you'd go away. You have no right to follow me."

His eyes narrowed and she could see him thinking. "Why did you come here?"

"That's my business. I don't want to talk to you." She

turned her back on him, ready to skip out of his range if necessary, and discovered that the bridge was empty. "Rats!" she exclaimed, and without stopping to think whether she ought to or not, she ran lightly across it herself.

Oliver was not about to let her get away, however. She heard him right behind her.

The Captain came into sight again beyond the statue, striding purposefully up the diagonal track toward the mansion. Charlotte slowed to allow him plenty of room: she had no desire to catch up with him.

"Look, why don't you go home?" said Oliver impatiently.

"Why don't you?"

"This is the way home for me."

"Tell me another one!" Charlotte was contemptuous.

"That's my house." Oliver pointed toward the Commodore's roof.

"I know that, but this isn't exactly on the way, is it?"

"More on mine than yours."

"I never said I was going home, though, did I?"

They reached the steps of the garden terraces. "Look," began Oliver, a hint of desperation breaking his voice, "it's getting late and dark and cold, so let's *both* go home." He took two steps up at once and blocked Charlotte's path.

"I don't want to," she replied stubbornly. "Get out of my way."

"Look—" said Oliver again. He was peculiarly agitated.

"I'll go around you if I have to."

He scowled at her, but allowed her to push past. The Captain was a dark, rapidly moving shadow just rounding the far end of the house. Wind blew handfuls of snow across the derelict garden like clouds of steam. The matted grass was turning faintly white and flakes caught in the tangled bushes. There were no lights in the house; it was a cold, dead bulk brooding over the river.

Only her deep-rooted stubbornness drove Charlotte along the patio past the vacant french windows and into the remnants of the orchard, beneath contorted apple trees. Once she looked over her shoulder and was disconcerted to find that Oliver had disappeared. It seemed highly unlikely that he had given up; most probably he was sneaking along somewhere behind her, and that made her even more uneasy. She found herself dodging from tree to tree although she was in little danger of being seen: the Captain was far ahead.

He left the park and crossed the road, then turned up the driveway to the Coolidges' house. There was nothing furtive or hesitant in his movements; he acted as if he owned the place.

The Coolidges, who actually did own it, were all in Jamaica, lying on a beach under straw hats and getting brown, Charlotte knew. The house was closed and dark. Mrs. Coolidge's "ANTIQUES" sign whined fretfully on its iron hinges, and below it the little board that said "Closed" hung precariously by one hook.

Paying no attention to the house, the Captain went past it and disappeared behind the big yellow barn. Cautiously Charlotte crept after him. It was a neat, well-cared for, old-fashioned barn, no longer used for anything as untidy as hay or horses or tractors. Mrs. Coolidge had turned two box stalls into an office and kept her antiques in the rest of the space. Charlotte's mother had helped her with the renovation.

When she reached the back corner, Charlotte paused and flattened herself against the clapboard wall, then with great care leaned sideways to peer around. There was no one there. Behind the barn the ground sloped sharply down to an uninhabited duck pond, and beyond it a long field stretched out to meet an uneven rim of evergreens. The view was as still as a landscape painting. Even if he'd run like a sprinter, the Captain couldn't have crossed the wide expanse in so short a time. Charlotte felt as if she'd fallen into a bad dream in which she was the only living thing. Baffled and suspicious, she stood in the silent afternoon. Unless he'd circled the barn and retraced his steps because he knew he was being followed, she didn't see where he could have gone. Unless . . .

She sidled along the wall of the barn to its narrow back door. Leading up to it was a steep concrete ramp which she climbed stealthily, then holding her breath, she inched up to peer in the tiny window set in the door. It was muffled with cobwebs and insect husks, and she discovered to her annoyance she couldn't see a thing through it. Emboldened by her irritation, she put a mittened hand on the doorknob and discovered that it turned; she felt the latch click back—it was unlocked. Her heart gave a lurch. There was a sudden glimmer of light beyond the murky glass. The light flared as a door opened, cutting through the darkness like scissors cutting through black felt. It was the door to Mrs. Coolidge's office, Charlotte knew. She'd been in the barn several times with her mother when they were working out the plans for it.

So the Captain was prowling around inside the barn; he'd come here knowing he could get in, in fact. He didn't strike Charlotte as a thief, but what other reason could he have for being there when the Coolidges were away? And what—she chewed her hair in sudden consternation—should she do about it? Unless she hiked back to the middle of town there was no one she could tell. She glanced down at the lock, but there were no scratches on the paint; it did not look as if it had been forced open. Could it possibly be that whoever the Captain was he had a key and was supposed to go in and out when he chose? In which case she would look pretty silly if she told the police and they came up here, not that she could actually imagine herself going to the police. But she could go to the DPW and find Eliot—he'd know what to do. At the thought of him, relief bubbled warm inside her. He was the solution.

Feeling very much better, Charlotte jumped off the ramp and jogged to the corner of the barn, then froze. Relief turned to dismay as she saw two men walking briskly down the driveway toward her. She ducked back out of sight, hoping they hadn't seen her. Frantically she looked for a place to hide, found none, then fled to the far side of the barn and waited, heart pounding, for whatever happened next.

She had been too startled to notice anything about either of the men except that they were coming straight at her, but she reckoned they must be some, or all, of the Captain's "others." As they reached the barn end and approached the door she could hear what they were saying.

" . . . can't honestly call it much of an improvement, old

chap. You are not a walking advertisement for Saville Row—you look more like second-rate Salvation Army."

"Aw, mash that!" said a voice Charlotte recognized.

"I don't see why you're feeling so bloody-minded, Tate. We're all in the same hole together, you know. Might as well buck up and make the best of it, I should think. Do you suppose anyone else is here yet? Hullo, there's a light on. Good, I'm parched, let's hope the kettle's on. Remember the password, Beaky?"

"Nark it, wullee? I'm fair zneesy."

Charlotte was positive. The man called Beaky was the one who'd fallen over her bicycle the night before. She didn't recognize the other, though he was English.

"I'm cold too, old boy, but we've got to play the old man's game, now that he's brought us here. It's his show."

Screwing up her courage, Charlotte slid to the corner. One of them knocked resoundingly on the door: thump-thump, pause, thump-thump. She had to look. *Both* men were familiar. She was right about Beaky, but the other one she had last seen walking in circles across from the Paige house, waiting for Deb. The pieces were coming together.

A voice from inside the barn answered the knocks, two muffled to be intelligible from where she stood. But Deb's admirer replied, "To the King across the water!" in a loud, cheerful voice.

The door opened, she could hear it creak, and two pairs of boots scraped on the barn's wooden floorboards. The door clicked shut behind them.

Questions buzzed in Charlotte's head like a swarm of angry bees. What were they doing there? Who were they? How long had they been using the barn? What did Oliver know about it? She shifted her weight from foot to foot and wondered what she ought to do. She wasn't particularly brave—in fact, she wasn't brave at all. Independent, yes, and that often made people *think* she was brave; they were the people she didn't know well enough to let them see what scared her. Eliot knew of course, and her mother, but they were both family and she was glad they did.

Now she stood debating. Half of her wanted to race off at

once in search of Eliot. That half told her reasonably that this was none of her business and she oughtn't to get involved. She should clear out before anyone saw her.

The other half, however, was dying of curiosity thinly disguised as virtue. It argued that something obviously suspicious was going on in the Coolidges' barn. She had discovered it, and it was her duty to find out what it was and report it to the proper authorities. All the peculiar characters in Concord seemed to be congregating on this spot.

That being true, her good sense countered, it would seem to be smart to leave them to it and get herself home safely. Let someone else—older and more capable—handle the problem if there was one.

And suppose something dreadful happened like the theft of Mrs. Coolidge's antiques or a fire in the barn? Wouldn't she feel guilty knowing she might have prevented it?

Prevented it how? By bursting in and telling all the men to leave because they were trespassing? They wouldn't listen to a twelve-year-old girl.

Well, she could go home and call the police from there and they could investigate.

Having backed herself against a wall of common sense, Charlotte didn't know how to escape. It was the logical thing to do: put the whole matter squarely in the hands of adults who would know exactly how to handle it. She had heard her mother suggest the same solution to Deb this noon.

What was the point in standing here turning blue with cold? She knew she'd never have nerve enough to go through that little back door by herself, into the dark with three strange men. The real question was whether or not she would tell anyone else about them. It was a very long way back to the library where she'd left her bike and she was tired. The afternoon didn't seem to have had much point.

As she passed the door, she glanced at it apprehensively as if it might suddenly be flung open, but it wasn't. It looked quite ordinary.

She never got round the barn, however. Just as she reached the corner this time, someone her own size came hurtling the other way at tremendous speed. The person—Oliver, of course—was moving fast enough to knock Charlotte clean off her feet onto the hard ground. She lost her wind. His legs tangled painfully in hers and, caught together, they plunged down the steep, short bank into the mucky shallows of the duck pond.

Gasping for breath and at the shock of the cold water into which she'd fallen, Charlotte, for one terrifying minute, lost the power to move. She felt the hostile ooze seeping into her boots, soaking through her pants, so cold it burned her skin, but she couldn't get herself out of it. Then she began to function again, air filled her squeezed lungs, and with it came outrage and fury. She rose, showering mud and water, and staggered to the bank.

"WHAT ARE YOU DOING?" she half-croaked, half-yelled at Oliver. "*Look* at me! Just look!"

Oliver, who had landed underneath her, was coated with semi-frozen black muck to the chest and had lost his hat. Charlotte would have relished his condition if her own hadn't been so awful. The wind bit viciously through her wet pants, making her legs sting.

"I can't believe it!" she went on loudly. "I have never done anything to you, Oliver Shattuck, and twice in one day you've attacked me. *Why?*"

Oliver struggled upright and squelched toward her making threatening gestures with his dripping arms. Charlotte ducked backward.

"You stay away from me. Wait'll my mother sees this. She'll be so mad—"

"Shut up!" cried Oliver in a hoarse whisper. "Just shut up, will you?"

"You can't talk to me—"

"Lissssen," he hissed through chattering teeth.

She realized he was in earnest and his urgency made her stop. With a shiver, not entirely due to cold, she heard other voices. The wind drove a flurry of words at them, mixed with snowflakes. More of the "others." Her eyes met Oliver's; they stared at each other for a tense second, then in unspoken agreement, they dropped to the ground and flattened themselves. With any luck the sharp incline would hide them from whoever was approaching.

The voices got louder, shoes scraped concrete and there were four more thumps on the door. The rough grass under Charlotte's cheek was unpleasantly stiff. Her feet were beginning to hurt. Beside her, Oliver lay completely still as if he'd frozen solid. Serve him right if he did.

"To the King across the water!" said several men together. A single voice replied crossly, "Pipe down, will you? D'you want to tell the town we're here?" The door opened and closed again.

"All right," said Charlotte after another minute, sitting up. "They've gone. Now what? I'm frozen to the bone because of you and I can't possibly walk home this way. What're you going to do about it?" She felt dreadfully close to tears and was furious with herself. She could imagine nothing worse than weeping in front of Oliver Shattuck.

"I told you not to mess with other people's business," retorted Oliver. "Anyway, I'm much wetter than you are."

"You can't be. I suppose you're going to say I was in your way again."

"You were. If you hadn't been there neither of us would be wet."

"It is not my fault!" she cried indignantly. "You never looked. How was I supposed to know you were going to come barreling around that corner without looking? I'm not a mind reader."

Oliver got slowly to his feet. "Well, I'm going home. And if you have any sense, you'll go home, too, instead of standing around in those wet clothes."

"It's miles to my house."

"That's not my fault."

Charlotte stood up quickly and wished she hadn't. Her feet screamed in protest and she almost fell over. Her pants were hard and crackly; they were beginning to freeze on her. "The least you can do after knocking me into the pond is take me back to your house and let me dry off," she declared as firmly as she could. The idea of going inside Commodore Shattuck's house, possibly even meeting the Commodore himself, filled her with dismay, but she couldn't think of an alternative. She knew she couldn't walk far as she was.

Oliver glared at her. "I don't want you to come home with me," he said bluntly. "I don't see why I should have to let you. You have been a pain in the neck all afternoon—I just want you to leave me alone."

"Well, I won't. Not until I'm dry again. You wait until my family hears about this." Then she added for good measure, "*And* the Commodore." Surprisingly, that was what seemed to work.

"You leave as soon as you're dry," growled Oliver. "And don't ever come near me again, you hear?"

"Don't worry, I won't!"

Chapter Nine

PAINFULLY THEY HOBBLED DOWN THE COOLIDGES' DRIVEWAY
wet, cold, and utterly miserable. At each step Charlotte could
hardly bear to put her weight down; her toes felt as if they
might simply break off if she bent them, and her mittens, she
discovered, were thick with mud. She would have liked to
wring Oliver Shattuck's scrawny neck if she had had the
strength to, but she had all she could do to keep moving.

It seemed like miles down to Monument Street, before the
Commodore's house came into sight. As they approached it,
Charlotte fixed her eyes on the brass name plate screwed to
the black front door, like a marathoner struggling toward the
wire. Someone had polished the metal until it was so shiny
the letters were hard to make out.

"We can't go in that way," said Oliver. "We can't track
mud all through the house."

"But—" protested Charlotte feebly.

"Either you do what I tell you, or you go home."

Passionate hatred lent Charlotte the energy to follow Oliver
down a flight of narrow brick steps and across the terrace
that spread between the house and the river. The kitchen door
was hidden behind a huge blue spruce.

It was unlocked. She was flooded with thankfulness as
Oliver opened it and practically trod on his heels to get inside.
Warm, dry air touched her tight cheeks like a blessing, but
made no immediate impression on the rest of her. She wanted

to collapse there, just inside the door, in a limp, boneless heap, close her eyes and forget everything until she'd dried out and warmed through again. Perhaps it was already too late; her feet were unfeeling lumps of ice. She searched her mind for scraps of information about frostbite.

"You're dropping mud all over the floor," said Oliver crossly.

"What do you expect me to do? So are you, if you want to know." With frozen, awkward fingers she unzipped her parka. The bottom edge was sodden, but underneath it most of her sweater and jersey were dry.

"It's my floor."

"No, it's not. It's Commodore Shattuck's. I've got to sit down." Her feet were starting to feel very queer.

Oliver regarded her with dislike. "Sit on this then." He pushed a vinyl-covered kitchen chair at her. "You can't hurt it. And keep your feet on this." He thrust a piece of newspaper under her boots. "Stay there," he ordered as if he were speaking to a dog.

"Where are you going?"

"Upstairs to get clean."

"What about me?" she wailed indignantly. She might have saved her breath: he was gone. She was abandoned on a plastic-and-newspaper island in the middle of Commodore Shattuck's unfamiliar kitchen. Abruptly the room around her blurred. She blinked hard, but she wasn't quick enough to stop two large wet tears from dribbling down her left cheek. Her pants were beginning to thaw and that was, unbelievably, even worse than having them frozen. Her skin felt raw and burned; the wet denim was sandpaper against her legs, and her feet ached and ached.

The kitchen went efficiently about its kitchen business, ignoring the sodden object in the middle of the floor. The refrigerator purred, the faucet dripped gently, the red-faced electric clock hummed, and on the stove a red enamel kettle whispered steam. An awful desolation overtook Charlotte, welling up from her boots. Oh, how she despised Oliver Shattuck!

How long she sat there by herself, she had no idea. The

clock meant nothing to her except a blob of color on the white wall. She stared and stared at it, but her numbed brain refused to make sense of the numbers.

She registered nothing except misery until a gruff voice made her jump violently. She turned to stare with wide eyes at the stocky figure in the kitchen doorway,

"Well, well, well, and what's this?" he demanded in a voice that years of use had worn the smoothness from.

"I-I—" she stuttered, unable to control the words in her throat.

"Gracious, you're remarkably wet, aren't you? That won't do! No place for you sitting there, no indeed." Was he going to throw her out? "You must come in by the fire at once! How on earth did you get in here? No, don't tell me now. What a perfectly wretched state you're in. All right, on your feet." She winced as she obeyed. "That's it, that's it. Down the hall and to your right." Like a sleepwalker, she let him guide her. "This wouldn't have anything to do with my great-nephew by any chance? Ahm, I thought as much— don't say a word. You don't need to. Forget the floor, it'll mop up. Can't have you falling ill of pneumonia in my kitchen!"

All the while he talked, he maneuvered her along the narrow, angled hall, past a staircase, and into a snug sitting room. There was a cheerful, domesticated little fire crackling softly to itself in a brick fireplace as it polished the room with an amber glow. The Commodore—for of course it was he— piloted her across the room to a chair by the hearth.

"Sit still while I relieve you of those disgusting boots. That's the ticket!" He grunted with each pull and a lot of mud fell out on the carpet. Charlotte wished he could take her feet off with the wet boots and stand them somewhere faraway to dry. They hurt dreadfully by this time.

Vaguely she was aware of other sounds in the room—an odd sort of twittering from just outside her narrow field of vision. She concentrated on it and gradually picked out two new voices.

"—but so *wet*, Samuel! She can't possibly stay in those trousers."

"Certainly not! Has she fallen in the river, do you think?"

"Don't know. Couldn't say. Just found her sitting in the middle of m'kitchen looking like something left by the flood. Most irregular."

"But how do you suppose she got here? Do you know her?"

"That doesn't matter, Vi. It's crucial that she not sit around in those trousers any longer. What have you got that she could wear, Samuel? You must have a dressing gown? There now, dear, you just sit still while we fuss. You'll feel better soon."

A hand patted her lightly on the shoulder, a thin, freckled old hand. Charlotte looked into a narrow, wrinkled face framed by crisp gray hair. A pair of violet eyes regarded her brightly.

"I'm sorry about the chair," she managed to say, glad to find her voice coming back. "I only came because I couldn't walk all the way home and it was Oliver's fault we got wet, and he said not to go in the front door."

"Yes!" exclaimed the Commodore. "Oliver. Exactly. He got wet too, did he? And left you to drip by yourself in the kitchen?"

"Oh, Samuel, will you stop ranting and get the child something dry to put on?" said the old woman impatiently.

"Dressing gown, you said, Ophelia. That do?" he asked Charlotte, and before she could answer he turned and strode out of the room and up the stairs.

"There now! Things'll be better when you're dry again, dear. What an unpleasant accident."

"But you might have drowned!" The room came into clear focus and Charlotte saw a second old woman, this one plump, round-faced, and comforting. She had silver hair done round her head in a braid. "Dear me, what an *awful* thing, Ophelia! Perhaps we ought to telephone the police?"

"Why on earth should we telephone the police now, Vi? Don't be silly. She's quite safe and will be good as new very soon. There's *no* sense in upsetting anyone at this stage. The best thing you can do, dear, is go fix her a big cup of your special Russian tea. I'm sure Samuel still has some. And you might fix Oliver one as well. He'll be down soon, I expect."

"What a marvelous idea! Just the thing to ward off chills. I shall make enough for all of us. I feel as if I've had a chill myself."

The room went suddenly still except for the small hiss and snap of the fire. Charlotte felt very much as she imagined Alice must have when she plunged down the rabbit hole; she could never have forecast this afternoon. The concentrated heat drew steam out of her jeans that smelled remarkably like the gym locker room at school: damp clothes and used socks. Her mistreated body was getting over the shock it had been given and was starting to complain; Charlotte was reminded vividly of the summer day years ago when she had trod unsuspectingly on a wasps' nest in her bare feet. But the haze behind her eyes had evaporated and she realized suddenly that the haze in front of them was on her glasses. She remedied that by taking them off and polishing them on a dry patch of sweater.

When she put them on again she saw that the thinner of the two women—Ophelia, she'd been called—was sitting motionless on a very small part of the sofa opposite her, her pale eyes steady on Charlotte. "You feel better," she observed in her calm, dry voice.

"Um, yes." Charlotte was a little disconcerted to find herself under such scrutiny, but the woman's expression was kind.

"You picked a very cold day to get wet," said Ophelia.

"I didn't pick it, Oliver did."

Ophelia nodded. "He can be rather vigorous."

That was hardly a word Charlotte would have used to describe Oliver, but for once prudence prevented her from saying so. Instead she darted quick, curious glances around the room, trying to hide her interest.

"It would be nice if you became friends," continued Ophelia conversationally. "He hasn't really gotten to know anyone in Concord yet, Samuel tells us. Such a pity for a boy that age to spend so much time alone. He's rather difficult at first knowing, but . . ."

Charlotte allowed her attention to wander while the old woman talked. The room was comfortably provided with dark, heavy furniture of the kind that welcomes you as you sink into it and accommodates itself obligingly to your shape. There were a lot of bright crewel-embroidered pillows scattered about and a rainbow afghan tossed over one chair. On the walls shelves climbed to the ceiling like ladders, filled with books and a variety of other objects: beer mugs, mineral specimens, pieces of pottery, odd bottles, and other things Charlotte couldn't identify from where she sat. Wherever there weren't shelves there were paintings of various sizes in assorted frames which looked as if they'd all been painted by the same artist. The colors in them were very bright and clear: blue skies, green trees and grass, flowers spattered about. Houses were simply blocks of yellow, red, or white wearing black witches' hats for roofs. Charlotte wished she could go stand close to them and look, but when she shifted a little on her upholstered chair she noticed the edge of an ugly damp spot and decided she'd better sit tight at least until the Commodore returned.

He did so almost at once, stumping into the room with a red, white, and black plaid bathrobe over one arm and a pair of furry slippers under the other. "Here you are then. Peel off that wet gear and we'll hang it to dry. We'll have you shipshape."

Charlotte hesitated, overcome by modesty but not knowing how to say so.

But, "Viola's in the kitchen brewing her special tea for us, Samuel," Ophelia told him briskly. "Why don't you go along and see what she needs?"

"What? Hmmph. I thought I'd take the—"

"Or find your great-nephew." She took the things from him and gave him a firm little push toward the door.

"Oh," said the Commodore. "Yes, I see. Back in a tick."

When he'd gone again, the woman turned to Charlotte. "Now, dear, why don't you tell me who you are while you change? I'm Ophelia Wardlaw and that is my sister, Viola, out in the kitchen. I do think if we're to have tea together it would be nice to know one another's names, don't you?"

"Charlotte Paige," said Charlotte obediently, stepping out of her soggy jeans. Ophelia had everyone under control.

"Paige. Yes, I thought your face was familiar. I know your father, dear. He's doing a fine job with the museum, no matter what Ella Prescott thinks. Viola and I are just delighted with him. Not stuffy and old-fashioned like Fuzzy Stubbs. I like Gordon's approach."

The dressing gown was the right length for Charlotte, but she could have wrapped it twice around herself. The slippers were deliciously soft and warm. Ophelia matter-of-factly brushed the mud off the chair with the Commodore's hearth broom. The damp spot would dry. Charlotte's spirits were on the upswing.

"Why don't you sit there on the sofa, next to the fire, dear, and I'll go hang these up."

No sooner had Charlotte settled on the brown velveteen sofa than Commodore Shattuck reappeared, driving before him a glowering, damp-haired, clean-faced Oliver. He'd managed to change and obliterate all traces of the Coolidges' duck pond; he was neat and carefully tucked in around the edges.

"Hello," said Charlotte innocently.

Oliver muttered a greeting without looking at her.

"If you would like to use the bath," said the Commodore, "it's at the top of the stairs. I've left the light on and a clean towel. Don't be long, I hear sounds of progress in the kitchen."

The stairs were carpeted in faded blue with a track worn down the middle from hundreds of trips up and down. More paintings stepped up the wall to the second floor. Charlotte could see the detail in them: little stick figures in dresses, pants, and hats, gardens, dogs, and birds of the simplest kind. With delight, she recognized a painting of the First Parish Church, its graceful white steeple and moon-shaped clock unmistakable. A congregation of little sticks was pouring out of it, down the broad steps into perpetual sunshine. Blimplike fair weather clouds stood in the blue sky. The trees were scalloped lollipops of green, the tiny cars looked like matchboxes on wheels. In the next picture, sticks in long striped skirts sat about on daisy-tufted grass in front of the Alcott House under more lollipops—these had red spots on them: apples. Charlotte was enchanted.

But just then Ophelia and Viola bustled through the hall, Ophelia carrying an enormous tray on which Charlotte could see among the cups and saucers, plates of little sandwiches, slices of pound cake, and frosted cookies. Viola carried a teapot under a knitted cosy.

This vision of tea dislodged her from the paintings and she flapped hastily upstairs to wash her hands and face.

When she returned to the sitting room, everyone paused to look at her—three smiles, one scowl—and she experienced a painful moment of self-consciousness. Then Viola said, "Do come sit next to me, Charlotte," and patted the sofa with a quick, plump hand. "Falling in the water must have made you dreadfully hungry. All that fresh air and exercise."

Ophelia poured a cup of amber-colored tea for her. There was no sugar bowl on the tray, so Charlotte steeled herself against the bitter taste, but was pleasantly surprised: the liquid was already sweet, full of orange and cloves.

"Well," said the Commodore at length, beetling at Charlotte and Oliver in turn. "This is an unexpected pleasure."

She looked suspiciously for sarcasm in his expression, but found instead a fierce little smile. Years and years of living had sculptured his face: grooved and pouched it, and crazed it with tiny wrinkles like the glaze on an old pot. It was the bushy unkempt eyebrows that made him appear so formidable. Below them, his eyes gleamed, shrewd and friendly, from the depths of their slits, and his mouth had a humorous twist. On close inspection, she decided he looked neither sinister, cruel, nor insane; aggressive perhaps, but not dangerous.

"I didn't mean to bring her," said Oliver sulkily, "but she insisted on coming."

"You could hardly have left her in that state, Oliver," reproved Ophelia firmly. "It would not have been the least bit gallant."

Cradling his teacup, with his head sunk forward and his shoulders rounded, Oliver did not look gallant. "I told her to mind her own business long ago," he said. "I warned her— she can't say I didn't."

"Hmm," Commodore Shattuck said. "Where did you, shall

I say, run into one another?"

"He ran into *me*," put in Charlotte before Oliver could reply.

"I thought she'd gone home."

"I thought *he'd* gone home."

"That doesn't answer my question."

"Behind Coolidges' barn," said Charlotte, taking another piece of pound cake. It was extremely good—moist and rich with butter. "He knocked me into the duck pond."

"Oh." Viola sounded disappointed. "Nowhere near as exciting as falling into the river!"

"Just as effective, however," said Ophelia dryly.

"And what were you doing behind Coolidges' barn?" asked the Commodore conversationally.

Charlotte saw Oliver give his great-uncle an anguished look. "*You* know," he said.

The Commodore placed the tips of his stubby fingers together and blew into them thoughtfully.

"*I* don't!" exclaimed Charlotte. "Why were you following those two men? Who are they?" She turned to the Commodore. "I saw you in Woolworth's with—"

His eyebrows lifted and he coughed. "Perhaps you do need some explanation."

"I don't see why," protested his great-nephew. "She doesn't have to know anything. Tell her to go home and leave us alone."

Commodore Shattuck sighed. "It's a little late for that, m'boy. It might be prudent to find out how much Charlotte already knows."

"I don't see why," said Oliver again. "It's nothing to do with her."

"There's something very queer going on around here," Charlotte said. "I know there is, and I'm going to find out what it is whether you tell me or not, Oliver Shattuck."

"There, do you see?"

Neither Ophelia nor Viola Wardlaw had spoken a word for several minutes; they sat sipping their tea and listening with interest.

"Suppose you tell us what you mean by 'queer'," said the Commodore.

"Only if you'll tell me what's happening."

"Don't," said Oliver.

His great-uncle ignored him and nodded. "Go ahead."

"For one thing, Concord's full of foreigners. They're all over the place—I've seen them at the Bridge and in Gurney's and at the dry cleaner's *and*"—she glared at Oliver—"in the library."

"But certainly that's not peculiar," observed Viola.

"Some of them have got uniforms," continued Charlotte. "British uniforms. But no one official has heard of them. My brother Eliot's a Minuteman and he doesn't know anything about a company of British soldiers."

"So?" said Oliver. The Commodore silenced him with a look.

"And they seem to have taken over the Coolidges' barn," finished Charlotte. "I don't think, whoever they are, they're supposed to be in there, with the Coolidges away. I was going to go to the police until Oliver knocked me into the pond."

"Police, hey," said the Commodore. "Oh no, I don't think so, Charlotte. It's not really a matter for the police. But you seem to be an intelligent, observant young woman, and there are only the two of us, Oliver. Had you thought we might need reinforcements?"

"No!" cried Oliver passionately. "You said we could do it ourselves, just us."

"Yes, I did. But I didn't foresee the present complications. I might add that here is a very able ally and it is pigheaded to ignore Providence."

"I don't like to interfere in a family discussion," said Ophelia, "but I feel I really must."

"She always interrupts," Viola put in.

"So do you." Ophelia quashed her gently but firmly. "It seems to me that whatever is afoot"—she gave the Commodore a look that was almost a smile—"you'd do well to have a woman on your side. She would add a valuable point of view and many useful skills to your campaign."

"Indeed," Viola agreed. They nodded to one another. "Besides, she's been baptized. In a manner of speaking."

"True," said the Commodore.

"Wait a minute," said Charlotte. "You haven't even asked

me if I want anything to do with you." She was tired of being talked about as "she." "I just wanted to know what was going on, I didn't say I wanted to join in."

"A good point," remarked Ophelia.

"I don't know that I want to associate with *him*."

"That's mutual." Oliver thrust out his chin belligerently.

"Children," reproved Ophelia. "Don't bicker."

"The problem is t us," began the Commodore. "We have good reason to oelieve that our Patriots' Day ceremonies this year are to be hampered by a British offensive. No bloodshed—I doubt Jimmy will run to violence—but serious nonetheless. I've expected it for several years now; thank God he didn't pick the Bicentennial!"

"Offensive?" Charlotte seized the word. "Offensive? Do you mean *war*?"

"Oh war's putting it a bit strong. Sabotage, perhaps. Skirmish, maybe. Incident, even. Whatever it is, however, we can't ignore it: it's bound to be disruptive, and Jimmy's feelings would be dreadfully hurt if we did."

"How do you know about this?"

The Commodore drew his eyebrows together. "I have reliable contacts."

"Are you making this up?" she asked suspiciously. It hardly sounded possible. "Are we the only ones who know about it?"

"It wasn't even you before," said Oliver bitterly. "If you don't believe it, why don't you go home?"

Stories of the Mad Commodore danced across her memory. His explanation was so improbable. Yet she'd seen the strangers herself and guessed that something out of the ordinary was happening. "I don't know that I want any part of this," she said after a bit.

"Good." Oliver was genuinely relieved.

"But I haven't decided. Who's this Jimmy?" she asked the Commodore.

"Captain James A. McPherson. An officer of mine during the war. He served on my ship. The point is that it's entirely up to you whether you join us or no—we do not conscript. However, I hardly need remind Oliver that I am in command."

Oliver looked glum but didn't argue.

Ophelia set down her cup and saucer and stood up. "Fascinating as this discussion is, and pleasant as the afternoon has been, I'm afraid, Samuel, that Viola and I must start home before it gets any darker. Viola really ought not to be on the roads after dusk, no matter what she says. She is quite a risk."

"Nonsense! My eyes are as good as they've always been. You are jealous because they've taken your license away and you're not allowed to drive," replied Viola pettishly.

"Have it your way." Ophelia snuffed the argument like a candleflame.

"But," the Commodore said, heaving himself to his feet, "before you go, you really must come up and see the College. Now that I've got it installed properly it looks grand."

"That would be very nice, Samuel," agreed Ophelia.

"I did enjoy working on those buildings," put in Viola happily. "Such a fine institution, and I do so love doing red brick."

"I'm looking forward to Salem, myself. It's been such a long time since we did waterfront," Ophelia remarked. "And we've found four more of Father's ship models we can use."

Mystified, Charlotte listened to this conversation. She had no idea what they were talking about. But the Commodore looked round expectantly. "Come on, come on! Don't sit like lumps, the two of you. Everyone upstairs to admire. Bring your tea along if you haven't finished."

"What about my clothes?" ventured Charlotte.

"Clothes? Oh, yes. You can get them on the way down."

So, clad in the Commodore's voluminous dressing gown and slippers, teacup in hand, Charlotte followed the others out of the sitting room and up the stairs. Oliver's expression was mutinous but resigned.

From the second floor, the Commodore led the way up a narrow, steep staircase; to the attic, Charlotte thought, faintly alarmed. What she'd seen of the house so far had looked comfortable and ordinary, but there were those stories about lights in the Commodore's attic late at night.

She climbed the stairs apprehensively, but although the attic was like none other in her experience, she found there was nothing in it to fear. The top floor of the house was one long room, full of gray afternoon light which fell like water through great dormers on either side of the rooftree and windows in each gable. There was none of the usual attic clutter in it of trunks and boxes, old chairs, outgrown toys, dead flies and cobwebs, electric fans, boxes of dusty encyclopedias.

Instead, most of the floor was carpeted with a sort of three-dimensional scale map: clusters of tiny houses, papier maché hills, painted fields and rivers, twig forests, and sandpaper roads. It was like the model village for Max's old train set, without the train and ten times as vast. It was truly a wonder. Across the countryside and among the villages ran a network of narrow paths which full-scale people could walk on without squashing anything.

Only the far side of the attic, under the windows that faced the river, was undeveloped. An island of bare floor had been set aside there for two easels, stacks of stretched canvases, and an old kitchen cabinet covered with paints, rags, and jam jars of paint brushes. The paraphernalia was so familiar to Charlotte she didn't give it a second glance; Deb's studio held the same stuff.

But the models—! Commodore Shattuck and the Wardlaw sisters had taken one of the paths that wandered toward the far side of the attic. Ophelia and Viola pointed and commented knowingly to one another. Gradually Charlotte became aware that Oliver was watching her. She gazed incredulously around the room again, then met his eyes. "Is this yours?" she asked with a hint of awe.

He gave his head an unwilling shake.

"You mean it's *his*?" But she'd known at once it must be. It was far too well established; there were years of work spread before her.

Oliver continued to watch her, as if waiting for her to make a derisive remark about great-uncles who played with toy towns.

"It's—it's"—Charlotte groped—"incredible!" she finished inadequately. It explained the lights at night in a way no one would ever guess. "Why? Why has he done it?"

"Why not? It's his attic, he can do what he likes with it."

"Well, yes, but—" The longer she looked, the more familiar the pattern on the floor seemed; she ought to recognize it. The houses were not scattered at random, the hills and rivers had been fitted together according to some plan. At the end of the room, Ophelia Wardlaw stood with her black boots at the edge of an ocean: a wide expanse of green-blue painted floor bordered with a white sand beach and a jigsaw of docks and tiny warehouses. There were even several sailing ships in the "water."

"Come over this way," called the Commodore, "so you can see Harvard College."

"Don't step on anything," warned Oliver *sotto voce.*

"Of course not." Charlotte was annoyed that he though she might. She stepped forward and the pattern clicked in her mind. She realized that what she was looking at was a model of Middlesex County, Massachusetts, not as it was today, but as it must have been hundreds of years earlier. The stairs came up beside Lexington; she and Oliver were walking east into Boston. Behind lay Bedford, Lincoln, Concord, Sudbury. Max had made lots of models, but nothing like this, with so many tiny parts that fitted together to make an entire countryside, complete with real stone walls, trees of twig and dried moss, bushes made of green-painted sponge, wire-framed hills. Charlotte's hands itched to touch and explore.

As she inched slowly toward the Commodore, she noticed gaps here and there: bits of floor still empty. The model was not yet complete and that fact gave her a strange feeling of excitement. "It's not done," she murmured to herself.

Commodore Shattuck had sharp ears. "Done? Good gracious no! Lots of work left. It'll keep me going for years."

"Us," corrected Ophelia gently. "We all work on it."

A light dawned. "You did the bead flowers in the library!" exclaimed Charlotte.

Viola turned to her in delight. "Oh, you've *seen* them! I'm so glad you noticed. Ophelia said no one would pay any attention to them there."

"All those beads." She looked at the Wardlaws in wonder.

"And so many more all over the house," said Ophelia. "We're still sweeping them out of corners. They rattle in the vacuum."

"We copied the flowers from Mother's *Herbarium*. She always carried a flower press when she went walking."

"But don't you want to hurry and finish this?" asked Oliver suddenly, gesturing across the room. "Don't you want to see it done?"

"Good lord, boy, why should I want to finish it?" asked the Commodore in surprise. "What earthly use will it be to anyone completed?"

"I thought that was the point."

"No," Charlotte disagreed. "The point is to be *doing* it."

The Commodore's mouth stretched like a rubber band. "Exactly!"

"Well, I'd want to finish it." Oliver sounded hurt.

Chapter Ten

CHARLOTTE WAS SORRY TO LEAVE THE ATTIC. SHE HADN'T HAD nearly enough time to see everything; it was all laid out in such minute, careful detail, and she wondered if she'd ever have another chance. But Ophelia was insisting they start home and had firmly offered Charlotte a ride back to town, which it would be silly to refuse. She suspected Ophelia made her offers difficult to turn down anyway.

So, when they all trooped downstairs again, the Commodore stumped off to find Charlotte's clothes, while the Wardlaws cleared away the tea things. Oliver quietly vanished.

He didn't reappear to say good-bye and no one mentioned his absence; it was evidently not unusual. The Commodore came out with them, thanking Ophelia and Viola for Harvard College and reminding them they were always welcome. He stood at the end of the driveway, where he could signal Viola about traffic and waved his arms, his white hair raging like a snowstorm around his head.

Charlotte had no idea what time it was, but the afternoon felt late, and her clothes, though stiff and shedding a fine powder of dried mud, were not even damp. She guessed she'd been in the Commodore's house several hours.

Viola was in favor of taking Charlotte straight home, in spite of her protest that she had to collect her bicycle at the library. "I don't think, after your harrowing experience this afternoon, that you really ought to ride a bicycle, dear."

But Ophelia said, "Oh, nonsense, Vi! The young are disgustingly resilient. Charlotte probably found the whole incident quite stimulating."

Charlotte wisely kept silent and let Ophelia win the argument for her. Fortunately it wasn't very far from Commodore Shattuck's house to the library by car, for she soon understood what Ophelia meant about Viola being a risk. Viola was interested in everything they drove past, even though she'd seen it all hundreds of times and in all weathers. Their little car wandered slowly back and forth across the road as Viola peered out its windows.

"Now do go straight home, dear," she said as they let Charlotte out at the bike rack. "Perhaps we should drive behind her, Ophelia?"

"That," declared Ophelia, "would distract her dangerously, I'm sure. We will simply take ourselves home now and fix Welsh rarebit for supper, wouldn't you like that? Do give your father our regards, Charlotte, and tell him we think he's doing a marvelous job."

They waved and Charlotte waved back, then waited as the red taillights wove gently down Main Street. She got on her bike with a sigh and rode home. It would be very difficult to describe her afternoon to anyone.

Eliot, Mrs. Paige, and Jean were in the kitchen fixing supper. Mrs. Paige and Jean did the serious bits, while Eliot grated mounds and mounds of cabbage and carrot for coleslaw.

"Hey, Chuck!" he greeted her as she came in.

"Hi," she said, testing the air. Roast chicken. Her stomach responded eagerly.

"I'm glad you're home, darling," said Mrs. Paige over her glasses. "You're the last one. Eliot, my love, don't you think that's enough?"

"You can never have enough coleslaw," he replied.

"You're like the broom that wouldn't stop in the *Sorcerer's Apprentice*," observed Jean. "Hello, Charlie, how are you?" She stopped mashing potatoes and turned to smile at her sister-in-law. "You look as if you've had a hard day."

"I got a little wet," said Charlotte evasively. "But I'm perfectly dry now."

"Wet?" echoed Mrs. Paige vaguely, her mind on the pea pods she was sautéing. "Then you'd better run upstairs and change, Charlotte. Supper's in ten minutes."

"Where're Deb and Max and Dad?"

"In the living room arguing over low-income housing," said Jean. "I told Max I wasn't going to debate it with him anymore, so he's found some new sparring partners."

"I don't see why it isn't possible to do something imaginative with low-cost housing," Mrs. Paige said. "Why does it have to be cinder block?"

"Money." Eliot shoveled his gratings into a huge mixing bowl.

"You might consider a salad bowl, Eliot, it's a little more elegant," suggested his mother.

"Speaking of elegant," said Eliot as Charlotte started up the back stairs, "you ought to have seen the characters I saw rummaging through the Good Will boxes behind the supermarket this morning."

"Rummaging?" said Jean. "You mean taking things out?"

"And trying them on. Really. You can imagine the conversations: 'My, that's a smart outfit you're wearing! Do tell me where you got it.' 'Why thank you, I get all my clothes from Good Will. This is the very latest—from the top of the heap.'"

Jean stifled a snort of laughter. "It really isn't funny, you know. Poor people!"

"I don' think these guys were poor, that's the odd part. They were just *unusual*. Several of them looked as if they were wearing old uniforms."

"Here's the dressing, Eliot. Charlotte, please *hurry!*"

Someone had been in her room while she was out. Charlotte discovered a little pile of paperback books in the middle of her neatly made bed. She saw them immediately, but resisted the impulse to examine them right away. Jean had brought them for her; she knew without opening one to see the initials "JWP" which Jean always put in her books. Much as Charlotte hated to admit it, her sister-in-law did have a knack for picking out stories she would enjoy.

But these, she noticed, when she couldn't stand it any longer—after she'd changed her clothes and dropped the disreputable ones on the floor of her closet—these were brand new and had "CTP" written in them instead: Charlotte's own initials. *The Wolves of Willoughby Chase, Black Hearts In Battersea, Nightbirds on Nantucket*. Charlotte was caught in a crossrip of emotions. She wanted to pick them up, to start one, to feel free to like them as she knew inside herself she would. But that meant liking Jean, didn't it? Being grateful to her. Accepting her along with her gifts. The books were a bribe, weren't they? And yet they showed that Jean thought about her—Charlotte—and about what she would be interested in. The books were chosen especially for her—

"Char—lie!" Eliot bellowed up the back stairs.

"Coming!"

The dining room was lively with words as people brought pieces of their conversations to the table with them.

"—isn't zoned for that kind of thing, is it?" Mr. Paige was asking.

"But zoning can be changed," argued Max. "It isn't cast in iron."

"First you have to get people to vote to change it, and you never will in Concord." Deb shook her head emphatically.

"Sooner or later even Concord'll have to do something about the situation. Better to have it done by someone with fresh, good ideas and creativity than a cheap, pedantic architect," declared Max, his eyes alight with passion.

"Scallions. Much better than onion in the winter. Onion's too strong," Mrs. Paige told Jean.

"I'll remember. There's Charlie," Jean exclaimed, looking hard at Max.

"Hmm? Charlie!" Max responded by giving his youngest sister a resounding, hairy kiss.

"Ouch. It's like being kissed by a nailbrush," she complained, pleased by his attention.

"That's what I keep telling him," said Jean. "If I could grow a beard in retaliation, I'd do it in a minute."

"Naw." Eliot shook his head. "I'll bet it itches like mad. Bugs and things."

" 'There was an old man with a beard,' " quoted Mr. Paige, " 'Who said, "It is just as I feared;/Two owls and a hen, four larks and a wren/Have just made their nests in my beard".' "

"I do think it would be a nuisance in the summer," remarked Mrs. Paige. "Isn't it going to be hot? Especially in Cambridge?"

"For the love of Pete," said Deb. "If the man wants a beard, he should be allowed to have one without having to take a bunch of guff from his kith and kin!"

"Hear, hear!" cried Max from the depth of his luxurious black beard. "What have you been doing all day, Charlie?"

"Oh," said Charlotte, "errands. And this afternoon—"

Eliot beamed benevolently at her. "Chuck, what would I *ever* do without you?"

"Fall apart," she replied, half-joking, half-hopeful.

"Do you mean," Deb said, "that you've been doing Eliot's errands all day? Seriously? That's embarrassing. You should *both* be embarrassed."

"Why?" asked Charlotte. "I didn't mind. I didn't have much else to do and I've done other things, too."

"See?" said Eliot.

Deb made a disgusted face at them, but before she could work into a lecture, Charlotte asked her innocently, "What happened about the man who was following you?"

"He stopped," said Deb shortly.

"There was a man following you? Here in Concord?" asked Jean with interest. "Was he attractive?"

"No," said Deb.

"Yes," said Charlotte.

"Attractive is beside the point, and how do you know what he looked like anyway, Charlotte Paige?" demanded Deb.

"Tell me what you're working on right now, Max?" inquired Mrs. Paige.

"Oh come now, Mother," chided Eliot slyly, "you're usually much more subtle than that!"

"I want to hear what else Charlie did with herself," said Mr. Paige from his end of the table. "When she wasn't running your errands, Eliot."

"Well," said Charlotte, glad to be distracted from Deb, "I met two people who asked me to give you their regards. They said to tell you you're doing a marvelous job with the museum."

"*Two?* In one place?" Her father raised his eyebrows quizzically.

"Ophelia and Viola Wardlaw. They made the bead flowers in the library."

"You mean 'Miss,' " Mrs. Paige corrected gently, then frowned. "Or 'The Misses,' I suppose it must be."

"Ms," amended Deb.

"No, because then how could you tell them apart?" objected Max.

"Why do you need to?" asked Eliot. "The Misses Wardlaw always go everywhere together, so it doesn't matter which is which. And they're much too Old Concord to be Ms, Deborah."

"You could say Miss Viola and Miss Ophelia," suggested Jean. "What lovely names."

"How on earth did you meet them?" Mr. Paige wanted to know.

"If they like what you're doing to the museum they can't be hidebound conservatives," said Deb.

"A pair of very lively, strong-minded and intelligent women," pronounced Mr. Paige. "I hope I'm as good when I'm their age."

"But where did you meet them, Charlotte?" asked her mother.

It was on the tip of Charlotte's tongue to say, "At Commodore Shattuck's house," but she hesitated and the chance was lost.

"Do you know," said Max, abruptly changing the subject, "I dropped fifty dollars at the dentist's on a filling last week? *Fifty dollars!*" He was chewing his chicken with some care. "It's still sensitive."

"So am I," declared Jean. "It flattened our checking account and we're eating gruel this week."

"Fifty dollars, old son, is a trifling sum," advised Eliot. "Jack DiChico spent seven hundred dollars for root canal work and a plastic molar last month."

"I could have a baby for that," said Jean thoughtfully.

"A plastic tooth's much less trouble," Deb said firmly.

"Look at the time!" exclaimed Mrs. Paige with a hint of relief. "We really must move if we're going to get dressed in time."

"Be late and make an entrance," suggested Eliot. "They can't start without me, anyway."

"Sooner or later you are going to learn that you are not indispensible," Max told him soberly.

"None of us is," agreed Mr. Paige. "The trick is to fool other people into thinking we are."

Everyone rose together and began to sweep the table clear. Everyone except Deb and Charlotte who sat where they were.

"Aren't you coming, Deb?" asked Jean on her way through the dining room to the front stairs.

"No, I'm not, if you want to know."

"Alas!" cried Eliot. "She's sitting home among the cinders."

"Oh, Eliot, don't be such an ass!" Deb scowled at him.

"But what about Geoff?" asked Charlotte. "Didn't he invite you?"

"Even the great Geoffrey Reynolds cannot arrange to be in two places at once," Eliot pointed out. "He can't play Dr. Prescott *and* take Deb to the ball. I was supposed to be his stand-in at the dance, as a matter of fact."

"Oh." Charlotte felt a stab of jealousy.

"You mean you aren't going with Eliot, darling? You aren't ill?"

"She turned me down." Eliot pulled a mournful face.

"Don't, for God's sake, make a *thing* of it, Mother," warned Deb dangerously. "No, I am not going. Yes, Eliot did ask me, and no, I do not feel ill, but I am not going. That's it. The end. All right? You'd better go change."

Jean had prudently withdrawn already. Mrs. Paige gave her daughter a careful, considering, slightly perturbed look, but said no more to her. As she and Eliot went upstairs together, Charlotte heard her say, "I do hope they haven't quarreled."

Deb cast her eyes upward in exaggerated despair. "Why does everything in this family have to be made public?"

"It simply isn't fair!" declared Charlotte. "You don't want to go to the ball and I do—you've been asked and I haven't.

I think that's rotten. I don't care at all why you aren't going."

"That makes a pleasant change!" Deb stalked out to the living room.

Charlotte went into the kitchen to find herself some more dessert.

Eliot was first to leave. He bounded down the stairs, pulling his uniform together, threw his music into a heap, and sped off to join the rest of the orchestra at the armory for a warm-up.

"Can't wear civvies if you're a dyed-in-the-homespun Minuteman. Don't forget, Charlie, I'll be back at quarter of twelve to collect you, but there won't be any time to spare, so be ready. I'll have to drop you by the flagpole, then race back to join the Minutemen. *If* you still want to go to the square tonight, that is."

"I guess so." She tried to sound indifferent without much success. They both knew she wouldn't miss going with him to see Dr. Prescott ride in on his horse, but she was still filled with a sense of injustice at being left home.

"At least this year you've got Deb to keep you company, darling," Mrs. Paige said, almost an hour later as she and Mr. Paige put on their outdoor clothes. She wore an elegant blue evening dress with a square neck and long sleeves designed to look suitably Colonial without being a costume. Over it she wore a heavy melton cloth cape with a beautifully romantic hood. Mr. Paige had gone all out for the Bicentennial a year ago and looked splendid now in velvet knee breeches and a brocade tailcoat made specially for that occasion. He relished being dramatic when the opportunity presented itself and carried it off with aplomb.

Max and Jean were more conventional in carefully preserved evening clothes befitting their modest income. Moodily Charlotte watched the four of them make last minute adjustments to one another in the front hall before they departed.

"Jean," she said suddenly as her sister-in-law was about to go out the door.

"Mmm?" Jean turned back.

With an effort she had to make, Charlotte pushed the words

out quickly: "Thanks for the books."

Jean's smile lit her round face like a candle. "They'll be something for you to do, anyway," she said.

It was snowing again, this time steadily. The flakes fell like glitter through the front porch light. As Charlotte stood in the open door, watching them leave, Earl Grey curled around her legs like smoke, out into the shimmering dark. There were haloes around the street lights and each passing car drove twin spears of silver before it. The wind had dropped and the cold made a deep, still pool around the house.

Charlotte shivered and went inside.

Except that she could feel Deb's presence in the house, Charlotte decided her sister might as well not have been there. Deb had abandoned the living room for the privacy of her own bedroom. Resigned, Charlotte settled into a chair and began *The Wolves of Willoughby Chase*. Rather in spite of herself, she soon became absorbed in the unhappy plight of Bonnie and Sylvia.

She reached the part where they were being pursued by wolves through the snow-filled park, and suddenly there was Simon to help them—when the telephone rang. She ignored it at first, but it rang and rang and she heard no movement upstairs, so at last, resigned, she put down her book and went to answer it. She knew it wouldn't be for her, it never was.

The voice at the other end identified itself as Stephanie Kruger, who was one of Deb's friends. Eliot couldn't stand her; he said she was an abrasive, man-devouring Amazon, a description Charlotte didn't completely understand, though she caught its drift. She had met Stephanie once or twice herself and had been intimidated by her large, forceful manner and penetrating sarcasm. In fact she was, if possible, even more devastating than Skip.

Stephanie asked if Deb was home and when Charlotte said, "Yes, just a minute," she replied, "Right on, Deb!"

Charlotte frowned at the receiver, then went to the foot of the steps and yelled for her sister, but got no answer. She had to go up and beat on Deb's closed door.

"What?" Deb sounded irritable.

"Telephone."

"If it's Geoff, tell him I'm not available. Tell him—"

"It's Stephanie."

"I'm coming." Deb took the call in their parents' room and Charlotte, before she hung up downstairs, listened unabashed for a minute.

"—serves him right. He's always taken you for granted."

"Let's not talk about it." Deb's voice was emphatic. "I'm sick of the whole subject!"

"If you aren't doing anything else tonight, come and have a beer with us then. Chris and I were thinking of going—"

Charlotte put the receiver down with a tightening in her chest. Deb mightn't be much company immured upstairs, but at least the house wasn't empty. That counted for a good deal. Charlotte cast herself despondently into her chair and tried to submerge in *The Wolves* again, but the words kept sliding into meaningless lines on the page as she listened for the thud of feet on the stairs, the rattle of hangers in the hall closet, and Deb's abrupt "Bye." For a long time nothing happened and Charlotte's apprehensiveness dwindled. Hu Kwah, the least domestic of Eliot's cats, came sneaking into the living room, moving suspiciously from one piece of furniture to another as if fearing attack. He was a wild tiger with extra toes on his front feet; when he raked someone with his claws he went for blood with all twelve.

Time drifted; Charlotte drifted. The long, unusual day behind her dissolved into dream. She really was very tired . . .

She woke with a jolt to hear Deb pounding down the stairs. Hu Kwah leaped into the air, spitting curses, and landed on all twenty-two claws in Charlotte's lap, which greatly surprised them both. He dug in, took off, and vanished. Deb put her head around the door.

"I'm going out," she said and pulled a knitted cap over her ears. "Keep the doors locked."

Charlotte wondered resentfully if Deb really expected her to go racing around the house once her sister had gone, *un*locking them. It was just after ten: at least an hour and a half before Eliot would come for her. She looked at her limited, dismal options: no point in going up to her room, she'd only worry about the emptiness downstairs; pointless to try the television, violence and rude jokes would only add to her feeling of insecurity; she wouldn't be able to doze now that she knew she was alone; and she couldn't concentrate on her book. At last she decided to make herself a cup of cocoa—that sounded comforting.

She worked hard to believe that she wasn't afraid, creating an island of light and warmth and safety in the kitchen. But outside the windows, darkness pushed relentlessly against the house, hiding all manner of things that were much more threatening hidden. When it began to overwhelm her, she searched frantically for distraction and fixed on Oliver and the Commodore. For a moment she was back, standing in the attic, gazing down like Gulliver on the Middlesex countryside spread around her feet. What a marvel that Commodore Shattuck should have created such a world under his roof! And what a marvelous story she could tell about him at school with the ring of authority. Except she knew perfectly well she wouldn't.

It was disturbing to find someone she had already categorized turning out to be in the wrong cubbyhole; it was like hearing a word she thought she knew pronounced quite differently by a person who really *did* know: not easy to accept and get used to.

In addition, there was the extraordinary story Commodore Shattuck had told about a British attack. She wished now she'd grabbed an opportunity to talk to Eliot about that, to ask what he thought. The odd thing was that when Eliot had been here to talk to she was reluctant to try. Now that he was inaccessible she found it urgent. She was beset by contradictions.

She drank two successive cups of cocoa, slowly, as she sat at the kitchen table and drew little faces on the sketch pad Deb had left there. Then she washed up because it took more time.

When the telephone rang again, a little before eleven, it scared Charlotte as much as Hu Kwah had earlier when he'd dropped onto her lap. She couldn't imagine who would call that late at night, unless . . . It might be some kind of crank. Or a burglar checking to see if anyone were home . . .

Chapter Eleven

CHARLOTTE STARED FEARFULLY AT THE TELEPHONE AS IT CON-
tinued to ring. Then suddenly she thought of Eliot; yes, of
course it would be Eliot calling to check on her and remind
her to be ready when he came to get her. Her breath evened
out at once, and when she answered the phone she sounded
quite normal in her own ears.

It wasn't Eliot. The voice at the other end was familiar, but
somehow distorted. For a moment she couldn't make any
sense of what it was rattling on about, then she caught the
name "Deb" and realized it was Geoff Reynolds.

"Wait a minute, wait a minute," she begged. "Go slower.
Deb isn't here right now and I—what? No, she isn't at the
ball either. She told Eliot she wouldn't. Then why did you ask
me if you knew? Well, she didn't go with Eliot either, I told
you. She went out with Stephanie Kruger."

A loud groan echoed down the wires, then Geoff started to
talk again, his voice urgent.

"Aren't you supposed to be on a horse somewhere?" she
interrupted. He told her not very politely to shut up and listen. Offended, she did, and by the time he'd finished she felt
as numb as she had after she'd fallen in the duck pond.

"Um," she said after a long pause during which she could
hear Geoff breathing heavily. "Eliot's coming home to get me
pretty soon. I can tell him when he gets here, but I don't
know what else to do. Where are you? Yes, I know where the

Dunkin' Donuts is in Lexington. Yes, I'll try to. There really isn't anyone else here."

Geoff released a final avalanche of words and hung up. There was a click and Charlotte stood holding an empty yellow receiver. Her mind felt like a clothes drier: tumbling over and over, pieces of information falling about like socks that didn't match. Two things were clear. One: Geoff Reynolds was stranded on the outskirts of Lexington, with a sprained ankle and no horse. He would *not* come riding into Concord center shortly after midnight this year. Two: she—Charlotte —was the only person, aside from the counterman at Dunkin' Donuts and Geoff himself, who knew that.

Geoff had wanted Deb to come and get him; he'd thought at once of her because she'd told him so emphatically that she was staying home tonight. But Deb, of course, wasn't home and Geoff's disappointment was obvious. All Charlotte could think to do was wait for Eliot, and by the time he came it would be too late to save the occasion. Fleetingly she considered phoning the armory—everyone in Concord who might help was there at the ball except Deb, but she balked at the idea. It would take ages to get through to her parents or to Max among all the people, and then there'd be a struggle to make herself understood. She thought feverishly for a moment.

Was everyone at the ball, though? She sorted through everything that Geoff had said about his "accident": how it had happened, where, and the fact that there were three strange men involved—three men who had disappeared immediately afterward *with Geoff's horse.* Then, amazed at her own temerity, she pulled out the phone book, paged through it with a hand that shook slightly, and pushed Commodore Samuel Prescott Shattuck's telephone number.

He answered on the third ring, as she was about to quickly hang up; he sounded wide awake, calm, and adult.

"Oh," said Charlotte with nervous relief. "C-Commodore Shattuck? This is Charlotte Paige." He knew her at once which made it easier. "Um, I'm calling about this afternoon —well, it's about tonight, really. Because I think those men, the ones we were talking about, in the barn—you know? I

123

think they've actually started something and I didn't know who else to call. Everyone's at the ball and I'm afraid it's important, and I—you will? Here?" She gulped. "Well, I guess —I mean there isn't anyone home but me and—yes. All right, I will."

This was the most extraordinary day. For one that had begun dull and lonely . . . Her head too busy for lurking dangers, Charlotte went back to the living room and took up a stand in one of the two big front windows where she could watch the traffic on Main Street. Her hands were damp; she played abstractedly with the curtain cord and tried to imagine Commodore Shattuck actually coming into her house. It struck her that she hadn't even told him where she lived. Suppose . . .

A pair of headlights came slowly down the street from the town center and turned, without hesitation, into the Paiges' driveway. Charlotte's heart shot up and caught painfully in her throat. She forced herself to go open the front door; as she did, Earl Grey slid inside like an icy shadow. Two people got out of the car: one short and stocky, the other short and thin. For some reason it hadn't occurred to Charlotte that Oliver would come along. It was logical, but she was annoyed. It was *her* business this time, not his. The Commodore marched briskly up the walk with Oliver slouching behind, collar up, hands thrust into pockets.

"Here we are," said the Commodore. He pulled off his watch cap and shook the snow from it onto the step. "Now, what is all of this, hey? Tell us carefully. Don't leave anything out."

As clearly as she could she recounted Geoff's astonishing tale while Oliver and his great-uncle stood in the front hall in little pools of melting snow.

Geoff had begun his ride as usual in Lexington, where Dr. Prescott had begun his in 1775, when he'd taken the message from Paul Revere, who'd been captured by the British, to the citizens of Concord, that the King's army was on the march. The snow made visibility poor for Geoff, and Baba, his horse, was skittish, so he'd concentrated on holding the mare together and staying out of the light traffic. He was fine until he'd reached the residential section near the Donut shop. Suddenly two men rushed out of the dark at him, waving their arms and shouting something. Geoff pulled Baba up to the right, away from them, then a third man materialized on that side and caught Baba's bridle. He refused to be shaken off, so Geoff began to dismount. Baba gave a snort and a skip, and the next thing Geoff knew he was on the seat of his pants in the snow and he'd twisted his left ankle in the stirrup coming down. The three men vanished, taking the mare with them. Painfully, Geoff managed to hobble in stages to the Donut shop, from where he called Deb. And got Charlotte.

When she finished they all stood silent, letting the story sink in. Then the Commodore said thoughtfully, "Hmmm. I suppose it might have been boys—out for what they call 'fun' these days. They do so many things I do not understand for 'fun.' "

"Oh, Uncle Sam!" cried Oliver impatiently. Charlotte was intrigued to hear the Commodore called "Uncle Sam." "You know it wasn't boys. It was *them*—it must have been. They've planned it—it's the first move."

Commodore Shattuck rubbed his head with a square hand. "Mmph. You may be right, Oliver."

"You know I am."

"What do we do about it then? Eh?"

"Storm the barn," said Oliver promptly.

That didn't appeal to Charlotte. It hadn't appealed to her in the middle of the afternoon; at night it was even less inviting.

"Well, Charlotte? What d'you say?"

Oliver gave her a look which said plainly, suggest something else if you dare.

She accepted the challenge. "I don't see that it would do any good to storm the barn. If it was them who stole the horse, they can't have gotten it back there yet. They haven't had time."

"So there won't be so many of them there to fight," said Oliver. "We could easily take the barn."

"Why do we want the barn?" demanded Charlotte. "What good is *that*?"

"Stop squabbling," ordered the Commodore. "Think a bit, will you? Use your heads. What are these men trying to do, hey? Disrupt the ceremonies. So they've knocked off our Samuel Prescott and stolen his horse. *I* think—Charlotte, get your boots and coat, we haven't got time to stand about jawing. I think we must find a stand-in for Geoffrey Reynolds. And we haven't a minute to spare if we're going to keep to schedule. We've got to make 'em fail, that's what we must do."

"How?" Oliver wanted to know. "We don't have a horse and anyway none of us knows how to ride one."

"A problem," agreed the Commodore, "but not insurmountable. We must be able to solve it between us. Charlotte, who do you know with a horse?"

Charlotte, struggling into her boots, said, "I don't know anyone. I can't—" Thunderbolt. "Unless . . . actually, I do sort of know someone. I don't know if she'd help, but—" Was this really Charlotte Paige talking, she asked herself.

"Of course she will. Don't be silly. Who is it? Come on, out to the car. No time to lose."

Parka, Deb's mittens because her own were still full of mud, hat. The snow still came; two inches on the ground and more accumulating. As her hand closed on the doorknob, Charlotte remembered her key and darted upstairs for it, then took an extra minute to scribble a note for Eliot. "We've gone to the Square," she wrote, "See you. Charlie." The "we" made it sound as if she'd gone with Deb. She tried not to think about what she was doing.

"Kath Schuyler," she said breathlessly as she ran after Commodore Shattuck and Oliver into the deep unfamiliar night.

"Schuyler?" repeated the Commodore. "George's girl, that would be. Has a horse, eh?"

"Not exactly."

"How can you not exactly have a horse?" snapped Oliver.

"She *knows* about them," Charlotte snapped back. She was sick of Oliver's perpetual bad humor. "That's more than you do. She works at Watts's Stables. And she runs the horse plow."

"The what?"

"The snow plow they use on the sidewalks in Concord. It's pulled by a horse."

"Does she indeed!" exclaimed the Commodore. "I should have known that." He sounded annoyed. "Seems to me I did once. Bother getting old! I keep misplacing things like that." He backed onto the street. "We'll need to make a slight detour."

Snowflakes flew like darts against the windshield. They had the town virtually to themselves at that hour; the center was silent and ghostly under the streetlights. Charlotte thought of Eliot going home for her and finding no one, just a note. She flushed hot. It was too late to go back.

Before driving out to the Bullard Farm, the Commodore stopped at his own house and left the car running while he hurried inside. In a couple of minutes he was back with a mysterious bundle which he threw into the trunk, then they were off again. He needed no directing from Charlotte; he knew the way. With his hands clasped wide apart on the steering wheel and his head thrust forward, he hummed to himself. It was a Sousa march, slightly flat. Oliver sat withdrawn and tense next to his great-uncle, his arms wrapped tight across his chest.

And beside him, Charlotte, who had in a rash moment suggested searching out Kath Schuyler, now wished she hadn't. She didn't even know the girl—not really. Fervently she hoped they would find the Schuylers had all gone to bed, or that Mr. and Mrs. Schuyler had gone to the ball and left their children with a sensible, unimaginative babysitter.

House lights burned warm rectangles of yellow through the blackness at the end of the Schuylers' road. Charlotte's hopes were dashed as she recognized the station wagon, Mr. Schuyler's pickup, and a lump that was Skip's tarpaulin-covered moped, parked side by side. Everyone was home and it didn't look as if anyone was in bed.

As the three of them scrunched up to the house through the snow, Alice set up a fearful row inside the french doors. Mr. Schuyler had nailed chicken wire to the frame to prevent Alice and the smaller children from breaking the glass in their enthusiasm. Alice beat on it with her front paws. A light sparked in the living room. Mr. Schuyler hauled Alice off the door, peered out, and called, "It's not locked—come in! Commodore Shattuck, what's got you out tonight? Not stuck up here, are you?"

"We've come to pay you a business call, George," said the Commodore. "Odd hour for it, but it's odd business. Didn't get you up, I trust?"

"Nope. I've been waiting for the phone to ring all evening. I'm on standby for the plows—looks as if we'll need to get 'em out tonight."

"George?" Mrs. Schuyler's voice came from the direction of the dining room. "Don't stand with the door open—bring whoever it is in, will you?"

"Right 'nough. Don't mind the dog, once you're in she'll be all right." Mr. Schuyler caught Alice around the neck with an enormous hand and whisked her effortlessly out of the way. She gave a little strangled "yurrp."

"In," ordered the Commodore. "Wipe your feet first. That's it."

"Don't mind a little snow in the house, it's seen worse. Go through to the dining room—we're all in there. Pat!" Mr. Schuyler raised his voice. "It's Commodore Shattuck and a couple of kids!"

A red curtain Charlotte hadn't noticed before was pulled across the open doorway that divided the two front rooms. On the other side of it lay warmth and light; a wood stove, glowing with heat, squatted on the flagstone hearth. The clutter on the dining room table had been swept haphazardly to one end, and at the other sat Skip, Mrs. Schuyler, and Andy. A younger boy was asleep in a compact ball in one corner of a small, bald sofa, while Kath occupied the other. On her lap a solid-looking book lay open to the diagram of a horse covered with little lines and numbers.

The others were in the midst of a card game. Their piece of the table was strewn with cards and heaps of vanilla wafers.

"Charlie!" exclaimed Skip. "What on earth are you doing here? Eliot not with you?"

Charlotte shook her head, overwhelmed. What on earth *was* she doing here?

"Commodore." He glanced from one to the other of them, his eyebrows questioning.

Mrs. Schuyler smiled at the three intruders, unperturbed and welcoming, as if it weren't nearly eleven on a snow-driven evening and she'd been expecting them all along. "Sit down, won't you? Just pull up some chairs—you can pile that stuff on the floor. I'm sorry, but if I put down my cards I'll forget what I'm supposed to do with them. They're teaching me poker."

"But she keeps eating her chips," said Andy with a snort.

"They're mine, after all," Mrs. Schuyler pointed out, offering Charlotte and Oliver each a vanilla wafer. "No? What about something hot to drink after this hand?"

Incredulous, Charlotte realized that no one had yet asked them why they'd come, unless she counted Mr. Schuyler at the front door, and he hadn't waited for an answer.

The Commodore cleared his throat abruptly. "Sorry to burst in and disturb you this way," he began, "but I'm afraid there isn't time for polite visiting. We've come to ask your help—"

The phone rang and Charlotte stiffened. Eliot. It must be Eliot this time. Or worse still, Deb! They'd found her gone and tracked her here and she was in real trouble. Her heart pounded and she felt sick. Mr. Schuyler went to answer it.

Mrs. Schuyler sighed with exasperation. "What a life!" she said. "God knows what time he'll be home. In time to dry out and shovel down some breakfast before he has to go out again, I suppose."

"You can't fight it, Sis," Skip told her. "That's what it is to be a public servant."

Mr. Schuyler was back in a minute, pulling on an old pea jacket. "Sorry, Patty. Foster's wife's having her baby tonight and he can't go out."

"I don't see why not," she replied with the trace of a smile. "*She's* the one doing the work, not Mike."

"He wouldn't know one end of a snowplow from the other right now, though."

"A Patriots' Day baby," Skip said, "red, white, and blue."

"I hope you didn't want me for anything, Commodore?"

Mr. Schuyler settled his peaked cap.

"No, George, not you. Actually," the Commodore looked at Mrs. Schuyler, "it's your daughter, Katherine, we need."

"Kath? Why in the world do you need her?" asked Andy throwing down his cards.

For the first time Kath looked up. She and Andy reflected each other like a mirror: two pairs of direct brown eyes, the same rusty hair and oval, freckled faces, the same single-minded set to their chins. "What?" she asked.

"It's somewhat complicated." The Commodore began an explanation of their errand with Charlotte's account of Geoff's story. "So he is stranded in Lexington without a horse or a way to get back to Concord. No good to us in any event, he can't ride."

"He fell off?" Kath's voice was heavy with scorn. "What about Baba? Where is she?"

"Gone," replied the Commodore without thinking.

"*Gone?* He doesn't know where she is?" Kath sprang up, dropping her book. "He's lost her? Do you know what Alan Watts'll *do*?"

"If Geoff's sprained his ankle," said Skip, "how's he going to get home?"

"He wanted Deb to go for him," said Charlotte. It was, after all, her story. "That's why he called our house."

"Umm," Skip grunted thoughtfully. "Look, George, if you can wait while I get my coat, I'll drive you to the DPW in the pickup, then go collect him in Lexington. How does that sound?"

The Commodore nodded vigorously. "Capital. There's half our problem solved."

"Half?" said Mrs. Schuyler.

"Baba's out there in the snow, scared or hurt, wandering through the streets of Lexington!" exploded Kath. "Who cares about Geoff Reynolds if he's dumb enough to fall off his horse! We've got to rescue Baba!"

"Not now," said the Commodore. He put a steadying hand on Kath's shoulder—she was as tall as he—and pushed her firmly onto the sofa again. In his corner the small boy remained obliviously asleep, curled like a snail shell.

Skip and George Schuyler stood waiting, doubtful, wondering whether they should go yet, but Commodore Shattuck nodded briskly to them. They shifted into gear at once.

"Now," said the Commodore again when they'd gone. "I understand your concern about the horse, Katherine, believe me. But I am sure it's all right. No harm will come to it. Or," he added mostly to himself, "heads will roll, I promise you! We can't spend time on the horse. We need you for something else."

There was a considering look on Mrs. Schuyler's pleasant face. She began absently to braid her hair. Charlotte sat very still with her hands clasped damply in her lap. Oliver, who had remained aloof throughout the conversation, had picked up Skip's hand of cards and was building a house with great precision.

"Why her?" Andy asked curiously. "What can she do?"

"Well," the Commodore began carefully, watching Mrs. Schuyler, "I wondered if she would be able to borrow a horse."

"At this hour of the night?" Mrs. Schuyler's fingers paused.

"Why?" Kath narrowed her eyes.

"Unless we find a substitute for Geoff Reynolds there will be no Dr. Prescott to ride into town tonight. No ceremony. No lights. No bells. It's very important that everything go as scheduled this year. We need a horse and a rider. Charlotte suggested you might be able to help."

"That's too bad, of course," began Mrs. Schuyler, "about the ceremony—"

"Only if I can ride the horse," said Kath flatly.

Mrs. Schuyler closed her mouth and continued to braid.

"Can you get one?" asked Charlotte, hardly able to believe her solution might work.

"I might."

"Phooey!" exclaimed Andy. "Of course she can get one!" He grinned suddenly. "You've come and asked my sister for the one thing in the whole world she can do for you better than anyone else!"

Charlotte saw Kath throw him an exasperated, tolerant, familiar look. It was the kind of look she knew from experience brothers and sisters shared and she felt a pang.

"All right," Kath agreed. "Nothing fancy. It'll have to be Cecil, the plow pony. I can't risk any of the others. Alan'll be furious enough when he finds out about Baba."

"Yes, yes," said the Commodore. "A horse is a horse. I do promise you the other one will turn up safe very shortly."

"How can you be so sure?" challenged Oliver.

"You will have to take my word for it, boy." Commodore Shattuck was firm. "We must get a move on if we're going to keep to time."

"I do think," broke in Mrs. Schuyler, unbraiding now, "that just as a matter of form you might ask me if I'll give my permission. It is my daughter who'll be risking her neck and someone else's property in the middle of a blizzard at midnight."

"My dear Patricia," said the Commodore turning to her at once. "I beg your pardon! The urgency of the situation, I do apologise."

"You'll let me go, won't you, Ma?" Kath was confident.

"Why on earth shouldn't I?" Her mother made a face at her. "It all sounds totally reasonable to me, and I'm only your mother! I know perfectly well I can't stop you unless I tie you hand and foot."

"Learned from thirteen years' experience," said Andy wisely. "And I'm going, too, of course."

"Now you wait just a minute, Andrew George Schuyler—"

"What?" The other boy unrolled. "What?"

"Now you've woken Dan. Andy, I can't let you go out in this with your ear; that's asking for trouble. You know what Doctor Mac told us."

"So I'll wear a hat. And a scarf. And earmuffs. But you *can't* keep me in, Ma, you just can't." Andy and Kath were both on their feet, looming over their mother. Dan pushed in between them, still demanding "What?" in a sleep-blurred voice.

"He can sit in the car with the windows shut," said the Commodore encouragingly. "But we really must get underway."

"Me too," said Dan. "Where're we going?"

"It's a stupid circus," complained Oliver crossly. "They don't all have to come. We're going to be late."

But Andy and Kath were off and running with Dan right behind. They dashed upstairs to collect outdoor gear and were back almost at once, flinging on their coats.

The Commodore gave Mrs. Schuyler a sideways glance. "I'm sorry to have disrupted your evening," he apologized gruffly. "This is important, believe me. I'd never have done it otherwise."

"Oh, phooey!" She smiled at him. "I'm just being a poor sport because I have to stay home with the babies while the rest of my family goes adventuring in the middle of the night. So long as you bring all three of mine back again just as soon as this is over. They're your responsibility, Commodore, and if that isn't enough to fill your soul with dread, you're a brave man!"

The Commodore actually smiled back at her. "Or a fool," he amended. "You'll have them back undamaged in a couple of hours. Word of honor."

She gave a little laugh. "Actually it's you I should worry about, not them. Watch out for Dan, and remember to keep your earflaps down, Andy!" she called after them through the open french doors as she hung onto a wildly struggling Alice.

Chapter Twelve

CHARLOTTE FOUND HERSELF SANDWICHED IN THE BACK OF THE Commodore's old Chevy between Andy and Dan. Up front, Kath gave the Commodore terse directions. The main road had been plowed recently: there were ragged hedges of snow along the sides of it.

The Watts's driveway, however, hadn't been cleared. A single pair of car tracks, made long since, barely creased the blanket of snow across it. "At least," said the Commodore optimistically as he swung in, "there are plenty of you to push."

"Won't they think," Charlotte ventured, "that we're stealing something?"

"Not we," said Kath. "Me. You're going to stay out of the way, and I'm going to tell them what I'm doing first."

"But then they won't let you, will they?"

Kath's shoulders lifted in a quick shrug. "Cecil's my responsibility. Anyhow, Alan and Liz'll be at the ball, and Paul's no problem. He knows zip about the horses—doesn't look at anything without spark plugs." Her voice held undisguised contempt.

"You'd better be right," said Oliver dourly.

"I am," replied Kath, "and you don't have any other choice."

"That's true, I'm afraid. Who's Paul?" asked the Commodore.

"Son," Andy answered. "He's a whizz with our tractor."

"Perhaps, Katherine, I should go with you to inquire?" suggested Commodore Shattuck as he braked beside the Watts's modern house. It looked incongruously flat next to the huge frame barn.

"Absolutely not. Paul's used to me—he wouldn't know what to make of the rest of you. Just keep out of sight and let me handle it." Kath scrambled over Oliver, who grunted in protest, and disappeared through the sifting snow toward the house.

"I don't know what we're doing," said Dan after a minute.

"I wouldn't admit that if I were you, kid," warned Andy. "You're lucky to be here at all."

"I don't know what *any* of you are doing," Oliver said, "besides complicating things."

"You couldn't think of anything useful," Charlotte pointed out.

"Enough," said the Commodore firmly. "Here's Katherine back again. Don't waste time quarreling."

"It's okay," called Kath. "I'm going into the barn."

"Then so am I," declared Dan and propelled himself out of his door before anyone could stop him.

"Hey!" cried Andy.

"Charlotte, you go with them in case they need help," ordered the Commodore. "We'll wait here. Don't argue, Andrew, I promised your mother."

"But—" began Charlotte. Andy sighed and Oliver sat still.

"It's getting late," said the Commodore. "Hurry!"

She hadn't the will to defy him even though she didn't find the idea of a dark barn full of horses very attractive. The situation was entirely outside her experience and beyond her control. Whirling blackness enveloped her, snow squeaked under her boots, home and family were alarmingly remote.

The air in the barn was warm and moist, pungent with unfamiliar smells, alive with strange noises: snorts, breathy sighs, shuffling and scuffling, scrapes and rustles, and a low, steady munching. Kath had switched on a light by the door, a single bare bulb fixed to the wall. Shadows crowded out of the corners. Charlotte felt surrounded. She clamped her teeth to keep from calling out to Kath in panic.

From the gloom ahead she heard Dan say, "But why? I don't understand *why*."

"Not now. Shut up and hold this, will you?"

Relieved, Charlotte scuttled over to them. "Can I help? The Commodore sent me."

"Know anything about horses?" Kath was busy buckling straps around the head of a large, dark animal.

"No," Charlotte hastily admitted.

"Then stand back."

Obediently, she shrank against the edge of the stall. Kath had called Cecil a pony, but for a pony he looked awfully big and solid. He shifted his weight and shook his head and Kath gave him a light smack on the nose. "Stop it, you brute," she said fondly. "Dan, pick up the halter, will you, before he steps on it? Hang it on that hook. Hold still, idiot, and don't blow down my neck!"

Wide-eyed, Charlotte watched Kath push the great, dangerous-looking creature around his stall; she bullied him fearlessly. Charlotte thought of her inanimate bicycle—she had used to pretend it was a horse when she was younger—while Kath slung a saddle on Cecil's broad back, stooped underneath him and pulled the cinch tight. "Look out," she warned.

Charlotte retreated as Kath forced Cecil out of his stall backwards. He jiggled up and down and minced sideways.

Dan emerged from the other side. "I don't see why I can't ride him with you. We've done it before."

"Because," replied Kath curtly. "Just because." She led the horse across the barn, his hooves thudding hollowly on the floorboards, and paused at the door. Cecil expelled a tremendous breath. It hissed through his nostrils like air from a burst tire. "Aha!" cried Kath and quick as lightning bent to pull up the strap around his middle. "Rotten beast!" she exclaimed without anger. "I'm much too smart for you!"

Out in the snow, Cecil shook his head violently from side to side, flinging his ragged mane about.

"Maybe he doesn't like snow?" suggested Charlotte.

"Nuts," said Kath. "He's just a show-off. Aren't you, Cece? He's perfectly used to the stuff, but he expects the plow not a saddle. It must be time to go—I guess I'm off."

"Wait a bit! Wait!" The Commodore's bulky figure materialized before them. He held out a bundle. "You'll need these. Best I could do on short notice. Otherwise no one'll know who you're supposed to be."

The bundle was a long dark cloak of some very heavy material wrapped around a battered tricorn. Kath flashed him a grin. She was pleased.

"Put them on. Hurry!" urged Dan, now resigned to staying behind.

"Yes, do," agreed Charlotte.

Kath flung the cloak over her shoulders and fumbled with the clasp.

"Hat's a bit big," remarked the Commodore as he set it on her head, "but it'll do."

Cecil eyed the billowing cloak with suspicion, but Kath held him firmly in hand. "All I have to do is ride into town yelling a bit, right? Canter up and down a couple of times?"

The Commodore nodded. "Exactly. Off you go now, Katherine. Don't take any risks, the important thing is that you turn up as scheduled. We've got 'em!" His face lit with triumph.

"Don't worry about me, but you'd better be right about Baba." Kath swung up onto Cecil and nudged him into a trot. She and the pony quickly disappeared in the blowing snow.

"Back to the car," ordered the Commodore. "We must be in town when she arrives."

There was a little trouble at the end of the driveway. The Commodore wasn't paying attention to the wheel ruts and Dan and Charlotte were forced to get out and push the car through the snowbank thrown up by the plow. Oliver sat impassive in the front seat and Commodore Shattuck forbade Andy to help even though he at least offered. As she climbed back into the car, red-faced and panting, Charlotte glared resentfully at the back of Oliver's head. But she hadn't the energy needed to sustain murderous thoughts, her head felt fuzzy on the inside. She slumped back in her seat as the whole long, eventful day caught up with and flattened her. She was suddenly incredibly tired—so tired her arms and legs and shoulders ached. The arches of her feet hurt. Her fingers felt stiff and swollen. The car was comfortably warm and dark and . . .

"There she is!" cried Dan from a long way off.

The Commodore gave a grunting chuckle. "Odd sight that must be for a stranger: figure in a cloak riding horseback hell-for-leather along a highway in the pitch dark. Make you think you're hallucinating!"

"She isn't going very fast," Oliver pointed out. "She'll never get there on time."

"They'll wait," Andy predicted. "They always do."

Charlotte caught a glimpse of Kath, picked out in the headlights. Cecil was jogging along the side of Lexington Road at a brisk trot, head up, ears pricked. Brimming with confidence, Kath waved her hat at them.

"I bless your mother for being such a reasonable person," the Commodore said to Dan and Andy.

"She's pretty good about this sort of thing usually," Andy agreed. "It's only my stupid ears."

"She can't really care much about you if she'd let you come," declared Oliver.

"Why did yours?" asked Dan curiously.

With her eyes closed, Charlotte listened for Oliver's answer, but when it came, it didn't tell her much. He only said, "She doesn't know where I am. She only knows that I'm visiting my great-uncle." His voice was brittle.

Neither does mine know, thought Charlotte with a little shudder. But she will soon, and Charlotte doubted Mrs. Paige would be as equable about it as Mrs. Schuyler. The idea of having to explain was too much for her right now; she couldn't think about it.

Talking softly across her, Andy told Dan as much as he knew about what they were doing and why Kath was riding Cecil into town through the snow. In the front seat, Oliver leaned close to his great-uncle, speaking in a low, urgent voice, but Charlotte didn't even attempt to untangle his words from Andy's. She concentrated hard on staying awake.

It was 12:03 by the First Parish clock when they reached

the Square. Normally, at this hour the town would be empty, folded and put decently to bed for the night, ready to be shaken out again in the morning. There were, as Max was fond of pointing out, no night spots in Concord.

But tonight the flagpole at the top of Main Street was ringed with a small, noisy, good-natured throng. They crowded together on the island in the middle of the traffic circle, under the white streetlights. They stomped and blew, talked and laughed, while the whirling snow glittered around them. A frisky wind tossed the flakes up again as fast as they came out of the sky. The air was in turmoil.

Commodore Shattuck drove slowly round the Square, hunting a parking place. Suddenly wide awake, Charlotte peered at the waiting figures. There was a disquieting flutter in the pit of her stomach, but it was too dark and people were too well muffled to be identified from a distance. She could only hope that worked both ways and she, too, could be anonymous.

"Right," said the Commodore, stopping the car. "Soon as Katherine's done her part, we'll plan to meet back here, so no one's stranded. Five bodies. Now then, quick march, and keep your eyes and ears open for anything unusual."

"Like what?" Dan wanted to know.

"Anything," replied the Commodore, with a glance at Oliver.

"I am not staying in the car this time, no matter what you promised Ma," declared Andy. "I'm so wrapped up I feel like a mummy."

A faceful of cold air revived Charlotte a little. She leaned against the car, breathed deeply, and tried to shake the haze out of her eyes.

Andy, his cap crammed down over his ears, caught her arm in a rough, friendly way and pulled her along with him and Dan. "Don't want to miss this!" She didn't resist; she let him tow her. Together they plunged into the milling crowd. From all sides she caught scraps of conversation punctuated with laughter; impressions came at her disjointed yet distinct, like snapshots. She jostled a woman wearing a black fur jacket and long gold skirt.

"My toes are absolutely numb! No feeling at all, John."

"Put them in your pockets."

Beside her a man in a tuxedo warmed his hands around a cigarette lighter. "Yes, but Nina, not like this since 1967—"

"I wanted to ask where she'd found it, but I hadn't the nerve," exclaimed a tall woman with a white stole wrapped around her head.

"—mean to say you *left* it there?"

"—dropped eight and a half points on the Dow Jones Average—"

"—most revolting shade of green. It made her look mauve."

"Charlie!" Charlotte froze in her tracks, bringing Andy up short. Cautiously she turned to find Max grinning at her from under a Persian lamb hat with the flaps down. "Glad you got here in time. Eliot made one of his spectacular last-minute exits and we were afraid you wouldn't make it. Did he just dump you?"

"Eliot?" She disengaged herself from Andy. "Oh, he must be with the other Minutemen by now," she said vaguely, hoping he was.

Jean appeared beside Max. "Just don't get lost in the blizzard." Snow had caught in the tendrils of hair around her face and melted in sparkling drops. She was smiling and pretty. "What a wild night! Did Deb come?"

"I think so." Charlotte hedged. "Where are Mom and Dad?"

"Near the flagpole, talking to the Harrises."

She marked the flagpole as an area to avoid and inched away from her sister-in-law and brother. "See you." If only it weren't so complicated and she weren't so muzzy. It would take considerable luck if she were to keep each member of her family thinking she'd come with some other.

"She'll be here any minute now." Andy broke into her thoughts. She'd forgotten him.

"Who?" she asked, startled.

"Kath, of course," said Dan. "Who were those people?"

"My brother, if you have to know."

"What kind of unusual things are we supposed to see?"

"Do you always ask so many questions?" demanded Charlotte.

"He does," Andy confirmed. "Always."

"I like to know things," Dan replied. "He's kind of old to be your brother, isn't he? He's an *adult.*"

"I can't help it," said Charlotte defensively. Dan shrugged.

Andy edged them through the maze of people toward the far side of the circle. From here they would be among the first to see Kath arrive. Something tugged insistently at the corner of Charlotte's mind; she ought to be looking out for other people besides her family, but she couldn't think who. She had the feeling she'd forgotten something important and just as she was on the verge of remembering, Andy shook her arm. "There she is!"

All around them, people spotted the horse and rider cantering toward them and set up an enthusiastic cheer. Behind Charlotte a man said loudly, "*Now* can we go home? That's it, isn't it?"

Kath gave her audience a good show, riding out of the snowstorm with her long cloak flapping. Cecil seemed to be enjoying himself as well. He arched his neck and picked up his feet like a professional performer as he caught the unfamiliar sound of applause.

"Neat!" observed Dan with approval. Everyone seemed to share his opinion. Shouting, "The British are coming!" Kath drew level with the spectators and waved her hat, and the cheers changed key as people realized she wasn't Geoff Reynolds, whom they had expected. There was no chance for questions, however, for the lights suddenly flared up along Main Street and bells in the church steeples all over town tumbled over themselves in joyful noise.

Out of the snowstorm marched the full company of Minutemen, flags high, fifes and drums playing. They swung up the Milldam, looking splendid, and circled the flagpole while people applauded enthusiastically. Eliot led his corps in the national anthem; its final notes were the signal to disband—the ceremony was over.

Slowly the crowd began to unravel. There was no point in standing about the square any longer on cold feet.

"Charlie, for the love of Mike!" Eliot, breathless, hat in hand, burst upon her. "I only wish I'd known Deb was going to bring you! I nearly broke my neck getting home in time. Did you walk?"

"Not exactly," said Charlotte. "We got a ride."

"Hey, Andy!" Eliot gave Andy Schuyler a friendly thump and got one in return. "Skip around somewhere?"

"He had to go to Lexington," Andy answered. Charlotte willed him not to give her away about Deb. He didn't.

"Lexington? Tonight?"

"And Dad's out on the plow," volunteered Dan. "Kath's being Samuel Prescott."

"Hold it," said Eliot. "Back up. Skip's in Lexington, and your *sister's* the one riding around on that horse? What's happened to Geoff? Where's Deb?"

Quickly, before they got in any deeper, Charlotte explained. "Geoff sprained his ankle in Lexington and Skip went to get him, so Kath's being substitute. That's all."

Around them people called good night to each other and drifted to their cars in knots of twos and fours.

Kath had ridden Cecil all the way down Main Street, as far as the bank, and came trotting back now.

"Where's Deb?" Eliot asked again.

Charlotte glanced around. "Max and Jean are here," she offered helpfully.

"And Mum and Dad, I see, but Deb—"

"There's our pickup!" cried Dan. "Look, he's got Geoff! Come on." Before Andy could catch him, he sped across the street to the truck. Eliot and Andy followed, but Charlotte hesitated.

"Not bad, was it?" Kath called as she trotted by to join the others. She sounded jubilant.

The Square was almost empty; no sign of Max and Jean, or Mr. and Mrs. Paige. Charlotte assumed they'd all have gone home, believing that Eliot and Deb would bring her. Commodore Shattuck, with Oliver in tow, was striding purposefully toward the pickup. It was like a magnet.

There was one other huddle of figures left; it stood in shadow beside the War Memorial, like an ill-assorted football team before the scrimmage. It was, she knew, precisely what the Commodore had meant by "anything unusual." If those were the men responsible for Geoff's accident, she wondered what they were thinking now; their sabotage had failed. And what had they done with the horse? But she was too tired to pursue the answers, all she could do was wonder.

Two more people joined the cluster at the truck: Alan and Liz Watts. Kath's voice, calm and clear, carried across the night: "I was sure you wouldn't mind if I took Cecil out, under the circumstances."

"Never mind Cecil, what's happened to Baba? That's what I'm interested in," declared Alan Watts. "Where's my mare, Geoff? If you've left her wandering around Lexington—"

"There was nothing I could do," Geoff defended himself. "I don't know where they came from, but all of a sudden these three—"

"There's no need to fear for your horse, Mr. Watts," interrupted the Commodore firmly. "She will be returned to you unharmed."

"How the hell do you know, whoever you are?" Mr. Watts said, rounding on him. "Oh, it's you, Commodore."

From the driver's seat of the pickup, Skip said, "He's quite reliable, Alan."

Mr. Watts snorted. "No doubt the Lexington police have been trying to reach me all evening—'We regret to have to tell you your mare is rampaging loose on the streets of our town'—or else she's lying somewhere with a broken leg. If I have to go out looking for her—"

"Believe me, please!" interjected the Commodore. "She will not have been injured. You'll have her back tomorrow, word of honor."

"Uncle Sam," objected Oliver, "how can you say that?"

"I know it's true," replied his great-uncle. "Damage to personal property is outside the rules. Jimmy'll have none of it, I'm certain. As certain as I am that Mr. Watts will agree there's no point in moving the animal tonight. Plenty of time tomorrow."

He certainly sounded convincing. Alan Watts visibly wavered.

"It does sound sensible," Mrs. Watts said. "Let's go home, Al. My feet hurt."

He gave in. "All right, but if I don't have my horse back tomorrow, you'll be the first to hear about it. Not sure why I'm letting you talk me into this. I ought to go to the police—if they don't come to me first! That's a valuable horse, you know."

"I'll take Cecil back and rub him down," Kath said. "Tell Ma I'll be along, Andy. You've had a grand time, haven't you, Cece. Didn't he look sharp? Did you see how he showed off for everyone? Marvelous pony!" She rubbed his ears affectionately. "Back to the snow plow in the morning, chum."

"But what glory this evening!" added Skip. "I'll take Geoff home and pick you up at the stables. Commodore, can you take Andy and Dan back? Thanks. God knows when George'll be off duty, they dispatched him out Lowell Road."

Alan and Liz Watts walked to their car, arm in arm, arguing comfortably. Skip started the truck. Kath remounted Cecil and headed back the way she'd come.

Eliot disentangled Charlotte. "Come on, Chuck. Enough excitement for one evening. Forgot my gloves and my hands is froze! Wonder where I left them—?"

"Good-bye then," called the Commodore, herding the others toward his car. "Thank you for your help, Charlotte."

"What's *that* mean?" asked Eliot.

"Oh," said Charlotte, "nothing much. Not really."

He gave her a calculating look. She remembered the group by the monument and turned back for an instant, but the men had gone. She'd forgotten to tell the Commodore; it couldn't matter, they'd lost the round anyway.

"I still haven't seen Deb," remarked Eliot.

"She must've gone home with Mom and Dad," Charlotte suggested.

That was plausible. They drove back together in silence. Now that the festivities were over, the snow capriciously slackened, almost stopped, though wind buffeted the VW.

Everyone else was in by the time Eliot and Charlotte arrived. They were standing about in the kitchen, drinking brandy or cocoa. Deb, in her long plaid bathrobe and moccasins, sipped herb tea out of a handmade mug. Charlotte's heart sank when she saw her.

"Quite a night, isn't it?" remarked Max. "Jean kept wondering if the whole thing wouldn't be cancelled because of the snow."

"We are made of sterner stuff," declared Mr. Paige, savoring his brandy.

Eliot stared thoughtfully at Deb, then at Charlotte. Charlotte held her breath. He must have recognized the anxiety in her face. He said, "It was almost cancelled. But not by the storm. Deb, your Geoff—"

"He is *not* 'my' Geoff," Deb contradicted him.

"Apologies, Sis."

Deb's expression showed clearly how much she disliked being called "Sis."

"Our friend Geoff Reynolds had an accident in Lexington and lost his horse this evening."

"He wasn't hurt, I hope?" asked Mrs. Paige.

"Sprained an ankle."

"Did anyone take his place?" In spite of herself, Deb was interested.

"I thought you were there," said Jean in surprise.

"Not me. I chose not to behave like a lunatic this year. Steph and I went out earlier, but I've been home since eleven."

"But I thought—"

"Me, too," said Eliot, "but I guess we were wrong, Jean. Anyhow, it was Kath Schuyler on the snowplow pony who saved the day."

The tension in Charlotte relaxed; she might have known she could count on Eliot. She smiled at him with gratitude and he gave her a wink.

"I wondered who that was," said Mrs. Paige. "Good heavens, you mean her mother let her do that in the middle of a storm? She can't be much older than Charlotte."

"Samatha Prescott!" Mr. Paige exclaimed. "What a blow for women's lib." He helped himself to more brandy.

"Not funny," said Deb judicially. "I'm going to bed."

"You're bitter because you missed a historic event," Max told her.

"Babble on, Gordon Maxwell," his sister replied.

"Much as I hate to leave the party," said Jean, "I am about to fall over. I worked all day, remember."

The silliness vanished from Max's face. "Of course you did, love. I'm sorry, you must be exhausted. Are you all right?"

His sudden concern startled the rest of his family, but Jean smiled. "Of course I'm all right. Just tired. And I'll bet Charlotte is, too. Come on, Charlie, let's beat them to the bathrooms!" She said nothing more about who was and who wasn't in the Square that evening, nor did Eliot.

Chapter Thirteen

THE WORLD BEYOND CHARLOTTE'S WINDOWS LAY MUFFLED IN snow. The air was clear and gray; cold winter light lay across the river. Charlotte looked out on it with distaste as she dressed Sunday morning. Winter had worn thin its welcome by March; it had no business at all in April. She was impatient for spring: gentle sun and the smell of drying earth; buds and flowers and new grass underfoot; open windows and sweaters instead of coats; and daylight far into the green afternoons. The snow was an affront.

It was late, but this morning she didn't worry about the rest of the family deserting her—everyone was slow. Only Eliot was out already: gone to the Episcopal church where he was acting organist until they found someone more conservative and sedate-looking. Not that that was an accurate measure of the inner man, as Eliot pointed out. The last conservative, sedate-looking organist had joined a Zen organic farming commune in New Hampshire, where she now played her music to pea vines and young corn.

By the time Charlotte came along, her parents were far less conscientious about her religious education than they had been about that of their other three children. As a result Charlotte had escaped Sunday school almost entirely, and if she went to church with any regularity, it was to hear Eliot either sing or play. He had taught her his love of church music, from Bach cantatas to "Amazing Grace."

Breakfast this Sunday was an extremely relaxed meal; it was going on all over the first floor of the house: the messier bits like eggs and grapefruit in the kitchen, but milk, coffee and tea, cereal, toast and cinnamon buns wherever anyone carried them.

Max was frying up last night's leftover mashed potatoes in huge pancakes, while Deb watched with undisguised disgust. She confined herself to a whole grapefruit and bowl of granola. "I don't envy your stomach having to cope with that," she remarked.

"My stomach is quite used to being treated to goodies like these, thank you," Max replied cheerfuly.

"Can I have one?" asked Charlotte, her mouth watering.

"Of course!" Max slid a golden cake onto a plate for her. "Great with plenty of butter and strawberry jam."

"Eeeesch. Charlotte is still a minor, remember! At least Jean has more sense than to ruin her digestion."

"Actually . . ." Max paused, spatula aloft. There was an odd excitement in his voice. "Actually, she'd be eating these, too, but lately she hasn't been very hungry in the mornings."

Deb finished her grapefruit and gave her brother a long, level look. "Really?" she said at last. "Like that, is it?"

Max's beard split in a wide, boyish grin. "Really! But don't say anything yet, will you? We agreed to tell everyone together."

"Tell everyone what?" asked Charlotte, mystified.

"Don't worry," exclaimed Deb dryly, "*I* certainly won't ruin your surprise."

"*What* surprise?"

"Well, congratulations, Max. I suppose you did plan to have one now?"

"Mmmmm." Max gave a noncommittal grunt. "It's a little earlier than we'd intended, but we'll manage."

"I hope Jean's pleased."

"Pleased about *what?*" cried Charlotte in frustration. "Manage what?"

Her brother and sister exchanged a knowing, infuriating glance and Max said, "Okay, Charlie, but you have to promise not to tell."

"Yes, all right, I promise. What?"

"We're going to have a baby!" Max looked ready to burst.

"Actually, Jean's going to have it," Deb amended, and added with a small indulgent smile, "You'd think it was an extraordinary event. Expectant fathers are insufferable."

"It is extraordinary—for us," declared Max.

"All this fuss is about a baby?" Charlotte was genuinely surprised.

"The fuss," her sister predicted, "is only about to begin. Wait until it's born. First grandchild." She rolled her eyes. "You'll be an aunt, Charlotte, how do you like that?"

"But I can't be an aunt," Charlotte protested. "Aunts are much older."

But Max, still grinning, shook his head. "Not always. Remember, not a word until we announce it."

"You're far more likely to blow it than either of us," Deb told him.

"Nonsense! I can keep a secret."

Taking with her two buns and a glass of milk, Charlotte wandered into the living room. It was hard for her to understand Max's excitement—from all she knew about them, babies sounded like more trouble than rabbits and were equally unsatisfactory. This baby would simply be one more thing to pull Max away from his family.

Mrs. Paige was comfortably settled in her favorite chair in the bay window, with the *New York Times* cascading around her. Only on Sunday mornings did she come to breakfast in her robe, and then she allowed herself all the time she wanted to sift through the newspaper. Of course, even in her robe, she managed to look well-dressed and stylish without visible effort.

Jean, on the other hand, was comfortably disheveled in her bathrobe; she had made herself a nest on the sofa out of pillows and the *Boston Globe* and wrapped an afghan over her feet.

"Want the funnies, Charlie?" she offered, looking up.

"Mmm," said Charlotte. Jean did not look any different to her. There was no obvious evidence of this baby that Charlotte could see, but Jean was plump and the bathrobe thick and shapeless, so it mightn't be easy to detect.

Jean returned her sister-in-law's gaze with one of amusement. "There isn't much showing yet," she said softly, "but she's coming along well, I'm told."

"Who?" Charlotte pretended not to know, but her face grew hot at the idea of being so transparent.

"It's all right," Jean assured her, misinterpreting the blush. "I didn't really expect Max to keep still for long. It was bound to come out this weekend. Don't worry."

Charlotte sat down on the floor and hid behind the funny papers. She ate the buns without giving them her usual careful attention and with only passing regret when they were gone.

Camomile and Lap played hide-and-go-seek with the Sports and Real Estate sections, creeping underneath the leaves and jumping on one another. The house drowsed in Sunday peace.

No one expected the front door bell to ring. Mr. Paige, who was just coming downstairs, answered it. Charlotte, Jean, and Mrs. Paige sat where they were and wondered while he held a brief conversation in the front hall; they could hear the sound of his definite, interested voice, and gaps when someone spoke in inaudible reply.

"Just a minute, I'll see." He appeared in the doorway. "Kit, do you know where Charlotte is?"

She was hidden from him by the sofa, but being asked for so startled her that she straightened up and peered over the back of it at him. "Me?"

"Oh, there you are. Good morning! Two of your friends are here."

"My friends?"

Mr. Paige nodded. "So they say. Schuyler—is that right? A boy in a funny-looking hat and a girl. Look like twins."

Charlotte snapped her mouth shut.

"Well, aren't you going?" Mrs. Paige prodded gently. She managed to conceal her surprise very well, but Charlotte detected the shadow of it hovering between her eyebrows. Friends did not normally come calling on the youngest Paige.

"I suppose," replied Charlotte with care. Her heart thudded

irrationally and her mouth had gone dry. She couldn't imagine what would bring the Schuylers to her house to ask for her.

"Gordon, while you're here, who in the name of heaven is 'the Big Bird of baseball'?" Mrs. Paige's pencil was poised over the crossword. She sounded totally disinterested in Charlotte's visitors, but Charlotte knew she wasn't.

"Fidrych," said Mr. Paige promptly. "F-i-d-r-y-c-h. Detroit."

Andy and Kath were waiting in the front hall. They swallowed whatever they'd been whispering to one another as soon as they saw Charlotte. Andy pulled off his cap and smiled.

"How are they?" Charlotte asked, meaning his ears.

"Better thanks."

Kath looked impatient. "I still don't see what she can do," she said to her brother. That didn't sound very promising and Charlotte was getting tired of asking "What?"

"But she *knows* him," Andy answered. "You do know Commodore Shattuck, don't you?"

"Yes," said Charlotte. She was not going to let Kath Schuyler intimidate her.

"I told you."

"All right then, get on with it!"

Andy took a deep breath, then let it out in a sigh. "It's kind of hard—"

"You make it hard," said Kath. "Just tell her what we want. Or I will."

"Somebody better," Charlotte agreed. "Does it have to do with last night?"

"Yes." Andy nodded. "And our brother, Dan."

"She already knows Dan's our brother."

"Stop saying 'she' as if I'm not here."

Kath shrugged. "Dan's gone. That's what we've come about."

"Gone? He went home with you in the Commodore's car— I saw you leave," said Charlotte.

"No, he didn't." Andy looked worried. "At least he started out with us, but then he disappeared. We thought he must have ducked out and gone with Skip in the pickup."

"But he hadn't," put in Kath. "He wasn't in the truck when Skip picked me up at the stables, so somewhere between the flagpole and the cars he vanished."

"And"—Charlotte stared at them as she realized what they were saying—"and you haven't seen him since last *night?* Did you call the police?"

"No."

"Well, you see, no one knows except the three of us," said Andy. "I thought he was with Kath and Kath thought he was with me, and we got home at different times, so we didn't know he was missing until this morning. He didn't sleep in his bed."

"What about your mother?" asked Charlotte incredulous. "*She* must know."

But Andy shook his head. "No school, so we all eat breakfast at different times. She hasn't missed him yet."

In silence Charlotte took this in.

"Now what?" Kath demanded of her brother. "We've told her, so what do you expect her to do? We should have gone straight to the Commodore. I said so, didn't I?"

"The Commodore?" Charlotte blinked. "Why?"

"Oh, come on," said Kath impatiently. "He's at the bottom of this. That business last night was no ordinary accident. Geoff Reynolds doesn't fall off horses. And Commodore Shattuck seemed to know all about Baba; he kept saying she was safe, and he knew she was, he really did. He's in this up to the eyebrows. If anyone can tell us where Dan is, I'll bet he can."

"Why didn't you go to him then?"

"We don't know him," Andy said. "Skip does, but we haven't even talked to him about this yet. We decided we'd try to find Dan on our own first. Anyhow, I thought maybe you'd go with us to see Commodore Shattuck. I feel funny just going by myself."

"I don't. And I want Baba back, too. I didn't mind doing that bit last night with Cecil, but this has gone far enough. Will you help us, or not?"

Kath's abrupt question caught Charlotte off guard. "Well, I—" She hesitated then plunged. "Yes, I will." She accepted

Kath's outright challenge, to her own surprise. "I'll tell Mum I'm going out."

Kath and Andy had brought bikes, so the three of them rode through the Sunday-slow town. Gifford's Market, which sold Sunday papers, was the only focus of activity. The sky hung low and ominous; the world was fast in winter again, looking like everyone's idea of New England in December: a neat Colonial town with white frame churches and a snowy green.

Their bike tires hissed on the wet pavement. A stream of gritty spray soaked the ankles of Charlotte's clean jeans. It irked her a little that Kath should be leading the way after the Schuylers had come to ask *her* for help, but she had to admit, if only to herself, that Kath was a stronger rider. It took some effort to keep up without letting it show. Andy didn't seem to mind bringing up the rear.

With Kath setting the pace, they soon reached the Commodore's house. They left their bikes in the driveway—still unshovelled—and trooped up to the front door. Goaded by Kath's proprietary attitude toward the expedition, Charlotte rang the bell before anyone else could.

"Ring it again," said Kath after a long interval of silence.

Charlotte did. At last there were scuffling sounds on the other side of the door and it opened about six inches.

"It's you," said Oliver as one stating an unwelcome fact. "What do you want?"

"To see Commodore Shattuck," Kath responded promptly.

"He's not in." Oliver moved to shut the door, but Kath's foot was in the way.

"Car's in the driveway," observed Andy.

And Charlotte added, "We'll wait," with unexpected firmness. Oliver and Kath between them called out every ounce of her stubbornness.

Oliver shot her a look of resentment. "You'll get cold standing around outside."

"Then we'll come in." Charlotte pushed past him before he could stop her. Yesterday this had been unfamiliar territory;

she'd been awed and intimidated by it and the Commodore and she'd been on her own. Now she knew where she was, and Andy and Kath were watching. Besides, she was fed up with Oliver.

"You can't!" he said indignantly. "You can't barge into our house this way!"

But the Schuylers had followed on her heels, and Kath said, "Look, cut it, will you? This is important. When's he coming back? We've got to talk to him."

Oliver's eyes narrowed; he acknowledged her tone of voice. "What about?"

"We want to ask him—" began Andy.

"We want to ask *him*," interrupted Kath with the kind of rudeness tolerated between brothers and sisters.

Oliver thought for a minute, his face a careful blank, then made up his mind. "Okay," he conceded, coming to a bargain with them but not telling them what it was. "Follow me, but hurry up. And don't stop to snoop."

"Nice kid," remarked Kath. She didn't bother to lower her voice.

Oliver led them through the house, through the kitchen where Charlotte had sat forlorn and thawing—only yesterday afternoon?—and out a back door. It opened onto a screened porch with a sloping roof, quite private from the road. Outside the fine mesh walls was a small backyard punctuated with dark evergreens and snow-humped shrubs. To the right lay the river, behind a narrow ridge lined with yellowing willows looking like giant forsythia and a wilderness of bushes.

Oliver gave them no time to look around; he crossed the porch, unlatched the door, and took a well-trodden path that burrowed deep through the coarse grass. It followed the curve of the river, lost sight of the house, and fetched up on the bank of a wide inlet, a river pond. Snow, like white flowers, caught in the bushes and softened the angles of a rowboat turned upside down above the waterline. Sitting on its hull, where he'd brushed a clear patch, was the Commodore, with his back to them. He wore his navy cap and great coat, and a trickle of smoke climbed the still air in front of him, rising from a thick black cigar. A bucket stood empty at his feet, and all over the bank around him a flock of Canada geese stalked and muttered as they gobbled cracked corn off the trampled snow.

Whatever Charlotte had expected to find the Commodore doing at the end of the path, this wasn't it. Nor, evidently was it what Kath and Andy had expected, for they all came to a silent halt at the sight. It was Oliver who broke the spell. "Uncle Sam."

"Mmmm?" said the Commodore without turning.

Kath took a step forward, but Oliver hissed, "Stop it! You'll scare them!"

The Commodore did turn then and nodded. "Doesn't matter, boy. This is the last of the corn and they always come back. They're too greedy to stay away long. Eating me out of pocket this winter, aren't you, troops?"

"Do you clip their wings?" Andy wanted to know.

"Good gracious no! Why go to all that trouble? Then I'd only have to feed the silly things year round. Been a bad winter for geese—no open water for three and a half months. And that one—" He waggled his cigar at a bird standing quite close to the boat, its neck coiled back, one leg tucked under its breast feathers. "That one's a gander I found with a handful of buckshot through his wing three Novembers past. Been stopping in ever since. He brings the others." Commodore Shattuck smiled to himself. "Makes us old friends as geese go. But—" He clamped his teeth on the cigar stub and stood up, scattering the birds who uttered loud curses at being disturbed. "You haven't come on a social call, I can see. You'd better tell me what it is."

"Well—" began Charlotte, feeling she was expected to explain.

But Kath cut across her. "We have a problem, and you're part of it."

"Now wait a minute," challenged Oliver hotly. "Who d'you think you're talking to?" He went to stand beside his great-uncle, as if they were choosing sides.

The Commodore handed him the bucket. "Only way to find out is to listen, boy," he said and put a hand on Oliver's arm. "Might as well listen in the house while we're at it, long as you don't have a coat on."

Chapter Fourteen

"NOW," SAID KATH, LEANING FORWARD PURPOSEFULLY. THEY sat in a lopsided circle in the Commodore's front room. "I don't know what was going on last night, but it was something fishy. That wasn't an ordinary accident Geoff had— I'm not stupid enough to think it was, in spite of what you told us."

"No," agreed the Commodore. "I never thought you were. But I hadn't the time to explain just then."

"Now it's over so there isn't any need to," put in Oliver who sat on the floor by his great-uncle.

"Oh no it isn't," contradicted Kath. "There's a *lot* of explaining necessary. Because of all that business last night, our brother Dan's missing, and we've come to find out where he is."

"Why did you come here? We don't have him," Oliver retorted. "He isn't our responsibility; we didn't even want him along."

The Commodore put a restraining hand on his great-nephew's shoulder. "How long has he been missing?"

"Since last night when we left the Square."

"And what have you done about it so far?"

"Nothing." Andy's face wrinkled with worry. "We should have, Kath, I told you we should have."

"Shut up," she said briskly. "We didn't know until this morning because we went home separately, but we know

now, and I'll bet you can tell us where he is."

"We can't," Oliver stated flatly.

"Hmmm," said the Commodore. "Interesting."

"Is he with Baba?'

"As a matter of fact," Commodore Shattuck admitted, "most probably. But I'll be damned if I know why they took your brother. I can understand them taking Oliver, but not Daniel."

"Why Oliver?" Charlotte asked.

"Because he's my great-nephew," replied the Commodore as if that explained everything.

Oliver said nothing; he sat tight where he was.

Kath said, "You know the people who took Dan, don't you?"

"Assuming he was taken."

"Well, he didn't get lost," declared Kath. "He's ten years old and *very* smart. I think he's been kidnapped."

"Oh no." Andy looked stricken. "What can we do? We'll *have* to call the police."

"Police again!" exclaimed the Commodore. "Can't people ever solve their own problems these days? If you haven't called them, I urge you to leave them out of this. It isn't that kind of business—not at all. I can't understand why MacPherson isn't doing a better job of this," he added to himself. "*I* gave him his training!"

"Look," said Kath, "I don't know what kind of business this is, but I do know that if we don't get Dan back my parents are going to be furious. We can't hide the fact that he's missing very much longer even if I could see a reason to, which I still can't. And Alan Watts is going to be furious if Baba doesn't turn up. You're going to have the police involved whether you want them or not."

The Commodore regarded her shrewdly for a minute or two. "Oliver m'boy, stand up."

"Why?"

"Just stand up. That's it. Now then, tell me. Daniel about `at size? Thinnish? Brown hair?"

"Yes, but—"

"Then there's your answer. MacPherson's got the wrong

boy. He wanted my great-nephew and got your brother. Careless mistake. No doubt he was upset when the horse and rider turned up in spite of his efforts, but that hardly excuses it. Never mind that. Daniel will come to no harm where he is, I assure you."

"That's what you say each time something disappears," said Kath, "but how do we *know?*"

Andy and Charlotte nodded.

The Commodore sighed. "It's a very long story, Katherine, but if you're going to insist, I'll do what I can to shorten it. In the Second World War, I was given a command in the British Navy."

Kath frowned impatiently and Oliver glared at her.

The Commodore went on. "I took charge of a small convoy in the Atlantic and the captain on my ship was a Scotsman by the name of James MacPherson—Jimmy, he was." A curtain of memory dropped between him and his listeners. Charlotte saw Commodore Shattuck sitting on his sofa in his sitting room in Concord, but though he seemed to be looking back at her, she could tell he didn't see her. His eyes were on something far different, invisible to the rest of them. "We had good days, Jimmy and I," he said from a distance. Then he gave his head a little shake and came back to the present. "Kept in touch ever since—some forty years now. I've been to visit him twice, but he's never come here."

"Until now." Charlotte's mind made the connection. "It's him, isn't it?"

"Mmmph." The Commodore fixed her with his eyes and she swallowed what she'd been going to add about the man in Woolworth's.

"You mean he's here in Concord?" asked Andy. "And what's he got to do with Dan?"

"Everything."

"If he's visiting you," said Kath, "and he's got Dan for some reason, then Dan must be here in this house." She rose from her chair.

"Wrong conclusion! Jimmy MacPherson is not exactly visiting me, not the way you mean. He isn't staying here. It's more that he's *invading*."

Kath looked blank.

"Back on that ship in the Atlantic we used to spend our off-duty hours arguing," explained the Commodore. "We refought all the greatest British and American wars, debated military strategy into the early watches! After the war, we did it by letter—still do. Spent months winning the Boer War properly. The lives and resources we might have saved! The suffering we could have eliminated!"

"Yes," said Kath, "but I don't see—"

"Then sit down and listen!" ordered the Commodore.

She did.

"You're all too impatient these days. You miss so much," he complained. "*Now's* when you've got the time, but you don't understand that, do you? Point is, Jimmy spent several weeks on that ship trying to convince me that given the right men and the right strategy the British would've *won* the Revolution. Our Revolution. What'd you think of that?" His cigar had gone out some time ago and now he puffed furiously to relight it. Clouds of evil-smelling smoke enveloped his head. "Said he'd prove it to me one day." He sat back, arms crossed, and waited for them to understand.

Oliver looked miserable. He didn't want us to know, Charlotte realized with surprise. He's known all along and he wanted to keep it just between himself and his great-uncle. She didn't want to sympathize with Oliver Shattuck, but she couldn't help it, just a little. She knew how unwelcome intrusions could be.

"No," said Kath at last, but the "no" sounded uncertain. "That kind of thing doesn't happen. People can't just refight our Revolutionary War. That's what you're saying, isn't it? That the British are trying to win it this year?"

Andy said slowly, "I think I believe him."

"But Captain MacPherson is the only one you've named," said Charlotte, "and there are others. I've seen them—so's Oliver."

Oliver's expression was wary, but he didn't contradict her.

"Jimmy'd never come alone," the Commodore replied. "Don't know who they are, but he's recruited them somewhere. We'll find out soon enough, I've no doubt. In the meantime, I suppose the question is, what shall we do about young Daniel?"

"Right!" agreed Kath, on firm ground again. She was in favor of immediate action. She wanted to plunge in and get Dan back, no matter what that involved. What was there to sit around and discuss? If the Commodore would just tell them where Dan was being held prisoner, they would do the rest.

Charlotte, listening to her, believed absolutely that Kath could manage the rescue if anyone could. She was so sure of herself, and Andy would back her the whole way.

But the Commodore wouldn't agree. He favored a delay. "What's Daniel like?"

The unexpected question disarmed Kath momentarily and it was Andy who answered. "He's a good kid. He doesn't hang on and slow you down even though he's younger, and he does lots of things by himself. That's why we knew he couldn't have gotten lost last night. Sometimes he gets weird ideas—"

"He isn't the only one." Kath looked meaningfully at the Commodore.

"Is he independent? Fairly brave?"

Andy nodded.

Kath asked suspiciously, "Why?"

"You'd say he can take care of himself?"

"Hold it!" demanded Kath. "Why do you want to know all this?"

"Because I have an idea, Katherine. Suppose instead of charging in to rescue Daniel, we do this."

When he'd finished outlining his plan, Kath didn't look exactly convinced, but she wasn't dead set against it, either. "I don't like the idea of using Dan like that. It puts him right in the middle. He really ought to say whether he wants to be there or not."

"How will you arrange to ask him?" demanded Oliver. "March up there and knock on the door?"

"Where? What door?" Kath pounced on the words.

But Oliver wouldn't answer.

"I think," said Charlotte, "that you—we—could make it

work. I'd like it much better than fighting people."

"Of course we could make it work," Kath affirmed. "That's not the point. The question is whether or not it's the best plan."

"Why don't we try it," said Andy. "We could give ourselves an hour or two to see if it works, and if it doesn't we can try something else."

"That's not much time," warned Kath.

"They were all over town yesterday," Charlotte put in. "We ought to be able to find at least one today."

"All right." Kath capitulated. "An hour and a half. Absolute deadline is twelve noon. We'd better divide up and we'll need some equipment for this."

Ten minutes later they were ready. It was decided they would go in pairs. Though Kath declared she didn't need help, the others weren't all that sure. Besides, Oliver and Charlotte were the ones who could identify the quarry. So Charlotte found herself with Andy for a partner and a coil of clothesline over one shoulder. The rope made her feel foolish, but it was easier to carry it than to argue with Kath.

Commodore Shattuck watched them off from his front porch. "Need a control at Headquarters," he said, "just in case. Good luck."

If any of them had good luck, Charlotte hoped fervently it would be Oliver and Kath. She could not see herself capturing a hostage, rope or no rope.

"Where first?" asked Andy.

"We'll take the Old North Bridge," said Oliver at once.

Charlotte was relieved; that seemed the likeliest area. "Then we'll try town," she decided.

"Twelve o'clock," warned Kath. "Don't you two be late."

"Don't worry about *us*," replied Charlotte.

She and Andy set off down Monument Street at a brisk pace. The route between the Commodore's house and the middle of Concord was beginning to look excessively familiar. The peculiarity of the situation struck Charlotte anew: never had she expected to become personally acquainted with the eccentric Commodore Shattuck and his weird great-nephew, or Andy and Kath Schuyler. It was as if someone mighty and invisible, with nothing better to do, had decided to shake up Charlotte Paige's life just to see what would happen. She wondered how long she would have to put up with the chaos before she could return to her familiar, comfortable existence, an existence that didn't include all these difficult people.

But an unsettling doubt had crept into the picture. The changes had begun coming, subtly, gradually, long before this. There couldn't be any going back—life didn't work that way, and this new perception frightened her. Ahead was the unknown dark; what light there was in the tunnel lay behind her.

"Weren't those geese terrific?" said Andy, shattering her disturbing thoughts as easily as ice on a puddle. "So tame! I'd love to have some of those in our pond. I wonder if he'd tell me how to get them to come."

"Find one with a broken wing," Charlotte suggested, but Andy missed the sarcasm.

"There must be other ways to do it. Where should we start looking?"

"For geese?"

"For whoever it is we're supposed to find this morning."

"Why did you want to come with me?" Charlotte asked curiously. For Andy had chosen her as partner as soon as they'd decided to go in pairs.

"I didn't want to go with Oliver," he answered bluntly. "He's kind of strange, isn't he? Do you mind that I picked you?"

"No. I suppose not." Better Andy than Kath, come to think of it. But it annoyed her that he'd made a negative choice rather than a positive one, and that annoyed her still further because she oughtn't to care what Andy thought.

They trudged on, past houses deep in Sunday silence. Few people had bothered to shovel their driveways and front walks yet. Only two cars passed them all the way to the Square. Andy pulled his cap over his ears to protect them from the raw, unfriendly air, and that made conversation too difficult to bother with. Charlotte gave it up without a struggle. She had no premonitions of success about their mission; instead she was beginning to think of this exercise as a pointless waste of time.

The men could be anywhere in Concord. What real chance did she and Andy have of finding one? And suppose they did walk around a corner to come face to face with one—what would they do? She had never captured anyone in her life, and she didn't want to now. She glanced covertly at Andy, to see if she could tell what he was thinking, but he looked so unconcerned she only felt worse. What's the matter with him, and how did I get into this? she wondered irritably.

For three-quarters of an hour they scouted the near-empty town. They went into Gifford's and both the drugstores. They searched the municipal parking lots and went as far as the library. They even climbed to the top of the steep Burying Ground at the head of Main Street, where Deb had encountered her admirer the day before. All to no avail. There was not a sign of the foreigners anywhere. Andy began to look doubtful and Charlotte congratulated herself. They would be able to report honestly that they had tried to find a hostage.

As they came out of the Burying Ground, Andy said regretfully, "I guess we ought to start back. I thought you said they were all over town?"

"Yesterday they were. They must have gone somewhere else."

"And taken Dan. What am I going to do about him?" Andy sounded so discouraged Charlotte felt sorry for him. "You know," he went on, "Commodore Shattuck's story sounded so—so believable when he was telling it, but now I'm not sure."

Charlotte said consideringly, "I don't think he's making it up. It fits too well."

"But there couldn't really be an invasion, could there? I mean, Kath was right, that kind of thing doesn't happen outside of books."

Charlotte shrugged. "We're going to be late if we stand around here. The others have probably caught someone by now—we'd better go straight back."

"Straight back" seemed like a very long way. With each step, Charlotte found herself wishing harder she didn't have to go; she would much rather have headed for her own house instead of the Commodore's. Her family must wonder where she was all this time, perhaps they'd even begun to worry a little. And who knew what they were doing, what she was missing out on, at this very moment.

She made up her mind. She would go back to the Commodore's with Andy, admit they'd had no luck and explain that she was expected at home. She had no more time to play someone else's games, she had a family who needed her. They had plans of their own—

" 'Scuse me, 'old on a tick, will you? Can you tell me 'ow to find this Walden-Pond-thing? I've lost me bearings some-'ow—can't seem to get the right road."

Charlotte jolted to a stop. Of all the miserable luck! Now that they'd stopped looking, now that they were safely on their way back empty-handed! With a sinking feeling she recognized the man who smiled engagingly at her and held a battered map under her nose. She wished she didn't, but she knew him at once as the man she'd spoken to in Gurney's drugstore the day before.

Andy didn't notice her dismay. He peered over her shoulder at the much-folded, dog-eared HISTORIC MAP OF CONCORD MASSACHUSETTS, thoughtfully printed up in quantity by one of the savings banks.

"Walden Pond?" repeated Andy as if he hadn't heard the man's peculiar accent. For a blinding moment, Charlotte considered pretending she hadn't either, but realized that wouldn't work. She thought of Dan and Commodore Shattuck and couldn't.

"Well, for one thing," Andy began helpfully, "you're going in the—oooop!" He rubbed his side in surprise where Charlotte had given him a sharp dig with her elbow.

"What's that then? Going wrong, am I?" The stranger looked up from his map and caught Charlotte making faces at Andy. " 'Ere," he said with concern, "you all right, luv?"

Andy seemed determined to be thick; he would not understand her message. In exasperation, she abandoned subtleties

164

and blurted outright, "You idiot, he's one of them! We want him!"

Andy's mouth opened but nothing came out for a moment. Then he demanded, "Why didn't you say so?"

"Oh, for Pete's sake!" cried Charlotte. "*Grab* him!" And before she could give herself time to hesitate, she caught the man by one arm.

" 'Ullo, 'ullo," he said in surprise, "what's this then?"

Looking somewhat perplexed, Andy took his other arm. "Now what?"

"You think of something. *I* caught him."

"We could tie him up." Andy sounded doubtful.

"D'you mean me?" said the man. "Why'd you do that, mate? 'Ave I said sommat amiss? All's I asked—"

"Do you think we have to?" Charlotte asked Andy. The idea didn't appeal to her. Suppose someone saw them doing it, mightn't they get into real trouble? Then too, if the man chose not to be tied up, he was big enough to make it very awkward for them.

"I don't know," said Andy.

" 'Ere," the man put in, "if you mean tyin' up with rope, I'd really rather not, if it's all the same. Seems a bit off to me."

"Are you going to struggle?" Andy asked.

"Or try to run away?"

"Crook me elbow an' 'ope it never comes straight! Trust me 'onest face, will you?"

"I think he means he won't," said Charlotte, "but we'd better hold onto him just the same." To the man she said, "We've caught you fairly now, so you have to come with us."

"Right you are, then," agreed the man.

All three of them much relieved, they set off again, Andy and Charlotte on either side of the hostage.

"If it ent too much to ask," he said after a bit, "could you tell me what all this is in aid of, 'ey? Where'm I going?"

"You're a prisoner," replied Charlotte. "We don't have to explain." But that sounded terribly unfriendly after he'd been so obliging about being caught, so she added, "We have to hurry because we're going to be late."

"What does that matter?" Andy demanded jubilantly. "I

never thought *we'd* be the ones to get a prisoner. It's always Kath who does things like that, not me!"

That cheered Charlotte up a little. "I knew we could. Why shouldn't it be us?"

The man between them cleared his throat noisily. "Me name's Cheavy. Friends calls me Fred." He looked from one to the other of them encouragingly.

"Are we friends?" asked Andy dubiously.

Fred shrugged. "Why not? 'Oo says we can't be?"

"Won't do any harm, I suppose," he conceded. "I'm Andy and she's Charlotte."

" 'Ow do," said the hostage. "Tidy village you've got. Mind you, I 'aven't seen all of it yet. But that bit last night with the 'orse and marchin' was all right. Me Uncle Sid would've thought that was grand, 'e would. It's 'is business, y'see. 'E's a turf accountant in 'Ammersmith, me Uncle Sid is."

"What's a turf accountant?" asked Andy.

" 'E takes bets on the 'orses. Done real well for 'imself."

"I didn't see you there last night."

"I did," said Charlotte. "All of them were there."

"The old man weren't 'arf mad about it gettin' messed up. Proper cheesed off, 'e were! Glad it weren't me told off to nobble that bloke on the 'orse. 'E was still steamin' this morning."

"Who's this old man?" Andy wanted to know.

"Captain MacPherson—'im that paid for us all to come 'ere. Though why 'e did, I'm still not clear. Nick says it's a joke on someone, but seems a pricey kind of joke to me. Still I'm not one to look a gift 'orse in the mouth. 'E paid me plane fare and I'd not 'ave got 'ere otherwise."

"You mean you don't know why you've come?" Charlotte couldn't help asking. "You came all the way from England without knowing why?"

Fred shrugged. "Sommat to do with me dad, 'e says. Me dad was in the Navy with 'im, see. Chums, they was. When 'e comes to me with a plane ticket in 'is 'and, I says to meself, Fred old lad, I says—'ere—" He broke off, his attention caught by the long yellow house they were passing. "What's in that little frame-thing by the door of that 'ouse?"

Charlotte, who'd been fascinated by his story and way of telling it, glanced up. "Oh, it's just a bullet hole. Nothing exciting."

"Bullet 'ole? All done up fancy in a frame?"

They couldn't move him further until they'd taken hin right up to the side of the Park Director's house and shown him: a small diamond-shaped pane of glass fixed to the clapboards over a tiny hole. During the battle at the bridge in 1775, a bullet had embedded itself in the wall of what was now known as the Bullet Hole House. Charlotte hoped fervently that no one inside would look out and see them trespassing. Apparently no one did, for they went unchallenged.

Back on the sidewalk, they hustled Fred—mildly protesting—past the Manse and the North Bridge, across the river, and up to the Commodore's front door. It opened as they stepped onto the porch, and there were Kath and Oliver, looking impatient.

Chapter Fifteen

"YOU'RE ALMOST TWENTY MINUTES LATE," SAID KATH.

"But we've got a hostage!" exclaimed Andy. "Did you?"

"That's a hostage? Are you sure?" Oliver inspected Fred critically.

"Of course, he is," Charlotte declared. "His name's Fred. Are you going to let us in?"

"Splendid!" cried the Commodore coming down the stairs. "I knew you could manage it. Come along in, don't hold the door open like a ninny, Katherine." To everyone's surprise, he strode forward and shook hands with Fred, who beamed at him. "So glad you could come!"

"What are you doing?" said Oliver. "That's the enemy."

"True," his great-uncle conceded. "Slipped my mind."

"Enemy?" said Fred. "Me, you mean? 'Oose enemy?" His voice rose an octave in disbelief.

"Ours," replied Oliver. "Aren't you?"

"*Me?* What rubbish! I've never clapped me eyes on you lot before! 'Ow can we be enemies, then? Gorblimey, you're 'aving me on, mate."

"What kind of hostage is this anyway?" demanded Oliver. "You didn't even tie him up! He comes in here like a guest, shakes hands with people, denies he's our enemy—"

"He's better than any you got," Charlotte countered. "No one said we had to find a hostile one. You ought to congratulate us—you're just mad because we caught him and you didn't."

"Cut it out," ordered Kath. "It doesn't matter who caught him, does it? Now that he's here we have to figure out the next move, so stop yelling at each other and think for a change, will you?"

The Commodore took charge. "Sounds to me as if we could all use a little lunch. Amazing how a sandwich or two restores equilibrium. Let's carry this discussion into the kitchen, shall we?"

"Right-o, guv!" agreed Fred enthusiastically. "Rare famished, I am. Meals 'aven't been quite so regular as I'm used." He shed his duffel coat and the Commodore hung it over the newel-post at the foot of the stairs.

"What's your name?" he asked the hostage as he led the way.

"Frederick R. Cheavy, guv. Friends calls me Fred."

"Cheavy—Cheavy—seems to me I knew a Cheavy during the war. Donald, would it have been?"

"Aye, me dad, 'e was. Fancy you knowin' 'im. 'E passed on three years ago August. 'E was a greengrocer in Claygate— left me the shop. Tidy little business it is, I don't complain, mind you. But I always wanted to see a bit a the world," Fred ran on cheerfully.

Commodore Shattuck turned out to have a surprisingly well-stocked refrigerator; the sight of food reminded everyone how long it had been since breakfast, and though they glowered a little at one another, they did it silently. All hands turned to and assembled thick ham and cheese sandwiches, while the Commodore and Fred mixed up a double batch of tomato soup. Fred's attention wandered easily, however. He was fascinated by unfamiliar appliances and equipment—had to try the Waring blender, have the disposal demonstrated, examine the toaster oven, and explore the refrigerator. He was overcome by the food-processor.

Kath tapped her forehead with a finger. "I never thought of England as a *backward* country."

"Indeed it's not," said the Commodore, "but it is foreign and things like kitchens are bound to be different."

Charlotte wondered what Fred would make of Deb's natural foods: wheat germ, toasted soybeans, spinach noodles, bean sprouts.

For ten or fifteen minutes after everything was ready, no one said a word. They were all too busy eating: pickles, potato chips—Fred called them "crisps"—carrots, and hard-boiled eggs besides the soup and sandwiches. It was an impromptu picnic, right there in the middle of the Commodore's kitchen—an odd assortment of people thrown together by irregular circumstances.

Then Kath rapped with her spoon on her soup bowl to call them to order. "Okay. We've got to come up with a plan now. "He"— she nodded at the Commodore—"said get a hostage, so we got one—more or less. Now what do we do with him?"

"I thought we were going to exchange him for Dan," said Andy.

"Some one of us is going to have to tell *them* that," Charlotte pointed out. "They probably haven't even missed Fred yet."

"She's right," Oliver conceded reluctantly. "Specially if he's been wandering around sightseeing."

" 'Ere," put in Fred who'd been following the discussion with interest. "You nobbled me because our lot nobbled one of your mates, that it? You want to trade us off?"

"Yes," said Andy. "Your gang has my brother."

"That your brother? Nice kid, right as a trivet." A frown creased Fred's round face. "But the Captain says 'e was the only kid we'd run into 'ere—the Commodore's nephew, 'e says. Where'd you lot come from, I'd like to know?"

"What did I tell you," said the Commodore. "Jimmy's luck seems to have turned. That's where Dan disappeared to, is it?"

"Dan—that's right. Safe as 'ouses, 'e is, Guv."

"We aren't getting anywhere!" Kath complained as the front doorbell rang: two loud, long buzzes.

"Party's livening up," commented the Commodore. "Who d'you suppose that is? Oliver—"

But Oliver was already out of the room, gone to see. Charlotte felt a spasm of sympathy for him; what a chaotic muddle this had become, with people leaping in all directions beyond his control. He'd wanted so badly to keep them all out of it. But it wasn't as if she'd asked to join in—she'd been pulled in against her will. The sympathy evaporated.

"Uncle Sam?" Oliver was back, his thin face tense but un-readable. "I think you'd better come."

"Oh?" The Commodore heaved himself upright.

Kath and Andy exchanged a glance and rose to follow. Charlotte and Fred brought up the rear. A tall young man stood in the front hall looking nonchalant and holding an enormous white handkerchief.

"Commodore Shattuck? Nicholas Boutwell-Scott, at your service, sir. Flag of truce." He shook the handkerchief. "I've come to parley with you. I think I was chosen because I'm rather less sorry-looking than any of the others." He had a handsome, clever face and there was a spark of amusement in his blue eyes. "I've been commissioned to negotiate your sur-render, I do hope you don't mind, but if you would like your great-nephew returned to you all alive-o, I'm instructed to tell you to come to terms without delay."

"Ah," said the Commodore, pressing his fingertips together and nodding.

"Captain James MacPherson sends you his compliments and deepest sympathy. He fears you are losing your grip, sir."

"Does he indeed."

Nicholas Boutwell-Scott smiled pleasantly. "Would you like to hear the conditions?"

"Perhaps," replied the Commodore, "it would be as well to examine the entire picture before we discuss conditions."

"I don't believe the Captain has 'discussion' in mind, sir. He led me to believe he expects nothing short of complete capit-ulation. He mentioned items like ears in matchboxes, finger joints, that kind of thing."

"Ears in matchboxes?" echoed Kath. "You mean *Dan's* ears? Now wait a minute—" Her eyes flashed dangerously.

"Shut up!" whispered Oliver fiercely.

The Commodore paid no attention to either of them. "You tell Captain MacPherson that he had better think twice be-fore he does anything rash," he said calmly. "To begin with, he should be sure whose ears he will be removing."

Nicholas Boutwell-Scott sighed. "That, sir, I'm afraid, is a time-honored bluff."

"Oh, no it isn't!" exclaimed Kath pushing forward. "It's

not his great-nephew you've kidnapped at all, it's *my* brother, Daniel Schuyler. And if he does anything to hurt Dan there'll be real trouble!"

"Hmm." Nicholas looked thoughtful. "Is this possibly true?"

"Regrettably it is," affirmed the Commodore. "My great-nephew Oliver just now opened the door for you. That means Captain MacPherson has made a serious mistake and taken the wrong boy hostage. You tell the Captain for me that I'm sure I need hardly mention 'international incidents' and the 'CIA,' will you?"

In spite of the talk of severed ears, international incidents, and unconditional surrender, Charlotte was aware that what was going on was actually an elaborate game, played out like a chess match between two people relishing every move. She was not at all worried about the outcome, only fascinated to see how far it would go.

" 'Ere, Nicky," broke in Fred, "what's this rubbish about ears and all?"

"Well, as the actress said to the bishop, that tears it!" exclaimed Nicholas, catching sight of his countryman for the first time. "What in the name of heaven are you doing here, Fred? Jack and Bobby have been out scouring the town, and you turn up, having a visit with the enemy! Haven't you any sense at all, old man? D'you know what the Captain'll say?"

"He is not here by choice," the Commodore told him smugly.

Andy nodded. "He's *our* hostage. Charlie and I caught him this morning and we're going to trade him back for Dan."

Without warning, Nicholas gave a sudden whoop of laughter. "Oh, I say, this was worth coming for! Wouldn't have missed it for a fortune! Frederick, old son, I'm glad I shan't be in your boots when MacPherson hears about this. He's got a tongue that would blister paint."

"I remember," agreed the Commodore. "Don't know what I would have done without him during the war. Kept everyone in line for me."

"He's still doing a fair job of it," said Nicholas. "Well, if you've got a message to send back to him, I'll toddle on up with it. This round looks suspiciously like a draw to me."

"Doesn't it." The Commodore rubbed his stubby hands together. "I expect, if the wind's right, we'll be able to hear Jimmy's reaction from the front porch. It remains for us to decide on a place to exchange hostages. Oh, and you might tell Captain MacPherson that we expect to have the horse back as well."

"Bless you!" Nicholas said fervently. "Only old Beaky will be sorry to see the back end of that brute. Nasty-tempered devil!"

"She's a thoroughbred mare," Kath informed him sharply. "She'd better not have been injured."

"Believe me, that horse has had better care than any of us."

The Commodore unearthed a large-scale map of Concord and everyone, including the hostage and the enemy messenger, poured over it.

"North Bridge is out," said Oliver. "Too close and too familiar."

"Better not in the middle of town," decided the Commodore, "that's too public. We need somewhere less conspicuous."

Andy suggested Walden Pond and Fred nodded eagerly, but Nicholas vetoed that when he saw how far away from the middle of Concord it was. "We have to get there on foot, you know. Can't spend hours marching hither and yon."

Charlotte, who had been studying the map with care, said, "That leaves Sleepy Hollow or the Calf Pasture."

"Well, we can't use Sleepy Hollow," declared Kath.

"Why not?" asked Oliver unexpectedly.

"You can't trade hostages in a cemetery, can you?" Andy said. "It doesn't sound right somehow."

"Private and accessible," observed the Commodore. "Sounds like just the thing."

"Looks all right to me," Nicholas agreed. "Then when the Captain gets through with old Fred here, we can bury him on the spot."

"Not 'umorous, mate. Still wish it was the pond."

"We could use the end by Authors' Ridge," suggested

Charlotte. "Then Fred could see Louisa May Alcott's grave, and Thoreau's. It's a great place for tourists to go."

"That right?" Fred brightened. "This Thoreau bloke's the one lived by the pond, isn't 'e?"

"Settled." Commodore Shattuck consulted his watch. "Shall we say two o'clock at Authors' Ridge? There are signs at the cemetery. Good idea, Charlotte."

"Right-o," said Nicholas, preparing to leave. He gave Charlotte a considering look. "I've seen you before, haven't I?"

Charlotte, who'd recognized him at once as Deb's admirer, tried to look vague.

"No? What filthy weather you've got in this country—and you tell us ours is bad! It's trying to snow again."

"Perhaps you'd like a cup of coffee before you go?" inquired the Commodore hospitably.

"How can you offer him coffee?" demanded Kath. "He's on the other side."

"Uncle Sam can do what he likes," Oliver said.

"Very kind of you, sir," Nicholas replied, "but business first or not at all. When I come back with an answer I may take you up on it. Cheerio!"

He returned with startling speed to report that the place and time of exchange were acceptable. He claimed his ears still buzzed with the Captain's fury and said he hoped temper had cooled a bit by the time two o'clock rolled round or Fred's life wouldn't be worth a farthing.

"Tell me," said the Commodore as they sat down over instant coffee and toasted bran muffins, "who exactly are you? How do you know Captain MacPherson and how have you come to be here? You're no Royal Navy, neither you nor Fred here."

"Told you, guv, I'm a greengrocer," said Fred.

"Came down from Cambridge myself three years ago," Nicholas admitted cheerfully. "Stay as far from the military as I can manage, I promise you! The old man's a London publisher and I'm his only son and heir. He gave me special leave for this lark. Then there's Beaky Tate, he's a stable lad in Yorkshire."

"It's him that's looking after Baba?" Kath asked.

"Only one who can lay a hand on the brute. They seem to speak the same peculiar language—And that, incidentally, explains a good deal about Beaky. We've got a Manchester taxi driver, that's Jack Spooner, and Bobby Hardcastle, who's a plumber from Richmond. The only regular navy is Charles Day, known to his intimates as Happy. He's the one with the sour expression. We are not exactly a crack regiment."

"Then how did you all end up here?" Andy wanted to know. "Were you friends?"

"Never saw each other before." Nicholas stretched his long legs toward the fire and slumped comfortably in his chair. "Bliss, bliss, bliss! One is so apt to take degenerate creature comforts like heat and an indoor loo and a decent mattress for granted! I've found sleeping in a barn rather a rude awakening, if you see what I mean." He drank deeply from his mug.

"Tell me," said the Commodore, "did your father happen to serve with Jimmy MacPherson during the war?"

"He did indeed. Along with everyone elses'."

"I told you about me dad," Fred reminded him.

"So Jimmy's recruited himself a second generation army and brought you all here to celebrate the nineteenth of April." A smile flickered across the Commodore's face. He drew his eyebrows together frighteningly and looked round at Oliver, Kath, Andy and Charlotte. "Well, I suppose we're equal to that!"

Nicholas smiled back. "We'll see, won't we? Here's to the best army!" He drained his coffee and stood up. "Sorry as I am to leave civilization, I think I'd better return to the troops. I look forward to our meeting in the cemetery."

"Is he always like that?" Kath asked Fred when Nicholas had gone.

"Aye, Nicky's all right when you know 'im. Bit of a swell, but with 'is background 's' only what you'd expect."

Charlotte knew she was supposed to be home at three for Sunday dinner. She could have used that as an excuse long ago by being unspecific about the time her family expected her. She had fully intended to do that in fact, but when she and Andy had captured Fred her intentions had gone astray. It now seemed urgent to stay and see how the exchange of hostages went, even if that meant cutting dinner pretty close. She was too deeply involved by this time—part of the group whether she had wanted to be or not—and she had a stake in the outcome.

With surprise she discovered that Andy no longer made her nervous, and she was determined not to be intimidated by Oliver or Kath. As for Fred, she actually liked him, he was such an obliging prisoner.

Commodore Shattuck was harder to tell about. He was like an onion with a brittle outer skin which hid so many layers that they could only be guessed at. Charlotte was fascinated by him and shy of him at the same time.

The plan they worked out for the hostage exchange involved driving to the cemetery together in the Commodore's car. Then, once the swap was accomplished, Kath was to ride Baba back to Watts's Stables, while everyone else returned to the Commodore's house. From there Andy and Dan would bike to the farm, and Charlotte would ride for home like fury. The knots would be untangled, the incident finished. It sounded quite straightforward.

At ten to two, the Commodore parked his car at the north gate to Sleepy Hollow, and the six of them entered the cemetery. Inside there were no colors, everything was black or white or shades of gray: the wet, rough tree trunks, the snowy dips and hills, the gravestones. An absentminded melancholy overspread the place. Every now and then the fitful wind threw another handful of snow into the air.

They walked through the cemetery without a sound, turned in on themselves and silent. Even Fred, who had hardly stopped talking since they caught him, was wrapped in his own thoughts. He strode meditatively along the white paths, his big hands behind his back, his chin tucked into the collar of his coat.

Authors' Ridge was a long, tree-stippled mound at the edge of Sleepy Hollow; many of Concord's distinguished writers were buried on it, keeping company together as Eliot liked to say. Charlotte hadn't visited the Ridge since last November, but she knew it well: she had come frequently with Eliot, for whom it was a special place. They brought a bag of apples, or a book to read aloud, or he would bring his recorder to play in the sympathetic company of Henry David Thoreau's spirit. Eliot had a deep affinity for Henry David.

From her brother, Charlotte had learned to think of Sleepy Hollow as a peaceful, calm spot: green and full of shadows in the summer, smouldering with color in the fall, starred with new flowers and sweet with birds in the spring. In winter, however, it did not feel as if it belonged to the living.

There was no sign yet of the British, so the Commodore took Fred onto the ridge itself to point out Ralph Waldo Emerson's massive pink granite boulder, Hawthorne's grave-stone, the Alcott family's little cluster of markers, and Thoreau's modest stone. The others kept watch below.

"This has got to be one of the weirdest things I've ever done in my life," said Kath in an undertone to her brother.

"I only hope Nicholas Boutwell-Scott was right and Dan and Baba are both okay," Andy worried. "I haven't any idea what we do if they aren't, have you?"

Kath didn't answer. She blew into her hands and stamped her feet. Oliver stood still, hugging himself for warmth, his face pinched, his ears pink with cold. He'd forgotten his cap.

"They're late," said Charlotte. "That means I'll be late for dinner and there'll be a fuss. Nuts!"

"Not very late. Look." Andy pointed toward the gate. A small procession threaded through it in single file and along the meandering little road toward the ridge. Kath breathed an audible sigh of relief at the sight of Baba prancing skittishly at the end of the column. The tall, angular figure leading her seemed to have his hands full. Nicholas had said that was Beaky, and Charlotte could tell from his disjointed gait that he was the same man who'd fallen over her bicycle. She wondered if Deb's bandanna was still tied around his ankle. The men ahead of him kept a wary distance between them and the mare.

Dan was the shortest one in line, and the watchers could pick out Nicholas Boutwell-Scott: he was the man loping along with his hands in his pockets and the scarf around his neck. The other four were unfamiliar.

"Time for some action," exclaimed the Commodore sounding pleased. He and Fred rejoined the group.

The British halted some distance away and huddled for consultation.

"Well?" Kath was impatient. "What do we do now? Let's get this over with."

"We pick a representative to parley." Commodore Shattuck pulled a white linen table napkin out of his pocket and handed it to Charlotte.

"*Me?*" The word came out as an undignified squeak.

"None better. You are not related to the hostage and you are not my great-nephew. All you need to do is go talk to their emissary. Tell him we'll send Fred into the middle when they send Daniel and the horse out. Nothing to it."

There was a flash of white cloth among the other group; they had evidently worked out a similar arrangement.

"What are you waiting for?" asked Oliver. "Go on then."

They all looked expectantly at Charlotte. To preserve her air of indifference, she scowled back and started toward the British. Inside she felt a glow of satisfaction: she had been chosen, singled out for something special, and by the Commodore.

She met Nicholas Boutwell-Scott exactly halfway across.

"Heigh-ho!" He greeted her with an impudent smile. "Sooner we get this over the better—the Captain's ready to let you keep old Fred at this point."

"We can't. We have to have Dan back, and the horse. So whatever we're supposed to do, we've got to do it now."

"Right-o. Let's shake hands, that'll look good—and swap hankies like this. Mine's the one with the monogram—posh, isn't it? Then we slope on back to our respective armies and send out the hostages—safe conduct assured, *et cetera, et cetera*. And while you're here"—the smile deepened infectiously at the corners of his blue eyes—"tell me something about your enchanting sister."

"My en—Deb?" Charlotte was totally unprepared for such a request. "Why do you want to know about her?"

"She's a nice bit o' skirt, as they say," he replied with a wicked wink.

"She never wears a skirt," Charlotte said seriously.

He chuckled. "No? That in itself is interesting. What did she say about me—she must have said something."

Charlotte had the feeling this conversation would make Deb simply furious. She wouldn't want Nicholas Boutwell-Scott to know she'd said anything about him. "Only that you were bothering her. She was really mad."

"Was she indeed!" He nodded, satisfied. "Well, let's get this over with, shall we? And you might remember me to your sister, if you think of it."

The rest of Charlotte's group was waiting for her with ill-concealed impatience. Trouble had developed among them; Fred had decided that he didn't want to be exchanged, and Kath's reaction to that was explosive. "*You* don't have anything to say about it! It isn't up to you what happens."

"We really do have to get Dan back," Andy was saying apologetically. "That's why we captured you."

"Ah," said Fred, "but I didn't give you no trouble, did I? I could of made it nasty for you, if I'd flippin' well wanted."

"That's not fair!" Charlotte retorted. "That was up to you —we didn't make any bargains with you."

"Why don't you want to go back?" asked Oliver curiously. "They're your friends, after all."

Fred looked round at them, his normally good-natured face redrawn in lines of obstinacy. " 'E's only going to 'ave me 'ead soon's I get there. 'E 'asn't 'arf got a temper, that Captain, and I didn't join up to be shouted at. I only come on this junket to see a bit a the world before going back to me turnips and cabbages. If 'e 'ad 'is way, I'd be sitting on me duff in some flippin' barn waiting for 'im to say as when I can so much as stick me nose out the door."

The Commodore listened to this tirade with a thoughtful expression. He offered no help or advice.

"Right," said Kath, taking charge. "There are five of us— well four anyway—and if we have to, we'll force you to go.

Oliver, you and Charlie take his arms and Andy and I'll push."

"Won't work," Oliver stated flatly. "Look at him."

Fred had planted his feet and folded his arms; he looked solid and immovable.

"Well, you can at least try!" Kath exclaimed.

The Commodore chose this moment to intervene. "We'll have to tell them why we're delaying—they must be ready. Charlotte, you and Andy take the white flag and go out again."

Charlotte snapped her mouth shut on what she'd been going to say and snatched the napkin. "This is crazy," she muttered crossly as she and Andy went. Nicholas approached them from the other side shaking his head.

"And here we are again! I say, we must stop meeting like this. Sorry, but we seem to have hit a snag on our side—it appears our hostage would prefer *not* to be returned to the bosom of his family. And all this time we thought we were holding him against his will!"

"You mean Dan? But—" Andy stopped, at a loss.

"Dan doesn't want to be exchanged either?" Charlotte supplied for him.

"Either?" repeated Nicholas. "What d'you mean 'either'?"

Charlotte stamped her foot. "This is ridiculous—the whole thing! I'm going to be late home for dinner."

"I think," said Nicholas, "that we ought to call the hostages from both sides out here to discuss this. It does seem a bit awkward, but none of us have had very much practice in this sort of thing. Perhaps if I could talk to old Fred and you could persuade Dan—?"

"Well?" Andy demanded of Dan as they were reunited. "What do you mean you don't want to come home?"

Self-possessed and determined, Dan faced his brother. "Why should I want to? I'm having a neat time." He gave a sudden ten-year-old grin. "Andy, you should *see* their camp, it's nifty! They've got a stove and sleeping bags and masses of other stuff. I don't want to go home yet, honest I don't. Why can't I stay at least one more night—it's not dangerous or anything. Mom wouldn't mind."

"Like fun she wouldn't!" replied Andy with a snort. "She doesn't know you're gone yet. If you come back now we won't have to tell her."

"You can think of something to say that'll make it all right," coaxed Dan. "I might never have a chance like this again, Andy!"

"It seems unlikely," agreed Nicholas.

"Well, if 'e's not going, I'm not either, mate," put in Fred firmly.

Andy regarded his younger brother with a mixture of helplessness and exasperation.

"Now what?" Charlotte demanded of Nicholas. "What do we do next?"

"Damned if I know."

"Some help you are. Andy?"

But Andy only shook his head. "We're stuck."

" 'Strewth!" Nicholas looked suspiciously as if he were having trouble keeping a straight face. "We could call out reinforcements and *force* them to cooperate."

"No!" cried Dan and Fred together, and Dan pointed out, "It works out even so long as we both stay where we are."

"That won't make any difference to Ma," Andy told him. "She will not accept Fred as a substitute."

"Well, make the Commodore explain to her. This is all his fault anyway," Dan suggested.

Andy gave a defeated shrug.

"We aren't getting anywhere," declared Charlotte. "What about the horse? That can't refuse to come, and we've got to have it back."

"With joy and my blessing," replied Nicholas enthusiastically. "You can't take it fast enough—it's a nasty-tempered brute! It spends all its time kicking and biting and foaming. Beaky's the only one foolish enough to go near it, and he seems to have fallen in love with it. The difficult part will be separating them, but I'll get him to bring it out for you. Take my advice and don't walk behind it."

"I guess it's the best we can do," said Charlotte with a glance at Andy, who looked as near gloomy as she'd ever seen him.

"You've still got me," Fred pointed out.

"I don't think you're precisely what they want, old son," Nicholas told him. "But if that's it, there doesn't seem much point in standing about here waiting for chilblains."

"Are you sure you're okay?" Andy looked hard at his brother. "They're treating you all right?"

"Good heavens, what do you think we are anyway?" asked Nicholas offended. "Child molesters?"

"No," said Andy quickly. "I'm sorry, it's just—"

"We're all friends," Dan assured him. "They taught me this neat card game this morning—I keep winning. Look!" He held out a handful of coins.

"Your brother has all the makings of a hustler," observed Nicholas.

"Dammit, dammit, dammit!" stormed Kath, pacing up and down. "Who does Dan think he is? Does he know how much trouble we've already gone to for his sake? What're we going to tell Ma and Pa, did you think of that? How can we—" Her outburst was effectively stemmed at that moment, to Charlotte's relief, by the arrival of the man known as Beaky, with the horse. All of them except Kath climbed the ridge to higher ground. Baba flung up her head; her eyes showed wild white rings and her nostrils flared. She moved as if she were on springs.

"Hey, Baba. Whoa, sweetie. Take it easy, it's all right now. Here you are. Easy, easy, easy," soothed Kath, walking fearlessly up to the mare. Baba shook her head and jumped sideways like a crab, nearly squashing Beaky, who put a long bony hand on her neck. All the while he spoke to Baba, too, using the same tone of voice as Kath, but totally different words: "Todge it, y'footy wold gry. Yer all a tirret. I'll not fadge wi'yer, y'great lummox."

Together they calmed the mare until she stood between them twitching and suspicious, but with all four hoofs on the ground. She kept one ear laid back as a warning, and the rest of the group stayed out of range.

Kath said a little grudgingly, "She looks all right. You the one taking care of her?"

Beaky nodded. "Arr. Fit as a pud, the dilly."

"There'd have been trouble if she wasn't!" Kath said with feeling.

Beaky seemed reluctant to take his hand from Baba's bridle. She gave his shoulder a nudge with her great moist nose.

"She's not easy to handle—she must like you." Now that she had the mare back, Kath could afford to be generous.

"Aye, she's a chippy wold gry," Beaky agreed, rubbing Baba's cheek. There was a wistful look in his pale eyes.

But Kath was eager to be off. "Thanks for taking care of her," she said, swinging into the saddle. "I'll go ahead," she called to Andy. "You'd better be thinking of something to tell the parents!"

"I guess I better," he agreed glumly.

At the last minute Beaky released Baba and stood watching as Kath trotted her toward the gate. Clots of snow flew up from the mare's hoofs, her neck arched and her tail rippled. Without a glance at the group on the ridge, Beaky loped back to the British, his shoulders hunched dejectedly.

" 'E was really fond of that beast," remarked Fred. " 'E'll miss 'er terrible, shouldn't wonder. Don't like people much, Beaky, but 'e 'andles beasts a treat."

"And what," asked the Commodore, "are we going to do with you now?"

"Me, guv? 'Ow about goin' over to Walden Pond first off?" suggested Fred hopefully.

"I've *got* to get home for dinner!" Charlotte reminded them impatiently.

Chapter Sixteen

AS THEY DROVE BACK TO COMMODORE SHATTUCK'S HOUSE AFTER the unsuccessful exchange, they passed the British troops hiking along the wet road, with Dan marching briskly beside Nicholas. He had the insolence to wave to his brother.

Charlotte was out of the car as soon as it stopped. "See you later," called Andy as she wheeled out of the driveway and began to pedal toward home. The Commodore shouted "Good-bye!" after her and she heard Fred's "Tira!" but if Oliver acknowledged her departure, she missed it.

See you later? Not if she could help it! Her part in the game was over. How they worked it out from here on wasn't her affair. She'd done what was asked of her and that was enough—more than enough. Yet she couldn't help a sneaking desire to know what was going to happen next and how the whole thing would end. Hard as she tried to talk herself out of it, she felt an odd sense of belonging. It wasn't as easy to cut herself free as she wanted it to be.

In spite of her anxiety, it was just past three when she reached the house—highly unlikely that there'd be any trouble. Sunday dinner was seldom on time anyway, but setting an hour satisfied Mrs. Paige's need for organization. Nevertheless, Charlotte chose the front door. If she were lucky, she could get upstairs without being seen and no one would know how long she'd actually been gone. Questions about where she'd been were bound to be awkward—how could she possibly explain? She thought back over the day and couldn't help smiling to herself; it was rather fun to have a secret.

There was an explosion of laughter from the living room as she entered the house. She closed the door carefully and made for the stairs. Just as she reached the bottom, Eliot came bounding down them. "Charlie!" he cried. "Where've you been all this time. I just went up to get you."

"Mom knew I was out," said Charlotte carefully.

"She said you'd gone this *morning*—she was sure you'd come back by now—not that it matters."

"It does to me."

"I just mean no one's checking up on you, ungrateful child! Anyway we're all toasting the coming attraction and you're the only Paige missing. Come on in."

"The coming attraction?"

"Max and Jean's prospective offspring! The next generation! The grandchild! Our niece-slash-nephew! The infant!"

"Oh, *that*." Charlotte started up the stairs.

"Aren't you excited? Just think, you won't be the baby anymore."

Charlotte hunched her shoulders. "It won't be born for months, will it? How can you get excited now?"

"Well, for God's sake, don't say that to anyone down there, will you?" warned Eliot with a grin. "You'll be disinherited. It amounts to blasphemy." He looked hard at her as she passed him. "You feeling all right?"

"Fine," she assured him. "I'm just going to clean up."

Her brother nodded wisely. "I'll tell them you're coming."

It was nice to know that she'd been missed. But this baby . . . It wasn't even here yet and everyone was making a fuss. What would life be like when it was born? Charlotte shuddered to think.

Upstairs, changing her pants and swiping ineffectually at her hair, Charlotte found unexpected pleasure in thoughts of Commodore Shattuck and Fred, even of Kath, Andy, and Oliver. They were part of something interesting she was involved in *without* Eliot or Deb or either of her parents. She wondered if Fred had convinced the others to take him to

Walden Pond. Perhaps at this exact moment they were walking the narrow path around its great gray bulk, wrapped in the silence of evergreens and snow. If they were, she was missing it. On the way home, suspended between the Commodore's house and her own, it had been easy to dismiss the whole business. With distance, perversely, it became harder.

She studied herself thoughtfully in the mirror over her dressing table. She had a picture fixed firmly in her mind of a round-faced little girl with dark pigtails and glasses; it was the picture she was used to seeing whenever she looked at herself—it didn't change; but her real reflection did. She examined it carefully; she looked older, different somehow. It disturbed her—she was on the verge of understanding something, but it was still out of reach. The more she stretched toward it, the remoter it got. It wasn't easy to be patient—it was painful—but she would have to be.

Everyone was still in the living room when she came down. They all looked warm and happy, as if they were celebrating, and they all paused to welcome her as she entered.

"Charlotte, hon, would you like some sherry?" asked Mr. Paige, decanter in hand. "In honor of the occasion?"

"Corrupting youth," Deb said with a smile that contradicted the words. "You shouldn't toast a baby with alcohol in in the first place!"

"Sherry can hardly be termed alcohol, can it?" Eliot remarked.

"It's terribly genteel," Mrs. Paige said. "It's respectable, Deb. Perhaps that's why I like bourbon so much."

"Sherry's a bit rich for this baby, I can tell you," Max put in. "He'd better not get used to it, Jeannie."

"*She* won't," replied Jean.

Charlotte accepted half a glass. "Do you know it's a girl?" she couldn't help asking. "I thought you couldn't tell."

Jean laughed. "The baby and I have discussed it."

"It better be a nice kid, whether it's a girl or a boy," said Deb.

Eliot drained his glass. "With a family like this, how can it be otherwise?"

"Literate, musical, cultured, discerning: an artistic paragon from the cradle," Mr. Paige pronounced.

"Able to use a card catalogue before she can walk," added Jean.

"This baby will only occasionally cry, and *never* at night," Mrs. Paige continued.

"Born with a T-square in his hand," said Max.

"Lord, wouldn't *that* be uncomfortable!" exclaimed Eliot with a chuckle. "Poor old Jean!"

"Thanks," Jean said dryly.

"Drink up, gifted and eccentric family," Mrs. Paige told them. "I can smell the ham—it must be ready. No, Jean, you stay right where you are, we can manage beautifully. Charlotte, will you help?"

Gladly Charlotte abandoned her sherry and followed her mother out to the kitchen.

"Did you have a good time today, darling? Move those plates over, will you please?"

"Doing what?" asked Charlotte guardedly.

"I don't know—doing whatever you were doing. Eliot said those children are Skip Bullard's niece and nephew. I don't remember seeing them before—are they nice?"

Charlotte gave a noncommittal grunt.

"Are they in your class? What have I done with the mustard? Shall I put capers in the sauce?"

"I don't like capers."

Mrs. Paige gave her a quick nod. "All right then, no capers. Are you pleased about Max and Jean's baby? I must admit I've never thought of myself as a grandmother—I hope getting used to it isn't too traumatic."

"Why would it be?" asked Charlotte, stirring the green beans.

"Age." Her mother sighed. "Mortality. Time marching inexorably onward. I don't like getting old, my pet."

Charlotte was shocked. "But you aren't! I never think of you as getting old."

Mrs. Paige gave her youngest child a rueful smile. "Thank you, darling, but I'm afraid it's happening all the same. All I have to do to remind myself is look at you—you're no little girl anymore."

"But I want to get older. I can't wait. It seems as if Max

and Deb and Eliot keep getting further and further away, while I'm still stuck being young."

"Oh, darling—" Mrs. Paige's voice softened with sympathy. "It must be very difficult for you sometimes, I know. But don't be in a hurry, Charlotte. If you keep your eyes on the future, you overlook so many of the good things happening now. And you may find it isn't as wonderful as you thought to be older. Believe me."

With horror, Charlotte felt tears sting the corners of her eyes. She blinked furiously. It was one thing to stand up stubbornly to being misunderstood—quite another to accept understanding gracefully. "I just don't know," she said finally. "I have to try it first."

"I know, I really do, but the trouble is you can't go back if you decide you don't like it."

"Would you like to go back?"

"Sometimes," her mother admitted. "But maybe that's because I've forgotten all the unhappy parts of being young."

They shared a moment of quiet sympathy. Then Mrs. Paige said, with a return to briskness, "If we don't get this on the table quickly it'll be stone cold. Why don't you put the plates at your father's place and we'll serve in the dining room. Bring me the pewter vegetable bowl, will you?"

It was nice to see everyone sitting around the table. They were so scattered, so busy with diverse friends and activities, that they seldom could do more than pass each other and wave during the days. Today they had a chance to come home again as part of one family. Here they were, sharing, passing themselves around the table with the plates and salt and conversation. They interlocked like pieces of a jigsaw puzzle. Even Jean fitted. And when the baby came, Charlotte supposed it would have a place, too. Could it really be possible to add people to a family like hers without forcing anyone out to make room?

"—I said, please pass the muffins!"

She came to abruptly to discover Eliot watching her with amusement. "Gone to sleep with your eyes open?"

"Of course not, I was just thinking." She passed him the bread basket.

"Deep, solemn thoughts, Horatio." He selected the largest muffin, layered it with butter and devoured it in two bites. "Mmm. Nice taste in spite of all the little black specks. Potting soil or weevils?"

"Eliot," cautioned Mrs. Paige.

"They are alfalfa sprouts," Deb informed him, leaning over the daffodils in the centerpiece. "You are a nutritional illiterate, if you'll excuse my saying so."

"A sharper tongue hath no sister," observed Max as he cut his ham into neat geometric shapes.

"In an attempt to restore the intellectual level of communication at this table—" began Mr. Paige.

"What's that again? What'd he say?" interrupted Eliot irreverently. "All those big words . . . "

"He said he'd like a more meaningful interface," Max translated.

"Dialogue," amended Jean.

"I was simply going to ask you about tomorrow's scenario," said Mr. Paige, unperturbed.

"Aha," exclaimed Deb. "Game, set, match. You get full marks for 'scenario'—it sounds like fingernails across a blackboard."

"I might ask who made you umpire," Eliot said. "But to answer the question—it's the usual. Struggle out at dawn for the twenty-one gun salute on the hillside. Brief inaudible ceremonies at the Bridge. Pancake orgy at Monument Hall. Parade at nine. All fall down at noon. I've got to be off at five thirty."

"A.m. or p.m.?" inquired Max.

Charlotte said, "I'm going with you."

"Max and I'll be there," Jean declared.

"Max better not go to bed then," warned Deb, "or he'll never make it."

Max just groaned.

"I made special arrangements at the library to have tomorrow off and I'm not going to miss any of it. Besides, it'll be good practice for five o'clock feedings," Jean said firmly.

"We'll opt for the parade, I think," decided Mr. Paige. "Nine isn't such a shock to the nervous system. Deb?"

"Don't know yet. I haven't made up my mind."

"Of course, Geoff won't be there after last night," observed Eliot, "but perhaps that's an advantage?"—Deb's eyes narrowed in warning, but he plunged blithely on—"or you could go be Flo Nightingale at the wounded patriot's bedside."

"Eliot"—Mrs. Paige raised her eyebrows—"you're making a good case for fratricide."

"Don't worry, Mother," said Deb, dangerously calm, "he's made up my mind for me. I shall skip the entire occasion and spend the day in my studio. Eliot can play soldier without me."

"That certainly tells *me*," said Eliot without contrition.

Deb refused to rise further to his baiting.

Dessert was every bit as rich and fattening as Deb had predicted. Jean had made a wickedly delicious cheesecake with strawberries glazing the top. She listened to their cries of delight with obvious pleasure. When it came to the slicing, even Deb couldn't resist a modest piece. Of Eliot, leering at her rudely from the other side of the table, she remarked, "Considering the time and effort spent on his upbringing, his manners are deplorable."

"Yes, well, it just doesn't take on some people," replied Mrs. Paige dryly with a smile in Eliot's direction. "Goodness knows we tried, your father and I."

Eliot scraped up the last of his cheesecake, sat back in his chair, folded his arms, and smiled benignly at them all. "Go ahead, have your little jokes at my expense. I can afford to be generous today; I have a special announcement to make."

"You're going to have a baby!" said Deb.

Eliot shook his head. "That announcement's been made— I've got a new one, twit."

"You're tired of being laughed at and unappreciated so you're leaving home," suggested Max.

"Warm, warm, but not right."

"You've got a new job," guessed Mrs. Paige.

"Sorry, Mother, not exactly."

"You've got a raise," offered Mr. Paige.

"On the contrary."

"You can't have been fired!" exclaimed Charlotte. No one would ever fire her brother.

"Nope. Actually I intend to quit."

"You do?" Jean said.

"Are you going back to school?" asked Mrs. Paige. She didn't disguise the hope in her voice.

Eliot nodded, his smile growing broader and smugger.

"Just look at him," said Deb. "He's saving the clincher for last, aren't you, dear brother?"

"When do you start again?" Mrs. Paige wanted to know.

"Not until next fall."

"Doesn't the Conservatory run a summer session?"

"I'm not going back to the Conservatory."

"What did I tell you?" crowed Deb in triumph. "Here it comes!"

"Spill it, for God's sake," demanded Max. "Don't keep us hanging by our thumbs."

"Very well." Eliot was enjoying himself. "I've been accepted for graduate work in the University of Montana's wildlife management program."

Charlotte froze in her chair.

"You what—?" A slow grin parted Max's beard.

"Yep! In June I shall pack my car and head west. I want to take a good look at some of that country out there, then find myself a graduate-student-type hovel in Missoula. Skip's going along with me for six weeks or so. We've been planning the trip for several months."

"Wildlife management?" said Mrs. Paige blankly. "*Wildlife management*, Eliot?"

"Mmm-hmm. It's been in the back of my mind for a long time, Mother. I finally decided it was time to act."

"How exciting," said Jean warmly. "Congratulations, Eliot!"

He gave her a brilliant smile. "Thanks!"

"Montana have a good program?" Mr. Paige asked with interest.

"Very. And it sounds like a great place to spend a few years."

"But what about your music? What about the Conservatory?" Mrs. Paige said. A frown pleated itself between her eyebrows.

"It was good experience—I'll always have what I learned, Mother, but this is what I really want to do. It's right, I know it is."

"Since when have you wanted to do it?"

"Since I left Boston last year." Eliot was firm; he sounded sure of himself. "Listen, Mother, I was always much more interested in how many different instruments I could learn to play passably than I was in learning to play *one* masterfully. That was my biggest impediment, you know: myself. I'm just not a dedicated musician. I love to mess around, but to be honest, though it pains me to admit it publicly, I am not a brilliant musician." He pulled a long face.

"You could be if you kept at it," objected his mother.

But Eliot shook his head. "No," he contradicted gently. "I'd get better, of course, but I'd never be exceptional. I don't want to spend my life teaching people to play better than I do. I have enjoyed working for the DPW this year, hard as that may be for any of you to believe. I've discovered I relish physical work and I like being outdoors—that's what I wanted to find out."

"Hard to get into, this program?" Mr. Paige inquired. "When did you apply?"

"It's competitive. I sent my forms off last fall. Thought I couldn't lose anything by trying. If I changed my mind in the meantime and they accepted me I could simply withdraw. But I haven't and they have, so here I go." He looked round at his family, exuberant at the prospect of a new venture. "It isn't so bad once you get used to the idea, Mother, really it isn't. It's more respectable than digging ditches!"

Mrs. Paige gave him a doubtful smile. "I suppose," was all she'd say.

"I think it's marvelous," Jean told him warmly. "Oh, you'll love the West, Eliot! You make me homesick just thinking about it."

"That's all part of my plan. If you start working on Max now, maybe you can persuade him to bring you and my niece or nephew out to visit me. I want everyone to come! I'll show you all around. Skip and I want to spend a week or two in the Tetons. Isn't that near your family, Jean?"

"Thermopolis. It isn't far. They'd love to see you again, I'll give you their address. My little sister thought you were wonderful!"

"God help her," said Deb. "Why didn't you tell us before this?"

"Thought I'd wait until it happened."

"Cagey beast," remarked Max. "You're just trying to up-stage our baby, that's all."

"Not a bit. In fact I'm relinquishing the spotlight to him."

"Her," corrected Deb.

"Well"—Mrs. Paige sounded resigned—"this isn't what I expected from you, dear, but I don't know why that should surprise me. You have almost never done what I expected. My son, the concert musician."

"I want to know what you'll be studying," Mr. Paige said. "Will you be doing field work out there?" He had seized the new idea with interest and wanted to know everything Eliot could tell him about it. The other members of the family had to slide their questions into odd chinks and gaps in the interrogation. Eliot's face was suffused with delight and enthusiasm as he answered them.

All but Charlotte. She'd been silent throughout the whole discussion and now she stopped listening altogether. She felt as if she'd been kicked in the stomach: winded and numb with shock. All she could absorb was that Eliot, her special friend— *Eliot*—was going to Montana. In a matter of months he'd be gone, leaving her behind literally this time. He'd be gone, not for weeks or months; he'd said it himself: for years. Montana was unimaginably far away.

So she sat in her chair devastated, gripping her napkin with stiff fingers. Just when she'd begun to find a path through the bewildering maze of contradictions that crowded her life, Eliot dropped a bomb on her and suddenly nothing looked the same.

Locked in her own private misery, which was already souring toward resentment, Charlotte ignored everyone else. They didn't miss her anyway; they were too busy being interested and excited to notice she was upset. A bad taste rose in her throat and her eyes began to burn dangerously. She hated feeling this way, really hated it, but what could she do?

"—coffee in the living room," she heard her mother saying from a long way off. "Darling, don't you want the rest of your cheesecake?"

"No," said Charlotte, "I don't. I want to be excused." She was aware that her mother and father exchanged a glance down the length of the table.

"It's somebody's turn to clear," Deb said pointedly.

"She helped me get dinner on."

"I'll clear," Jean volunteered. "Max'll help me. Come on, you slug." She gave him a gentle dig in the ribs.

"Can I go?"

"Yes, Charlotte. All right, you may."

She was up and out of the room in an instant, not looking at anyone; especially avoiding Eliot's eyes, but she knew her whole family was watching her.

"What's got into Charlie?" asked Eliot in genuine surprise.

"—should leave her alone for a bit."

"—she's tired. She was out so long—"

She didn't wait to hear more. *No* one knew what was wrong with her. They thought it couldn't be very important—being tired was all. She just wanted to get away from the lot of them, be by herself, nurse her hurt, build up some kind of protection she could use against them later. She took refuge in her room. Today no one had magically tidied it up while she was out; the bed was a tangle of sheets and blankets and limp pillows. Her pajamas lay where she'd left them on the floor. Lap had made herself a nest in them and was curled in an arc with all four feet touching. Her oblivion aggravated Charlotte's raw mood and she shook the cat out, then hung up her pajamas. Lap yawned and scowled, showing a great many little pointed teeth, then stalked out and down the hall to continue her nap elsewhere.

Charlotte threw herself across the bed, but the rumpled bedclothes made it impossible to find a comfortable position. She wept a few hot tears of frustration and unhappiness and felt worse—as if the inside of her head were too big for her skull. It would be awful to have any of her family come up and find her here, crying. That made her even more vulnerable. And yet the other side of her longed for comfort, reassurance, sympathy. How could she be so confused? Why wasn't anything simple, the way it had been only last year? She couldn't be the only one who didn't understand, but she felt so isolated, so cut off. The other people she knew were so sure of themselves: in control and satisfied with what they were making out of their lives.

Panic swept over her in a rough, clammy wave, shaking her up, immobilizing her. She couldn't visualize life without Eliot. He was a part of every one of her twelve years; she had shared so much with him, depended on him in a way she never had on Max or Deb.

For a frightening, stifling minute, Charlotte couldn't move. It was hard to breathe, as if the air around her were too heavy and thick. Dinner solidified sickeningly in her stomach and she was really scared. She forced herself to sit upright, her heart thundering. What was happening to her? She was afraid to lie still any longer so she got up and paced, and gradually her heart stopped pumping so hard and her breath came easier.

It was no good staying where she was. She needed to get away from the house and all the people in it—they seemed determined to respect her privacy without asking her whether or not she wanted it respected. Probably they had forgotten about her over their coffee: out of sight, out of mind. Well, they weren't important to her either.

There was a knock at her door. She stiffened.

"Charlie?" It was Eliot. "Charlie, can I come in?"

He was the last person she wanted to face. "No." The word was said before she could stop it. A reflex. And once she'd spoken it she couldn't take it back.

There was a pause, then Eliot said, "Charlie, what's wrong? Why won't you talk to me about it?"

"You know what's wrong."

"I'm not sure I do. Is it my going away?"

The tears gathered in a lump in the back of her throat. She

had to swallow hard several times before she could speak. "I don't know what there is to talk about," she managed finally.

"We've always talked before," Eliot replied. "Let me in?"

Charlotte wanted to say, "You've never done anything like this to me before," but she couldn't. "It won't do any good," she said instead. "I don't want to talk to you now."

"Oh, Charlie." Eliot sighed loudly enough for her to hear him through the door. "I'm feeling so good about Montana I wanted everyone to share it with me. I wish you'd let me explain it."

"How can you? There isn't anything to explain. It's done."

"Well, I can't go on talking through a door, Chuck, it's silly. When you want to come out or will let me come in, we'll see if we can work this thing out between us. All right?"

"Sure," said Charlotte bitterly.

"Charlie—" He broke off and there was a moment's silence, then she heard his footsteps retreat down the hall.

That was what she wanted, wasn't it? To have him leave her alone, to let him know she was unhappy and upset and he was the cause? There was no comfort in it at all. If anything, she felt still worse now that he'd gone, but she couldn't fling open her door and run after him and tell him she hadn't meant it. She was too proud and stubborn, and she wasn't even sure it would do any good. So she let him go and hardened her heart. She would *not* cry. She wouldn't.

After a safe interval, she opened her door to listen. There were no sounds on the second floor, but a faint drift of voices came up the front stairs. Making up her mind, Charlotte snatched the parka she'd left lying over a chair before dinner. Its being there was lucky—that meant she could sneak down the back stairs and out the kitchen door.

Chapter Seventeen

SHE HAD NO IDEA WHERE SHE WAS GOING, SHE JUST WANTED to get outside by herself and walk. The frightening panic she had felt upstairs, lying on her bed, was bound to come back if she didn't do something to prevent it. Furtively she avoided the driveway which was visible to anyone looking out of the side windows of the living room and took instead the over-grown path around the far side of the garage.

It was after five and Sunday; she had the town to herself except for a pack of dogs nosing around, companionable and aimless, and a few cars drifting through. Charlotte struggled to make her mind a painless blank, to force all thoughts of Eliot out of it. When that didn't work, some animal instinct told her to run. She ran and ran, up Main Street and through the big parking lot behind the banks, as if by going fast enough she could outdistance her unhappiness. She ran until she had no more breath left and a stitch throbbed in her side, then she paused to catch up with herself, to ease the stabbing agony, only to discover she'd reached the DPW yard with its mounds and deserted dump trucks. This time, instead of making her uneasy, it simply reminded her of Eliot when she thought she'd gotten away from him. She kicked furiously at a chunk of snow in the road and missed it. Sunk in misery, she mooched on.

The bushes edging the river looked as if some giant hand had dropped popcorn among them. Bits of snow clung to the twigs, making the water appear black as India ink. The weather was an accurate reflection of Charlotte's present mood: bleak, wintry, comfortless. She leaned over the cold cement parapet of the bridge and watched the current eddy and race below her. Every now and then a dead, waterlogged branch swept by, going wherever the river chose to take it, helpless to plot its own course. She was like that, being carried along against her will by things happening around her. She had no choice. Panic threatened again—she had to keep moving, and it was somehow inevitable that she should continue up the hill toward the Buttrick House.

As she approached the top, she remembered the Coolidges' barn. That was a place she definitely did not want to go to, not if the British soldiers were using it as their headquarters, so she altered course and climbed over the stone wall into the park. It was utterly deserted. The long sloping field caught and reflected what was left of the light; it lay blank and white like an unused sheet of paper. At the bottom the willows laced their branches against the gloomy sky.

Without direction, Charlotte wandered down the field, leaving her footprints scattered behind. But once she was out on it, she discovered hers weren't after all the first tracks to be written across the snow. Everywhere there were distinctive signatures and little flourishes made by feet of many shapes and sizes: threadlike italic script where tiny creatures had bulldozed runways; a neat dotted line of paw prints running straight across the hillside; rough circles stomped down by dozens of sets of small feet; scratches and strokes that reminded Charlotte of a pen running out of ink. Attentive now, she stepped among them with care, trying to sort out the patterns.

The smallest tracks were probably made by field mice, and the trampled patches, she knew, were rabbits—she recognized the brown oval pellets only too well. Birds must have left the scratches—pheasants?—arrow-shaped claw prints and a long brushstroke of tail feathers. She was surprised to find she could identify such a lot of the tracks, until she remembered who had taught them to her. So many of the things in her life had been put there by Eliot. It simply wasn't fair! What was she going to do without him?

Deliberately she scuffed through the snow, destroying the prints until she reached the middle of the field and a new set caught her eye. She turned hastily to give the park a careful survey, but the only movement she could detect was the flap and glide of a blue jay, skimming the distance.

The tracks at her feet looked recent, however, not blurred by blown snow. They were almost exactly the size of her own, she discovered, putting her boots in them. She felt an uneasy curiosity about their owner and detoured to follow the trail toward the Buttrick House. It wandered into the winterbound garden and across the terraces, arriving indirectly on the patio overlooking the river where Charlotte had stood—only two days ago?—and glimpsed spring.

Someone was sitting hunched on one of the benches, a dark figure with its shoulders drawn up around its ears and its arms wrapped across its chest. It expressed Charlotte's own gloom so well that instead of turning and melting away, she lingered. She saw the figure become aware of her: it stiffened and went very still, like an exposed rabbit, then it turned its head and looked at her.

"Oh," said Oliver. "It's you." He relaxed just a little.

Now that she'd been seen and recognized, there was no point in fleeing, and when it came to meeting Oliver, Charlotte was reluctant to be the one to retreat, even though in this case he had claimed the spot first. Her streak of perverseness made her choose the other bench and sit down. He went back to contemplating the river.

"What did you decide to do with Fred?" she asked after a silence.

Without looking at her, Oliver said, "He went home with Andy and Kath. After he made us walk all the way around Walden Pond."

"I wondered if you'd gone. Did he like it?"

"How should I know? He took a photograph of all of us at Thoreau's hut."

Charlotte felt a sting of jealousy at not being in the photograph.

"He doesn't amount to much as a hostage," Oliver commented.

"Well, this doesn't amount to much as a war, either," she retorted.

"It was all right until all of you came barging in. Uncle Sam and I were doing very well."

"I didn't ask to join it, any more than Dan asked to be kidnapped," pointed out Charlotte. "If you'll remember—"

Oliver cut her short. "Don't want to argue."

Charlotte drew her mouth straight. "Where's your uncle anyway? I thought you never went anywhere without him."

Oliver turned to regard her coldly. "I do what I want. And he does what he wants, and it's nobody's business but our own. *Nobody's.* I don't care what any of them say around that stupid school."

"How do you know they say anything about you? They've got better things to talk about."

"I know," said Oliver. "It always happens; they always talk about me."

Charlotte had no ready answer for that. She wondered how many schools he meant by "always."

"I usually don't put up with it for very long," he continued after a pause. "I make them send me to a new one." There was grim satisfaction in his voice.

"Who?" Eliot forgotten, Charlotte returned his stare with interest. "Your parents, you mean?"

"One or the other of them."

"You mean they just let you change school whenever you want to?" She was skeptical.

"They don't *let* me, I make them. I have ways of doing it. When a school gets unbearable, I do something about it."

"But—how long do you usually stay?"

"Depends. Months. A year sometimes. Once only three weeks."

"I don't see," objected practical Charlotte, "how they can find enough different schools in one place for you to change so often."

"They don't have to. They mostly send me to boarding schools. Since I was eight and they got divorced."

Charlotte contemplated that in silence for several minutes. She couldn't imagine being away from home since age eight, and not having a home either—or not a regular one. He couldn't if his parents were divorced. The prospect was awful. "If they send you to boarding schools, why aren't you at Fenn, then? Why are you in the public school here?" she asked, veering from the unpleasantness.

"Fenn wouldn't take me," he said flatly. "Besides, Uncle Sam said I had to go to public school if I was going to live with him in Concord. So I said I'd try it. Don't like it much, though."

"It's a very good school," replied Charlotte, sounding like her mother. "The high school has an extremely high rate of college acceptances. If you've been to so many schools, I don't see how you'd know a good one if you found it anyway."

"I don't expect I'll stay much longer," Oliver said.

"That doesn't seem like a very good way to get an education," Charlotte observed primly.

"Why should I care? *They* don't. They just want me out of the way somewhere. It upsets them to have to find me a new school each time because then they have to remember me."

"I don't believe your parents are like that." Charlotte couldn't believe any parents were like that.

"*You* don't know anything about them."

"Your uncle doesn't seem that way."

Oliver frowned. His face tightened unhappily. "But he doesn't want me here. Not really. He'd rather live by himself. Besides," his eyes hardened, "I don't want to spend all my time with an old man like him in this kind of town. No, I don't expect I'll stay much longer." He kicked the ground with his heel.

"What do you mean 'this kind of town'?" Charlotte challenged.

Oliver shrugged. "Not very exciting, is it? If it weren't for us, Uncle Sam and me, nothing would be happening, would it?"

How terribly conceited, thought Charlotte, but she didn't say it. Something about Oliver made her reconsider. Dozens of questions suggested themselves to her, but she sensed that he had told her all he was going to—perhaps more than he'd wanted. "I *like* living here," she said at last, pointedly.

"You would," he countered.

"Maybe if you tried liking things you'd find you did."

"That's a stupid, grown-up thing to say. You don't know what you're talking about."

"No," she agreed, "and I don't think I want to, either. You have no reason to be unfriendly to me, I never did anything to you. You're just being obnoxious."

The chink in Oliver's armor showed again, briefly. Somebody else has told him that, she thought with a sudden flash of insight, and it hurts. "Once tomorrow's over," she said, "you can do whatever you want and see if I care. But you won't keep me away from the Bridge and the parade no matter how much you want to. You can bet Andy and Kath'll be there, too."

"I can't stop you."

Charlotte stared at him a moment in perplexity. What a strange person he was, and how unhappy. Their conversation was obviously over; he'd drawn into himself again, and there wasn't much point in continuing to sit on a bench near him, so she got up and started home. No "Good-bye," no "See you tomorrow." She left in silence, steeling herself not to look back; she didn't know if he was watching her.

In the darkness of her room, Charlotte sat up in bed hugging her knees. She was tired enough to sleep; she felt tired all over, inside and out, but her head refused to stop working. It churned out an endless string of disturbing thoughts and kept her wide awake.

All afternoon she'd been hard and full of anger, like a balloon ready to explode. Now it was as if instead of bursting, she'd developed a slow leak: the anger seeped away from her, she went soft. The frustration and resentment dissolved in unhappiness. There was a long dull ache inside her caused by the thought of Eliot's departure; it settled in the pit of her stomach as if it intended to stay permanently. Without the fire of anger, she was lost and scared and she didn't know what to do.

There was a wall between her and the rest of her family,

too high to climb over and too long to go around. And the worst of it was that no one seemed to see it there but Charlotte. She couldn't make them understand.

Eliot had done her an injustice: he'd left her out. She would never easily accept his going to Montana, but she wouldn't feel so awful now if only she'd known from the beginning. If only he'd shared this—his biggest secret— with her, but he hadn't. He'd shared it with Skip, and Skip wasn't even family.

A chasm yawned at her feet, and on the far side of it Eliot got smaller and smaller in the distance. She'd actually dreamed that, twice that she knew for sure, probably other times as well—when she woke up suddenly scared and very much alone without knowing why. It was a frightening dream; she tried calling out, but she couldn't make a sound. She jumped up and down and waved frantically, but Eliot's back was turned and he didn't see. In desperation, she'd finally tried to jump across the gulf, but it was too wide and she'd fallen . . . that's when she woke, cold and staring.

Only a dream, she told herself sternly, and pushed it out of sight in the back of her head, under scraps of daydreams and odd bits of information. But this time when it happened she was forced to acknowledge that it wasn't just a dream any more. It was really happening to her. She saw herself being twelve years old for the rest of her life.

The family had all still been in the living room when Charlotte had let herself in the front door. She'd been so muddled with thoughts of Oliver that it had slipped her mind that she hadn't told anyone about going out, so she'd forgotten to use the kitchen door and creep up the back stairs. She remembered with a jolt when she turned away from the hall closet and found her father standing in the living room doorway, watching her with a bemused, thoughtful expression.

"Yes," he said, "there you are," as if he'd temporarily misplaced her. "Not snowing again?"

"No." Guardedly, she returned his look.

"Eliot's made bushels of popcorn, come and have some."

The deflation had begun, even then. She felt too subdued

to refuse, so she trailed him into the warm, bright room. Max, Deb, Jean, and Eliot were crouched and hunkered and sprawled around the Scrabble board in front of a fitful little fire. They were all munching popcorn and drinking a variety of liquids from beer to cranberry juice. Max had made himself an admiral's hat out of the Real Estate section of the *Globe* and looked extremely piratical, lowering over his tiles.

"Charlie!" he hailed her. "I need advice. Help me scupper everyone, will you? What can I make out of five consonants and a vowel?"

"Pity you don't know Welsh," remarked Jean.

"Wouldn't matter if he did," said Deb, "it would be illegal. We ought to play with a time limit. Hurry *up*, Max!"

"Don't rush me." Max chewed his beard meditatively.

"Pass me Obituaries, Deb, will you?" Eliot asked.

"Anyone interesting die today, dear?" Mrs. Paige had progressed to the diagramless crossword.

"Me, waiting for Max to play." Deb rolled onto her back and pedaled with her legs. "Where have *you* been all afternoon?" she asked Charlotte.

"Out." Charlotte took a handful of popcorn and slouched into a corner of the sofa. She discovered she didn't really want the popcorn so she sat holding it.

"Been out a lot lately," pursued Deb, still bicycling. "What do you find to do?"

"Nothing much." Charlotte wished they would all just go on with what they were doing and not pay any attention to her.

"Deborah, how am I supposed to think while you're doing that?" demanded Max. "You're deliberately trying to distract me."

Deb retorted, "I'm deliberately trying to keep awake! Who'd you go out with, Charlotte?"

"No one. Why?"

"Just wondered. There are some odd-looking characters wandering around town these days."

"Charlie has sense enough to stay away from them, I'm sure," said Mr. Paige, systematically gutting the Sports section. "Hot damn, the Bruins won against Toronto last night! They've almost got it sewed up this year, Max, did you see?"

"Shhh," said Max. "I'm about to dazzle everyone. Look— G-N-A-T, goes right in front of CATCH. There."

"Does what?" Deb shot upright.

" 'Gnatcatch'."

"You can't do that!" she cried in outrage. "What kind of a word is 'gnatcatch'?"

Max was unruffled. "You've heard of gnatcatchers, haven't you? Large brown South American birds? Well, for a living, they gnatcatch. Perfectly good verb, if that's where you're at. Nineteen points please, Eliot."

"Hmm," said Eliot, pencil poised.

"Actually," elucidated Jean, "they're small gray North American birds, I think. I spent several days last month helping a very solemn little boy do a science project on the birds of Massachusetts."

"That's a gnat-picking children's librarian for you," Eliot remarked cheerfully, and Jean threw popcorn at him. Undaunted, he continued, "Deb, it won't make that much difference to the score, he's losing dismally anyway."

"And so he should," pronounced his sister righteously.

From her corner of the sofa, Charlotte watched them squabble companionably, her mouth set, her thoughts bleak. Eliot glanced up and grinned at her, inviting her to join them, but she stared stonily back and his grin flattened. She couldn't forgive him so easily—part of her wanted to desperately—but she couldn't.

If anyone noticed her odd, unfriendly behavior it wasn't mentioned. Several times she caught the tail end of a significant glance between members of her family, but after Deb's unsuccessful interrogation, no one asked her anything about what she'd been doing for the last couple of hours. That was what she had wanted, but now that she got it she felt neglected and ignored. Either way she lost; it momentarily revived her resentment. She picked at the funny papers and leafed unseeingly through the magazine section. In the teenage advice column, "Dear Edie" was offering help to a thirteen-year-old girl whose mother wouldn't talk to her, and a boy who wanted to find out if a girl in his class really liked him although she never spoke. They added to Charlotte's depression; she couldn't understand problems like these; they belonged to a life entirely alien that thousands of people seemed to live. Perhaps that was her trouble: she just wasn't *like* anyone else.

"There." Mrs. Paige put down the *Times*. "Anyone hungry? I'll get out sandwich stuff and you can feed yourselves—I'm not getting any more meals today."

"You shouldn't even have to put the food out," said Deb.

"Darling, I'd much rather organize things than have people scavenge through my kitchen!" her mother replied with firmness.

Deb shook her head disparagingly but didn't argue. "Eliot, you *won*? How could you have? Jean was way ahead a few minutes ago!"

Eliot had added the scores for each player and written the results in large figures. "Scorekeeper always wins, house rule," he told her smugly.

"You are beneath contempt!" she snorted. "Wretched cheat!"

"Charlotte, come out to the kitchen with me, love, and I'll make you some cocoa," said Mrs. Paige in a tone that did not invite refusal.

"Any hope of a sandwich?" inquired Mr. Paige, rising out of the basketball scores.

"Possibly."

"I'll have some cocoa, too," declared Eliot, throwing down his pencil. "Winning makes a guy thirsty."

"On top of beer?" said Deb in horror. "I don't know why your whole digestive tract doesn't go on strike!"

"Galvanized." He patted his stomach and tried another smile on Charlotte who'd gotten up to follow her mother. "I'll come with you, Chuck."

But Jean put out a restraining hand and caught his arm. Charlotte saw her give her head a slight shake, but all she said was, "You are staying where you are, Eliot Paige, until we've checked your arithmetic. You can't pull a fast one on a pregnant woman and get away with it. Can he, Max? Sit on him."

"Right!" said Max agreeably and threw himself on his younger brother.

"Gracious, children," remarked Mr. Paige with mild surprise. "I thought you'd outgrown that."

"Too much to hope," said Deb.

"Charlotte?" Mrs. Paige called.

"Coming." With a sigh Charlotte left her siblings rolling about on the floor and followed her mother into the kitchen. Cocoa was a comforting idea, but she knew there was more ahead than that and she quickly pointed out that she'd already done kitchen duty once today.

"What about me?" asked her mother. "I did breakfast as well. *And* supper last night."

"But that's different," objected Charlotte. "I mean, you have to."

"Mm-hm." Mrs. Paige began to pull white wrapped parcels out of the refrigerator. "Sometimes, my love," she said conversationally, "I get so sick of thinking up meals I can hardly stand to look at food. Do you know that?"

Stuck momentarily for words, Charlotte shook her head.

"Well, I do. But that's another story. In general I don't mind it because you're my family and I love you all very much, but every now and then I would jump at the chance to seal off the kitchen. Unwrap those, will you, darling? You can arrange them a little on those plates instead of leaving them in lumps."

Charlotte bent her attention to cold cuts and cheese, while her mother assembled mayonnaise, bread, butter, mustard, the remains of Eliot's coleslaw, and a big bag of potato chips. "Deb won't approve of those, of course, but your father loves junk food so." Her face softened in a smile. "All of you are so different—I sometimes wonder how your father and I did it."

"Are we?" asked Charlotte in surprise. "Really different? And me?"

"Goodness, yes! Of course you're different, and each of you is special."

Charlotte shoved the ham and Swiss cheese together on a plate. "I don't *feel* special," she said at last. "I just feel unhappy."

"Darling." Mrs. Paige sat down across the cold cuts from

her. "He didn't mean to do that to you. He didn't think, Charlotte."

"Well, he should have. He *should* have!"

"He was so pleased, he thought it would be a marvelous surprise for all of us. He didn't tell anyone else, either."

"He told Skip."

"Do you feel worse because he's going to Montana, or because he didn't tell you?"

"I don't know. Both."

"Darling, are you going to stay cross with him forever because of that?"

The tears dribbled miserably down her cheeks and she stared obstinately at the piece of ham she was shredding.

"Did it never occur to you before this that Eliot might leave?" asked her mother gently.

"I always thought he was happy here!" Charlotte burst out.

"Oh, my darling, of course he's been happy here! He's twenty-four years old. Most children leave home long before they're that old, it's a natural part of growing up. You let your family help you until you're ready to try life on your own and then you go out and do your best."

"But what about me?"

"It'll happen to you, too, in time."

But Charlotte shook her head violently. "I mean without Eliot? *Now.* He's my one best friend, but he never thought about me at all. He doesn't care."

"Now that's just silly, Charlotte. If he didn't care he never would have got to be your best friend. He's always cared a great deal about you—don't try to fool yourself into thinking he hasn't; that's not fair to Eliot."

"What'll I do?" whispered Charlotte, misery closing its fingers around her throat.

"You'll manage," said Mrs. Paige briskly. "You'll be lonely for a while, but you'll get over it. I don't say you won't always miss him, you do miss people you love, but that's not a bad, unhappy thing. It's been hard for you to find out he's leaving all of a sudden and that's too bad, but you'll adjust."

"I don't want to," declared Charlotte and knew as soon as

she said it that it was true and that it was not a good thing to say. She waited for her mother to scold her, but she didn't.

"Right now all you see is the great gaping hole in your life that Eliot will make when he leaves. You'll be surprised at how quickly it will fill up with things you haven't guessed at yet."

"But I don't see—"

Abruptly, Mrs. Paige turned severe. "*You* don't see. *You* don't want. *You.* I forget how narrowly children look at the world. Have you thought about Eliot at all, Charlotte? He wants to go to Montana, it's his choice. Do you really want him to call it off because it makes *you* unhappy? Even though he's excited and pleased? Do you want that responsibility?"

"No," said Charlotte in a small voice.

"That is to say," Mrs. Paige said dryly, "that you're not at all sure you wouldn't want exactly that. But try to imagine how you'd feel if Eliot came in right now and told you he'd decided to stay in Concord because of you. You might be glad at first, but I think afterward you'd feel sorry and guilty because you'd know you were the reason Eliot gave up something that was important to him. You'd never be quite the same kind of friends. You do love him very much, and I think knowing what you'd done would make you even unhappier than you are now."

"Oh, I don't know," cried Charlotte desolately. She seemed to be saying that a lot lately.

"One of love's hardest lessons is letting go, believe me. But we learn it and teach other other. We won't try to stop Eliot, either one of us, even though we want to."

"You want—*you* want to, too?" Charlotte asked in surprise.

"Darling, he's one of my children, just as you are. I hate to see any of you leave home. It hurts. It hurt when Max left even though I love Jean dearly."

"You mean you—*minded?*"

Mrs. Paige didn't answer right away, and when she did, she didn't look at Charlotte, she simply said, "Yes."

"I thought I was the only one who did. You never said."

She shook her head slowly. "Baby, you're so young," she

said and held out her arms. "I forget sometimes. I'm sorry."

In spite of her age and size and dignity, Charlotte went and sat on her mother's lap and found she still fitted there. It was comforting to be held safe again.

"Can you make it up with Eliot?"

She heaved a great sigh. "I don't know."

"Try," urged her mother softly.

The kettle whistled on the stove and Charlotte got up, rubbing her eyes a little. Mrs. Paige gave her an encouraging smile and began to make the cocoa.

Now, alone in the dark, Charlotte searched through all the words her mother had spoken; they were reasonable, sympathetic words, and she understood them with her mind. But they didn't yet touch her where it hurt. Perhaps they needed time to work: she'd have to be patient and see.

But the anger wasn't there any more. She felt empty without it, and relieved, too. She realized the anger had been destructive. It wrenched her still further from Eliot. Their friendship would never be quite the same, but it would grow back.

And she had learned something else today, something faintly disturbing that she wasn't sure she was ready to think about yet. That other people shared the same kind of feelings she had. Maybe not exactly, and maybe about different things, but they worried and ached as much as she—people like her own mother and Oliver Shattuck. She was used to thinking mostly about herself, but she felt a grudging sympathy for them.

Chapter Eighteen

SOMEONE WAS WHISTLING OUTSIDE CHARLOTTE'S BEDROOM door. Soft but insistent, the notes penetrated her unconsciousness, first at random, then as a pattern of sound, which finally wove together in a recognizable tune: "Reveille." Struggling out of a web of sleep, Charlotte opened her eyes. The room was swimming in early light, its corners shadowed, the shapes of furniture vague. Beyond her windows the sky was smudged gray; it was an unearthly moment to wake: neither day nor night, but the thin edge between. She lay in her own warmth and sleepily contemplated it.

The whistling stopped. "Twenty minutes, Charlie," Eliot called softly, then she heard him thud down the back stairs in his stocking feet.

She knew instantly the reason for being waked at such an hour. But it wasn't until she was almost dressed that she remembered there was something wrong between her and Eliot. Last night she believed she would never fall asleep because of it—certainly never forget it; this morning she was up and functioning ten minutes at least before it even crossed her mind. She paused, a sock in her hand, obscurely upset. Perhaps she should go back to bed and pretend she hadn't heard her brother—serve him right if she did. Trouble was, she knew it wouldn't, it would only serve *her* right because she'd miss the day she'd been looking forward to for so long. Her mother was right: she, Charlotte, would be the loser if she stayed mad at Eliot.

A shiver brought her back to the moment and roughly she pulled on the rest of her clothes—layers of them against the chill. She was giving in, not willingly, not with a good grace, but she was giving in, for her own sake. It made her feel extremely disagreeable.

In the kitchen, Eliot was shoveling down a bowl of instant oatmeal with raisins and cinnamon. He was inordinately fond of the stuff, to Deb's disgust. "Want some?" he offered between spoonfuls. "Not much time—you can eat it"—gulp —"in the car."

Charlotte shook her head. Face to face alone with her brother, she was uncomfortable. She didn't know what to say or how to act toward him. Eliot only made the situation worse by being normal. His presence didn't rekindle her anger, it wasn't that simple. Rather it was the memory of yesterday's anger, cold and hard, that came between them like a sheet of ice, and she didn't know how to break through it.

Instead, she busied herself rooting for breakfast among the cupboards. She took advantage of the lack of parental supervision to make a thick peanut butter and strawberry jam sandwich, then filled a bag with the rest of the brownies and took an orange for good measure. There was no point in going hungry. Eliot downed the last of his cereal, filled a Thermos with coffee, and stuffed his leather shot pouch with a large bar of fruit-and-nut chocolate. "Cold comfort this morning!" He gave his sister an encouraging wink, but she didn't return it, so he shrugged a little and picked up his fife case. "Time to shove off, Charlie, ready? Sutton'll have conniptions if I'm late."

It had snowed another couple of inches during the night, and clouds lay thick across the dawn. Charlotte nibbled her sandwich as Eliot piloted the VW through town. There was quite a lot of movement for ten past five in the morning: bicycles and cars, and small knots of people on foot, their faces still puffy with sleep. They were all being drawn like iron filings to a magnet, toward the park. In spite of the layer of snow, the air had a luminous freshness that had been missing on Saturday and Sunday.

"Lot of people out this morning," remarked Eliot with a

yawn as he pulled into the parking lot across from the Bridge past a uniformed and bearded park ranger. "Better with a good audience. And we're almost on time into the bargain. Good for us."

The Minutemen were assembling as they had Friday afternoon, but with a minimum of horseplay. This morning they had about them an aura of purpose. The plan was to have them march over the Bridge and up the hillside just before the cannon salute.

"Your family here, George?"

"You kidding? I got up at four and no one *moved!*"

"Easier not to go to bed at all—then you don't have to get up."

"Yeah, but can you march with your eyes closed?"

"The cannons'll wake you up, don't worry."

"Gotta go, Charlie, I'll see you back here when it's over," promised Eliot. "We'll walk to the breakfast together, all right?"

Reluctantly Charlotte nodded. Breakfast was another thing she'd miss if she stayed mad at Eliot: the tradition of pancakes with the Minutemen in Monument Hall before the parade. Being part of their group was a privilege that went with being Eliot's sister; she didn't want to surrender it. She gave herself a shake. She didn't know what she wanted, except for her life to stay the same. But it wouldn't because that depended on other people, and they were constantly changing.

She stood with the spectators and watched Captain Sutton pace back and forth, counting and inspecting. "Atten-*hup!*" he barked, and the company snapped to attention in three neat columns, handsome in their uniforms: white shirts with rust-colored stocks, brown breeches, fawn waistcoats and stockings, shoe buckles and buttons polished, black tricorns straight. Trim but not ostentatious. Authentic in detail but uniform as a group, they were aware of their importance as a symbol of patriotism and free-thinking in America. They represented those vigorous individuals who, more than two hundred years ago, had defended their rights as citizens of a new country. It was complicated and emotional, but it was far more than a game to the twentieth century Minutemen, and to most of the spectators. Originally the Militia had been mostly local farmers, determined and ready to fight in a minute if they had to. Now they were lawyers, doctors, shopkeepers, publishers, a veterinarian, a DPW worker, teachers —no longer equiped for actual combat, not really prepared to rout a British army and send it back to Boston exhausted and depleted. But then no one anticipated such a necessity.

Although she searched the somewhat sparse crowd, Charlotte could not find any of Captain MacPherson's men. Perhaps they'd gotten discouraged with what had, up to now, not been a very successful campaign and had given up? It wasn't a very convincing thought.

The Fife and Drum Corps, in place behind the Color Guard, began to warm up on "The York Fusiliers." Johnny Hawsbrook was scribbling a list of tunes, Peter Howe was shaking his fife irritably, Ray Simms and several other men were passing small flasks back and forth. Eliot glared at Ray over his instrument. They were all occupied; Charlotte drifted away on her own. Despite her gloom, she felt a faint thrill of anticipation. Something unexpected was going to happen this morning and she was determined to be in on it.

The best place to watch the proceedings from was across the river near the cannons, which were doubtless being set in place at that moment. Charlotte set off at a jog, keeping an eye out for familiar faces, but there were none in evidence.

The long white hillside beyond the river was spattered haphazardly with people; they streamed through the gaps in the stone wall along the top and wandered across the field in all directions, waiting for the ceremonies to begin and give them a focus. At this hour they were mostly local people, attracted by the idea of a mildly eccentric, authentic Concord tradition, which renewed in them a sense of belonging and pulled them together to make a community. This was what Eliot meant when he declared his affection for Concord; Charlotte could see it herself.

She trudged up the hill through the snow, searching the crowd with greater care. Lots of kids tearing around, laughing, roughhousing, showering snow at one another. Occasionally a parent would reach out a long arm and catch one who might be getting out of hand, but for the most part the adults collected together in clumps, shuffling their feet, yawning, talking sporadically, not fully awake. The kids Charlotte's own age kept aloof from the younger ones, demonstrating their maturity, eyeing one another self-consciously, afraid to be caught taking any of this too seriously. Charlotte avoided them. Babies slept suspended in canvas slings, fore and aft, from their parents, while two- and three-year-olds hung and twisted from adults' hands or rode piggyback safe above the turmoil. The dogs had a marvelous time chasing among the legs, playing tag with kids, barking, sniffing one another, skirmishing.

But there was something missing from the scene, and Charlotte studied it for a moment, puzzled, before she realized what it was. The cannons. It was almost time to begin the ceremony and the Concord Independent Battery was not yet on the field with the gun carriages and two brass cannons. The only people in uniform on that side of the river were several park rangers with walkie-talkies.

If all were well, the cannons should have arrived an hour ago to be installed on the plateau by the flagpole with a interested throng around them. The members of the Battery should be standing by with ramrods, buckets, and powder box, waiting for the Minutemen to march up. But they weren't. Charlotte felt a shiver of apprehension. Beside the wall by the field gate, she finally spotted two of the people she was looking for: the Commodore and Kath Schuyler. He was leaning forward, listening to Kath who gestured toward the Bridge with one hand and down Liberty Street with the other. Charlotte joined them.

"Ah," said the Commodore, looking up, "another of the troops. I suspect we'll need everyone this morning."

Charlotte went right to the point. "Where are the cannons?"

"Coming, with any luck at all," Kath answered.

"There's been a slight delay," added the Commodore. "Amazing thing is how few people seem to have noticed they're missing. Lazy sluggards haven't opened their eyes yet!"

"It's very early," Charlotte pointed out.

Kath was scornful. "Not really. I'm up and working by now most mornings."

"Most people do not have your equine responsibilities," said the Commodore. He glanced round impatiently. "All right, all right, we've got to get this thing moving! What's keeping them?"

"But you haven't told me—" began Charlotte, bursting to know what had happened. She was interrupted by the sound of ragged cheers from the bottom of Liberty Street, and the creak and clop of heavy equipment and horses.

"There they are!" Kath vaulted the wall and raced down the hill.

"Ah!" exclaimed the Commodore, smiling fiercely. "Now where the deuce is Oliver?"

"Right here." He materialized, breathless, by Charlotte's left elbow and caused her to jump. The look he gave her was neither welcoming, nor overtly hostile; he accepted her presence. "I found them, Uncle Sam. They're in the field next to the Old Manse, except for the lookout by the Buttrick House. Seven, counting Dan."

Commodore Shattuck nodded. "Look sharp, both of you. We need to know at once if they begin to move. *This* should give them something to think about!" He rubbed his stubby hands, cracking the knuckles.

The Independent Battery made its grand entrance onto the field: two gun carriages, one pulled by four mounted draft horses, the other by two; followed by a single horse drawing a covered wagon. Five uniformed men on horseback circled the little convoy watchfully, and a small army of civilians on foot escorted them. Skip Bullard was in his usual place, driving the second carriage, but next to him on the seat Charlotte was surprised and a little envious to see Andy Schuyler and Fred Cheavy. Pleased and cocky, Fred beamed at the spectators lining the wall and touched his cap to them. He looked as if he belonged, even without the khaki uniform of the Battery, but Andy grinned self-consciously as if he weren't sure. When he caught sight of the Commodore, Charlotte, and Oliver, he gave a sudden relieved wave. Instinctively, Charlotte waved back, and Commodore Shattuck gave a brisk nod.

Kath had wormed her way into the midst of the escort. She jogged next to Skip, talking earnestly to him. Charlotte saw Mr. Schuyler among the group on foot, looking vaguely quizzical.

"But what happened?" she cried in a frenzy of curiosity. "*Why* are they so late?"

"The carriages," said Oliver tersely.

"What about them?"

As the Battery lumbered and bumped over the hillside, people turned to look and began to move toward it like a tide.

Oliver nudged Charlotte. "The wheels."

She had been so busy looking at people that she'd given the carriages little attention. Now she noticed that there was something incongruous about them: instead of being mounted as usual on great iron-rimmed cartwheels, they rolled along on heavy rubber tractor tires.

"But where—"

"Hsst!" hissed the Commodore, slicing off her question. "Oliver, go find the lookout and see what he does. Jimmy MacPherson's not going to be pleased when he catches sight of the cannon, I'll wager. Thought he'd got 'em mothballed, the sly old devil."

Oliver hared off, leaving Charlotte to ponder the mystery of the missing cartwheels. But the Commodore caught her by the elbow. "No time to moon about, young woman. We've got work to do!"

"I'm not mooning," she retorted, but he ignored her.

They joined the people milling around the cannons, and Andy who'd detached himself from the Battery, greeted them thankfully. "Hey, Charlie! Hello, sir." He was still shy of the Commodore. "What a mess that was! If it hadn't been for Dad and Fred we'd never have gotten those wheels on. The cannons must weigh a ton each! Fred says it's just like heaving crates of turnips. What d'you suppose happened to them?"

"Not to worry," replied the Commodore briskly. "They'll turn up fast enough now they're not needed."

"Where did you get the tires?" Charlotte asked Andy.

"One's an old set from the DPW and the other came off our

tractor. Skip says they're a bit low for the carriages, but they got the cannons here."

"Can't have a twenty-one gun salute without the guns," agreed the Commodore.

Quickly and efficiently the members of the Battery moved to settle the cannons. They braced the wheels, filled the water buckets, put the powder box in place, and checked the guns over. Skip planted the red Battery guidon in the ground between the two carriages, where it fluttered bravely. It had crossed gold cannons and CIB 1804 on it. There were four men to each gun, to load, ram, prime, fire, and steady. The park rangers, working like sheepdogs, drove the spectators back out of range and held them there.

Commodore Shattuck watched the proceedings narrowly, as if he were in charge of the whole event. "Charlotte," he said at length, "I think we're ready here. You'd better go tell the Minutemen they can start."

"Me? But they're all the way over in the Monument Street parking lot," she protested. "It'll take me ages to get there!"

"Someone has to go," he replied sternly.

"I'll miss everything here if I do."

"Never mind," said Andy. "I'll go with you. If we hurry we'll see most of it."

He started down the hill, but Charlotte hung back. She thought she'd heard fifes in the distance. A moment later people turned their heads toward the Bridge and craned to catch a first glimpse of the Minutemen. The sound of "Yankee Doodle" rose through the gray morning air. Andy stopped partway down the hill and came running back. "Guess we don't need to go after all," he said, grinning.

Across the gently steaming river the column of Minutemen came marching with their flags fluttering, their muskets on their shoulders, their fifes and drums shrill and invincible. They made a splendid sight. Charlotte's pulse quickened as she watched them move smartly up the hill.

As he marched past her, Eliot gave her a wink, and she smiled a swift, embarrassed smile in return. They marched up to the flagpole and formed a semicircle behind it. The Concord Selectmen joined them and a minister delivered the Invocation while the adults looked solemn and the children fidgeted. Afterwards a high school student blew "Reveille" on a cold trumpet and Captain Sutton raised the American flag. Eliot's Corps played "The Star-Spangled Banner."

"Where's Oliver?" asked Andy. "I thought I saw him with you."

"His uncle sent him off to watch the enemy. Somewhere near the house," Charlotte told him. She thought Eliot had never played better.

Andy scanned the crowd intently. "There's one of them," he said suddenly, pointing. Grudgingly Charlotte wrenched her attention from the Minutemen and followed his finger. Nicholas Boutwell-Scott was stationed beside a dense jungle of ornamental shrubs at the edge of the gardens; he stood with his arms folded across the front of his red jacket, the black and yellow scarf still wrapped around his neck. There was a thoughtful frown on his handsome face as he surveyed the scene below him.

"And there's Oliver." Charlotte pointed to a spot behind Nicholas where a small figure lurked in the shrubs. "He's not very well hidden."

"Neither are we," said Andy, "standing around here in plain sight. Should we be doing something, do you think?"

"I don't know what." Charlotte was irritable because she felt she ought to have an idea.

"Hey," said Andy. "Look!" His face was lifted skyward. Above the people on the hillside the gray sky stretched higher and higher, the clouds pulled thin across it. In the east a hazy ember that was the sun burned steadily behind them. Strung across the new light flew a great shifting wedge of geese; over the confusion of noise on the ground their wild crying came faint, over the music, the rising voices, the bark of orders among the Battery. Andy and Charlotte stood rapt, watching until the geese disappeared beyond the trees, heading for the wildlife refuge downriver. Then they looked at each other and smiled at the wonder they had shared.

The world splintered around them. "Number one gun ready! Fire!" came the command, followed by a thundering explosion that shattered the morning and threw echoes down among the willows. Pigeons broke from the trees around the Bridge, clattering upward like a burst of applause. A great pillow of thick white smoke rolled from the cannon's mouth.

Charlotte swallowed to clear her ears of the terrible sound. Men were busy around the guns: thrusting a long wet damper down the muzzle of the one just fired, preparing the second with a charge from the powder box, ramming it home, setting the lanyard. "Number two gun ready! Fire!" This time she was watching as it happened and was better prepared for the deafening crack. She saw the spurt of fire, the bits of cartridge flying black out of the smoke, the violent kick of the gun carriage. She found she had her teeth clenched.

Beside her Andy cried, "Neat!" with enthusiasm, and there was a ripple of applause and "ah"s of appreciation as people pointed upward and exclaimed. Charlotte craned to look. The vigorous expulsion of smoke had taken sudden form overhead and become a perfect rolling smoke ring which melted slowly into the morning.

Someone called, "Hey, Skip, what'd you put in that bucket? Hundred proof?"

Skip grinned. "I'll never tell."

"Aren't you glad we got them here in time?" Andy asked Charlotte.

She nodded, less enthusiastic. The noise of the cannon sent shock waves through her, to the soles of her feet. She didn't much like explosions, though she didn't admit it. Eliot loved them, like Andy, the louder the better. He had taken her to a really terrifying fireworks display in Boston last Fourth of July. So long as he was standing close beside her, she managed not to flinch too much. This morning, however, it was a matter of pride; she was not going to let Andy Schuyler know that cannons made her nervous.

"Let's go closer," suggested Andy.

"We can see everything from here."

"But I want to see how they fire them."

Charlotte planted her feet, and with a sigh, Andy stayed with her.

"Number one gun ready! Fire!"

Two little girls, arms linked, and a park ranger standing

nearby clapped their hands over their ears and screwed their eyes up in anticipation. Charlotte would have liked to do the same, but restrained herself. By this time the accumulation of smoke which lay inert and heavy on the air around the guns enveloped most of the hillside. It smelled of bad eggs and heat. People sniffed and wrinkled their noses, but no one complained because it was a legitimate part of the occasion.

Charlotte, bracing for each new explosion, distracted herself by picking out the people she knew among the spectators. It was hard to miss Fred; he danced about on the edge of the Battery, hands tight clasped behind his back like a small boy told not to touch. He watched every move with rapt attention while firing off his own barrage of questions at the gunners.

Kath and Mr. Schuyler watched from a prudent distance. Neither of them turned a hair each time a cannon fired. Nor did Skip who stood by the powder box, counting out rounds of ammunition and handing them one at a time to the man loading each cannon.

The cannonade seemed to go on forever. The Minutemen stood at parade rest, their musket butts on the ground, their pennants flickering in the softening breeze. Charlotte lost count of the explosions halfway through and clenched her hands in her pockets waiting for it to be over. When at last the final round was fired, the Battery packed up its gear with the same speed and efficiency they had unpacked it. Eliot gave the Fife and Drum Corps the high sign, and they played "The Battle Hymn of the Republic." On all sides the crowd stood quiet, attentive, while curtains of gunsmoke frayed and blew apart, and the men of the Battery saluted. "Glory, glory hallelujah . . ." The familiar words clogged in the back of Charlotte's throat.

Eliot had a showman's instinct for programming and never overplayed his hand. As the last notes of the "Battle Hymn" drifted down over the river and faded, he led his men into "Aiken Drum." The lively and nonsensical tune was one of Charlotte's favorites.

The teams of draft horses were led up from a distant part of the field, and the carriages were rejoined to their front wheels. Kath couldn't resist lending a hand with the harnessing; she went from horse to horse checking straps and tightening buckles professionally.

"Can't keep her away from them," remarked Andy with a grin. "So far so good, Charlie. Maybe they've given up?"

But Charlotte shook her head. "Not that easily." Although she'd been thinking the same thing herself.

"I wonder where Dan is?"

"If he's anything like Fred, he's turned traitor to his side and you oughtn't to care," said Charlotte severely.

Andy shrugged, unbothered. "I've got to find him this morning. Ma thinks Fred is great, but she was pretty definite about wanting Dan home today."

"Oliver says he's across the river with the enemy."

"Thanks," said Andy gratefully. "I'll go look for him."

"You can't now," Charlotte pointed out. "It's too late—there go the Minutemen."

The Color Guard led off and the Minutemen fell into place behind to march back down the track to the bridge. The Battery swung round to bring up the rear, and the crowd dispersed to rearrange itself along the route for a good view. The patch of ground where everyone had been standing was trampled bare and muddy, the grass a sodden mat.

"Nuts," said Andy. "Hadn't we better stick with the Commodore?"

Charlotte glanced round. "He's gone."

"The Commodore's right over there—see?" Andy pointed.

"No, stupid." She nodded toward the rhododendrons. "I mean the lookout, and Oliver's gone, too!"

Together, she and Andy set off after the Minutemen, dodging slow-moving and wandering people. Kath joined them on the way. She'd done all anyone would let her do with the horses, so she lit out after Andy when she saw him, calling, "What's up?" But he didn't stop to answer. Commodore Shattuck was keeping pace with the head of the procession; he strode along keen-eyed and formidable, alert for signs of trouble.

"See anyone yet?" demanded Kath when they overtook him.

"Not yet. But there's time—plenty of time." He smiled grimly.

At the bottom of the field the track ran flat through a clump of brush and willow. Here it was built up above ground level, making an earth causeway that would stay firm when the low-lying river plain around it was flooded with rain or spring melt. Even though today the ground was coated with snow, it was thawed and spongy underfoot, soft with mud and waterlogged grasses. Keeping up with the Minutemen was difficult at this point because the Company filled the track from side to side and left no solid verge for civilians to walk on. But the Commodore seemed to think it urgent to reach the Bridge with, or before, the Militia, so Andy, Kath, and Charlotte squelched around the marching column after him. It was rough going and several times Charlotte caught her balance barely in time to keep from falling headlong into the melting ooze.

Just before it reached the bridge, the track opened out onto a kind of round, high island of hard-packed ground. In the middle stood the statue of the Minuteman, where his real counterparts had stood to face the British army, and fired, according to Ralph Waldo Emerson, "the shot heard round the world."

The Commodore and his group arrived at the statue well ahead of the Minutemen to find Oliver there already and three park rangers in a concerned huddle behind the statue, discussing something in low agitated whispers. Their chief function during the ceremonies was to keep the public safely out of the way, but at the moment they were so absorbed in consultation they didn't even notice the public.

"Uncle Sam, I thought you'd never get here!" Oliver's voice broke with relief.

"How did *you* get here so fast?" asked Kath.

"I ran. I was following Nicholas and when he took off, I went after him. He crossed the bridge, though, and I thought I'd better stay here and wait for you."

"Well?" said the Commodore. "What now?"

"Come and see."

They followed Oliver around the statue and the three park rangers, who now seemed to be arguing heatedly among themselves, and came face to face with the latest strategy: it stretched unevenly across the Bridge at the highest point of its arch. Captain MacPherson had deployed all his troops, including Dan Schuyler, in a line blocking access to the far bank. The British were armed with an imaginative assortment of weapons: a baseball bat; two rifles—one lethally new, the other rusty—an antique scimitar; one genuine rapier; a crowbar and hatchet; and a garden rake. The man with the rake —whom Charlotte recognized as Bobby Hardcastle from the dry cleaner's—also held a flagstaff flying a large Union Jack. All but Dan were in uniform, though only the Captain and one other man, a lugubrious individual, could really be said to look military. The others had a patched-together, miscellaneous appearance. Nevertheless, they presented an unexpected and imposing spectacle. It was no wonder the rangers were in a quandary.

For a long moment the Commodore and the Captain faced one another; although neither spoke, they were obviously communicating.

Andy was the one to break the loaded silence. "Hey, Dan, what do you think you're doing with that baseball bat? You aren't really going to fight us, are you?"

Dan frowned and pursed his lips. "Gotta."

Andy looked genuinely surprised. "What d'you mean, 'Gotta'?"

"Well," Dan explained, "for one thing there're more of you than of them"—he indicated his companions on the Bridge— "and for another I've won their money."

"I don't see—"

"What did I tell you," whispered Charlotte. "A traitor."

"Quiet!" barked the Commodore. "I need to think."

"Aye, well think awa', Sammy lad," called Captain Mac-Pherson.

"You're going to have to move," declared Kath. "Here come the Minutemen, and if you don't get out of the way they'll march over you. Serve you right, too, Dan Schuyler!"

"Ach, noo ye think so, lassie. Let them come agin us! The river shall run red wi' bluid first, I promise ye. Ma lads'll fecht tae the last drap!"

He means it, thought Charlotte in amazement. The Captain's face was set like granite; he stood ramrod stiff in the middle of his men, shorter than any but Dan, yet dominating them all. In his right hand he held the rapier. He was making his last stand.

"You won't win this one, Jimmy," the Commodore told him. "You can't. We've got the numbers with us today—hear them coming? And there'll be more Minutemen from the other towns before long."

The sound of fifes and drums, which had been growing steadily louder, burst into the clearing. With well-rehearsed precision the marching Minutemen divided to circumvent the statue, rejoined, then came to an unscheduled halt at the sight of Captain MacPherson and his troops. The music dwindled away raggedly. "Who are they?" someone said loudly. Heads shook. From the back of the column an indignant muttering rose, as those who couldn't see what lay ahead walked into one another.

Searching out her brother, Charlotte saw an expression of puzzled interest on his face. The Company Commander, Captain Sutton, looked put out. "What is this?" he demanded of the three park rangers who were observing the scene nervously.

One of them swallowed and said, "Um, we don't—ah—exactly know, sir. I mean they just—ah—*appeared*. I don't know what to make of them, sir."

"Well, did you ask them to move?"

"I did, sir," spoke up Ranger Two.

"And?"

"Well, ah, the one in the middle—the little one there, sir—he, ah, said . . ." Her voice trailed off miserably.

"Said what?"

Number Two looked at Number One and Number Three looked at his feet. The little island around them was rapidly filling with curious spectators as people edged into the clearing past the stalled Minutemen. It was becoming cramped.

"Tell me what he said," ordered Captain Sutton. "What's going on here?"

"I'll tell ye masel', ye damned upstart!" bellowed Captain MacPherson, brandishing his rapier. The metal blade caught the sun's first thin rays and flashed cold blue. "I'll tell ye, richt!

225

I telt 'em, 'Come forder if ye dare, ye villains—we fecht tae the bluddie death! For God, Empire, and King George's glorious memory, we sall hold this brig 'gainst the lot o' ye! Confusion to the enemy and death to traitors!' "

"Yes," agreed Ranger Two, "that was it. We don't quite know what to make of it, sir."

The Captain seemed similarly at a loss. He rubbed his chin, bemused.

" 'Ere," said Fred who'd pushed forward to join Commodore Shattuck. " 'E means me by that, 'e does. 'E's callin' me a traitor, the old brute. 'Oo does 'e think 'e is, chuckin' names about like that?"

"Well, you are one, aren't you?" asked Kath bluntly. "You did help us get the cannons here."

Fred looked hurt. "I was only doin' a good turn—me Christian duty, after the 'ospitality you lot give me."

"This is ridiculous," declared Captain Sutton vehemently. "Does anyone here know those men? What do they want? Where are the police? Damn it, we can't allow a handful of crackpots to bring the whole ceremony to a grinding halt like this!"

On the Bridge, the British shifted uneasily, darting sidelong glances at one another, but standing their ground. Captain MacPherson alone looked as if he were enjoying himself. "Ye daur call Her Majesty's finest fechtin' men crackpots, do ye? Ye sall rue that, I promise ye!"

Charlotte jumped as Eliot touched her shoulder. She'd been so fascinated by what was going on she hadn't noticed him leave the ranks. "Charlie, do you know what's going on?" he asked in an undertone.

"It's a battle, Mr. Paige," answered the Commodore who'd overheard. "Or if it isn't yet, it soon will be if I know Jimmy MacPherson. If you intend to cross that Bridge you'll have to fight your way through them." His eyes glinted beneath the tangled eyebrows.

"He's serious then?" Eliot sounded disbelieving. "He really means to try and stop us?"

"He does."

"But they're outnumbered," Andy protested. "They don't have a chance."

Fred scowled at him. "Aw, don't rub it in, mate."

"He's right, they haven't," Kath agreed matter-of-factly.

"But I don't want to fight anyone. I come 'ere to see a bit a the world, not get meself killed! 'Ell's bells!" With a great unhappy sigh Fred stumped forward to join his countrymen on the Bridge.

"Welcome, old Fred," said Nicholas warmly.

"Halt!" challenged the Captain as Fred set foot on the timbers. "What business hae ye wi' us?"

"Aw, stow it," said Fred disrespectfully. "Against me better judgment I've come to 'elp." He gave his former captors a helpless apologetic shrug as he took his place in line next to Dan.

Captain MacPherson watched him narrowly. "I'll sort ye oot later, Private Cheavy, dinna fear."

"If this bleeding lark don't kill us all first," muttered Fred.

In the meantime Captain Sutton and the park rangers had gone into a huddle. They were clenched together like fingers in a fist.

"What do you think they'll do?" Charlotte asked the Commodore.

"Wait and see."

"But will they really fight?" Andy wanted to know. "Will there really be violence?"

"Could very well be."

"Hey," said Eliot, "that doesn't sound like much fun, does it?"

Commodore Shattuck smiled his fierce smile. "War is hell, boy!"

Captain Sutton left the rangers and strode to the foot of the bridge, looking determined.

"Ready!" roared Captain MacPherson to his men.

"What's 'e mean, mate?" Fred asked Dan.

Dan flourished his baseball bat a little dubiously. "I think he means get ready to defend the Bridge."

"Oh crikey! What'll me mum say when I don't come 'ome?"

"Wheesht in the ranks!" Captain MacPherson glowered at him.

"Listen," Captain Sutton called. "Are you guys demonstrating for some reason? I mean, have you got a cause or a grievance or something? You know it's not legal to do this without a permit. You could get into serious trouble. The police have got to know about it first—technicalities like that. You *could* all be arrested." He sounded calm and reasonable. "The best thing you guys can do is clear off right now and we'll forget the whole business. Okay? Look, you've got uniforms on, and maybe we can fix it so you can be in the parade if you cooperate. How's that hit you?"

"Ach, get awa' wi' ye, ye rascal!" cried the Captain. "A place in yer parade, ye offer? 'Tis a bluddie sop—an insult tae Her Majesty's troops! Ye speak o' unlawful assembly an' look at yer ainsels. Ye've bin doing it for years, ye colonial rabble. Ye'll no get awa' wi' it this time, or ma name's not Jamie MacPherson! Ye'll no pass this brig wi'oot ye trample us underfit, ye great daft bunch o' haverin' upstarts!"

"Does that mean you refuse to move and let us cross the Bridge?" asked Captain Sutton in a dangerously level voice.

"Aye, ye've got the message."

Captain Sutton set his square, clean-shaven jaw and gave the Scotsman on the Bridge a measuring look. "Then we'll have to move you."

"Jist ye try it!"

Captain Sutton gave a nod, swung on his heel, and strode back to the waiting Minutemen.

"Round two," said the Commodore.

"Charlie," said Eliot, "who *are* those men?"

"British soldiers," she answered promptly.

"Yes, but—"

"Where are *they* going?" Oliver interrupted.

Two of the park rangers and one Minuteman pushed their way back through the plug of interested people who stopped the entrance to the clearing.

"Damnation!" exclaimed the Commodore in annoyance. "That'll mean interference, I'll wager. They're going for reinforcements."

"But they don't need them," objected Oliver. His face was even more pinched and white than usual; his green eyes were a startling contrast.

"If Jimmy's to have a chance at all, it'll have to be now. We'll have the police here soon."

"Why do we need the police?" said Kath. "This hasn't got anything to do with them."

"Ma's going to be cross if Dan gets mixed up with them," Andy predicted.

Oliver said with sudden passion, "It's not fair!"

"You're right, it isn't," agreed Charlotte. She suddenly knew she would hate to see the British soldiers ignominiously arrested by people who had no idea at all what was going on. It was none of the police's business.

Across the river, more people had gathered on the bank. They lined the shore, peering curiously over to see what was going on, doubtless thinking it was all part of the scheduled ceremonies. They couldn't see the grim faces of the British, nor the peculiar collection of weapons they carried.

But Captain Sutton, having dispatched runners for help, was evidently not content to stand about and wait for that help to come. After another brief consultation with the remaining ranger and a handful of Minutemen, he thumped his fist into his open hand, then put two fingers into his mouth and whistled. The company, which had been slouching at ease, passing around flasks and telling jokes, sprang to attention. Eliot snapped back into his place with the band.

"All right, men, we've hit a little problem here, as you can see. These characters on the Bridge say they won't let us march over it. I don't know who they are, or who they *think* they are, but I for one don't want to let them claim they've stopped us."

He was interrupted by a fragmentary but enthusiastic cheer. He looked gratified. "How many of them are there, anyway?" he asked rhetorically.

"Eight," called out some joker from the anonymity of the ranks.

"Very clever," said the Captain sarcastically. "You can count, but can you fight? What do you men say we show these guys whose Bridge it is?"

"Yes!" The Minutemen responded loudly.

"Paul O'Brien's gone for the police, but they won't get

here for a while, and I'm tired of twiddling my thunbs. I think we can clear 'em out ourselves. After all, that's what we're supposed to stand for, isn't it?"

This was greeted with an even louder "Yes!"

"All right then. Eliot, get the fifes and drums to give us something martial. Pull yourselves together!"

Chapter Nineteen

ELIOT SALUTED SMARTLY AND SIGNALED HIS MEN WITH THREE fingers. They struck up "The White Cockade"; the shrill, brave sound of the fifes pierced the brightening air and, underneath, the drums set a sharp tempo. The sun had, by this time, succeeded in burning a sizable hole in the cloud cover, and blue sky shone out. The Commodore and his little group stood by the railing just to the right of the bridge, all of them tensed with anticipation.

On command from Captain Sutton, the Minutemen began to mark time. The Color Guardsmen in the vanguard looked somewhat uncertain, but they hoisted the colors aloft in readiness.

On the Bridge, the Redcoats stood rigid, feet braced on the timbers, their faces expressing different emotions: several looked just plain scared, Beaky had turned a sickly greenish-white, Fred appeared distressed, and Dan anxious. Captain MacPherson looked invincible, and Nicholas Boutwell-Scott, with the great, flashing scimitar held high in his left hand, could only be described as swashbuckling.

Captain Sutton shouted, "Shoulder—*harms!*" in a mighty voice. "Forward, *march!*"

Obedient, the column moved forward, stomping through the wet snow.

"They really don't have a chance," said Kath, her voice unusually faint

"No, they haven't," agreed her brother. "And Dan's right in the middle. Look at him, the turkey! He's going to get *hurt!*"

"Uncle Sam," said Oliver urgently, "*do* something! Stop them!"

The Commodore turned and gave his great-nephew a long searching look. "I don't know that I can," he said. "I rather doubt I can stop Jimmy now, he's planned this for so long."

"But—but they've got guns and swords," protested Charlotte. "What happens if they use them? Lots of people will get hurt—even—even Eliot. He's right in the front!"

"Hey!" cried Oliver suddenly. "But it doesn't have to be that kind of a fight, does it?" He spoke so rapidly the words fell over one another, barely intelligible. "They don't have to use guns or swords—there doesn't—oh, hell! Come *on!*" He darted forward, bent, and quickly scooped up a handful of snow.

"Yes!" Kath understood instantly. "Yes, he's right. Come on!" She copied Oliver and a moment later her first snowball flew after his, outdistancing it, and plastering a circle of white on Nicholas Boutwell-Scott's chest.

His mouth made a surprised "O," but Kath didn't wait to see what he'd do, she was too busy packing a second ball. By this time Andy and Charlotte had caught on and were scrabbling in the snow. They straightened and threw—all four of them now—indiscriminately, not caring whom they hit, British soldier or advancing Minuteman. They fired them off as fast as they could make them.

For a long moment the whole scene, with the exception of the four children scratching frantically, was locked in place. Then people glanced around in astonishment as the idea began to take hold, and in another minute the air was full of flying snowballs. The Minutemen bent to it with enthusiasm. The Color Guard, getting pasted from the front where the British had begun to defend themselves, and from the back, out of their own ranks, withdrew hastily, still clutching their flagstaffs.

Charlotte saw Eliot stuff his fife into his back pocket and join the melee with a look of delight. The rest of the Fife and

Drum Corps followed his example. Even the one remaining park ranger leaped into the fray—in self-defense most likely, for no one in the clearing was safe.

The snow was perfect for packing. With the change in temperature it had begun to melt; it made beautiful snowballs. The only trouble was that the British—who held their ground surprisingly well considering their scant number—were quickly running out of raw ammunition on the Bridge. They scraped it bare and were forced to retreat in order to find a new supply.

On the other side of the river, the people didn't seem to realize what was going on yet. They stood about, looking puzzled as the red-coated figures moved backwards toward them. The Minutemen greeted the withdrawal vociferously. Their cramped space gave them a handicap which helped the British. The men who packed and threw from the rear of the company kept hitting their fellow Minutemen in front, who would then turn and hurl snowballs back in irritation instead of concentrating all their efforts on the enemy.

Panting for breath, Charlotte paused, wiped the hair back out of her eyes and surveyed the scene. Even Commodore Shattuck had entered the fray. He didn't bend very well, but he threw with gusto, his cheeks flushed pink and his fine white hair dancing wildly around his head.

As the British retreated across the Bridge, the first lines of Minutemen stepped upon it. The hail of snowballs began to reach the spectators on the far bank now and they moved speedily out of range.

Quite suddenly Charlotte became aware of a high distant wail overlying the shouts, war cries, panting, and cursing on the field of battle: sirens. She grabbed Andy's elbow making him miss his shot. "Police!" she bawled at him.

"We don't need them!" he shouted back. "This is fine!"

She shook her head. "Listen. They're coming."

The British finally relinquished the Bridge. It was swept bare of snow and they had no choice if they were to continue to defend themselves. As they gave it up, the Minutemen surged forward onto and over it with a loud cheer, Andy and Charlotte caught willy-nilly in their midst. Charlotte glimpsed

Kath bobbing up and down in the front line, and doubtless the Commodore and Oliver were somewhere else in the crush of bodies. She had no time to worry about anyone but herself, however. She had all she could do to keep her feet. She was jostled on all sides, squeezed so violently by moving bodies she couldn't lift her arms. It was like being forced through a funnel.

Once they gained the far bank, the Minutemen spread out and she gasped with relief. The British soldiers had already regrouped to make another stand, with Captain MacPherson jigging about in their midst, alternately pelting the Americans with nasty-sounding Scottish curses and yelling encouragement to his own men. Suddenly the British were picking up reinforcements of their own, Charlotte noticed. Now that the spectators on this side understood what was happening —even if they didn't understand why—they enthusiastically joined the fracas and many of them allied themselves with the Redcoats. The odds, though still long, weren't quite so one-sided. The snow battle raged fiercely around the granite column with its inscription commemorating that first battle in 1775. It and everyone within range was liberally coated with white. The overall effect was that of being in a storm of over-sized hail.

" 'Ey!" cried Fred, cutting in close to Charlotte for an instant. "Now this is more like it, mate, innit?" He beamed at her as he scooped up handfuls of snow.

Charlotte grinned back and puffed out her cheeks. She was getting hot under her jacket. They fought on. The British took up a defensive position behind the stone wall near the memorial to their fallen countrymen; its wreath was still in place, though frosted with snow.

She had forgotten about the sirens when suddenly a state trooper's car roared down the pedestrian walk toward them from Monument Street, its horn blasting and light flashing. Hard on its wheels came a small but dense mass of state police on foot. Several Concord officers jogged in attendance, looking faintly annoyed.

As the car jerked to a stop, the driver's door flew open and out leaped a large trooper with a bullhorn. If he was surprised at the sight that greeted him, he didn't show it; his men did, however. They gaped in wonder at the snowy, disheveled crowd. The trooper switched on his horn and shouted, "Cease and desist in the name of the law! We've been called in to arrest people here engaged in illegal demonstration and the disruption of scheduled commemorative events. If those persons so described give themselves up quietly there will be no trouble, but anyone offering resistance will be dealt with accordingly!"

Silence met this announcement; the combatants looked at one another like guilty schoolchildren.

It was impossible to tell where the snowball came from—even whether it was thrown by an American or a British hand—but it was hurled with force and deadly accuracy. It hit the bell of the bullhorn, which fortunately the trooper had taken down from his mouth. It efficiently rendered the instrument useless. "Who threw that?" the trooper bellowed, his voice thin and furious.

A number of people from all parts of the crowd shouted back, "I did!" and there was a ripple of surprised laughter. The trooper glared and shook his horn while his men nobly stifled grins. "It isn't funny, you realize, playing games with the law," he told them.

For several minutes everyone stood at stalemate, each waiting for someone else to make the next move. Then the trooper happened to focus on the lanky, unfortunate figure of Beaky Tate who stood clutching his rusty musket. They were no more than five yards apart. "You!" he cried. "You're under arrest for creating a disturbance! Do you have a license for that firearm?"

"Eh?" Beaky threw him a startled glance.

"I thought as much," said the trooper grimly. "I strongly advise you to offer no resistance. Marretti, take this man into custody and read him his rights." He glared round in triumph and the crowd rumbled disapprovingly.

Charlotte saw the man called Marretti mouth "Sorry" as he came forward and took Beaky's arm. It hardly seemed fair that anyone should be arrested merely for taking part in a snowball fight.

"He doesn't have a license, of course," someone behind her said. She turned and met Skip Bullard's level gaze. Although the gun-carriages and caisson were still on the Buttrick side of the river, the men from the Battery had surged across with everyone else.

"Charlie, where's Eliot?" Or Commodore Shattuck?"

"Don't know. Will they really arrest him and take him away?"

"They will unless we do something," Skip replied. "They'll arrest as many of them as they can find. Come on, stick with me, kid." He pushed his way through the crowd in search of Eliot and the Commodore. As luck would have it, they were together, conferring urgently on the steps of the monument.

Before Skip could interrupt them, the trooper with the defunct bullhorn found another troublemaker. Or, more accurately, was found by one. From the top of the granite platform that ran around the obelisk, Charlotte could see over the heads of people to where there was a sudden turbulence —a kind of whirlpool effect—right beside the police car. An angry Scottish voice rose out of the middle of it, demanding to know in whose authority the arrest was being made, and did the troopers realize they were abusing the rights of a free British citizen, protected by Her Majesty, Queen Elizabeth II?

"Oh, no," muttered the Commodore. "Ah Jimmy, Jimmy, you old fool! Whatever are you doing, lad?"

With satisfaction, the trooper declared his second arrest and told another officer to take charge of Captain MacPherson.

"This is serious," said Eliot. "If they arrest the lot of them, we'll win this fight by default and there's no glory in that!"

"It was going so well," mourned Charlotte. "It was, wasn't it? No one was getting hurt. Why did they have to come and ruin it?"

"Eliot, my old school chum," said Skip thoughtfully, "how many years do you suppose one gets for throwing snowballs at the state police?"

"You mean—?" Eliot's eyes lit and the Commodore gave an explosive snort.

Skip shrugged. "Do you see any alternative?"

Commodore Shattuck considered for a moment. "Not really, no. But we'll have to act quickly—here come the newshounds."

"What?" asked Charlotte.

"The media," Eliot translated for her. "They must have got wind of our 'Happening' on a radio scanner. Well, we may as well give 'em a good show, children!"

Skip nodded and gave the thumbs-up sign.

Behind the cluster of police, another small army was gathering. Instead of weapons, this one was armed with videotape and cameras, notebooks and portable tape recorders. Their equipment was emblazoned with the names and call letters of a Boston television station and two newspapers. And more were coming down the path.

"Hell and botheration! Why in Tunkett can't they leave us alone to fight our own friendly little wars?" demanded the Commodore irritably.

"Charlie," warned Eliot, "you stay back and if you throw any snowballs, whatever you do don't let the troopers see you doing it. Not until we find out what's going to happen."

Charlotte narrowed her eyes at him. "But—"

"Go find Andy and Kath and tell them what we're up to," put in Skip. "Eliot, now or never, I think!"

"Don't fire until you see the whites of their eyes!" cried Eliot and leaped off the platform. Skip hopped sideways down the steps. They paused long enough to pack a couple of snowballs each, then dove into the crowd. There was a moment's delay, then a yell, and another yell. Of the two, Skip was the better aim. His first two shots scored direct hits—one on the trooper, the other on the man who'd arrested Beaky Tate. Eliot's exploded against the car.

"E-e-e-e-e-ha!" someone hollered.

Charlotte sped off to find Andy and Kath as instructed and ran headlong into Oliver.

"Hey!" He caught her by the arm before she could slip past him. "What did they decide? What're we doing?"

"Fighting," snapped Charlotte trying to wriggle away. "Let go—I've got to find Andy and Kath." She was about to wrench free, when she remembered that it had been Oliver who had averted the real fight earlier. It had been Oliver who kept people from actually hurting each other. She paused and looked at him more carefully. "You could help me," she offered reluctantly. "Eliot and Skip are attacking the state troopers with snowballs. They need all of us."

Oliver pursed his lips, then accepted her overture. "They're over by the wall with Dan. I saw them a minute ago."

The crowd around them erupted once again in whoops and cheers and flying snow; Charlotte and Oliver had to battle their way through, shielding their heads as they went. As quickly as the Minutemen had caught on to Oliver's strategy back on the other side of the Bridge, everyone now caught on to Eliot's and Skip's. With enthusiasm they turned once more to the fray: spectators, Minutemen and British alike, fighting side by side against the intruders The state troopers were forced to retreat behind the cruiser which offered scant protection for them all, while their leader abandoned his bullhorn and dignity and dove for shelter inside the car. Before he could get the door open, however, he was pasted mercilessly from all sides. In haste he gave up the struggle and flung himself into the huddled mass of his men.

"Well, don't just stand there like a bunch of morons," he roared at them. "Fight back, dammit!"

They sprang into action and turned to packing and hurling as fast as they could. They did surprisingly well under the circumstances. The reporters and cameramen were receiving the same treatment but faring rather worse, encumbered as they were by their equipment. They spluttered and yelped with indignation. One hollered something about the neutrality of the press which rewarded him with a perfect hail of snowballs; another continued bravely to film the unexpected scene; but the others downed their cameras and recorders and joined the beleaguered troopers.

By the time Charlotte and Oliver reached the Schuylers, there was no need to tell them anything; it was obvious what was happening and all five of them plunged into the battle together. On every side townspeople, Minutemen, Battery, and Captain MacPherson's troops were pitching in, shoulder to shoulder.

Charlotte was elated. She ignored the snow melting down the back of her neck and her wet feet and the fact that she was steaming inside her parka. She forgot that she was mad at Eliot and that she didn't much like Oliver Shattuck and that Andy and Kath made her uncomfortable. She gave herself up to the knowledge that she was part of this extraordinary morning, that she belonged, and the joy of it bubbled inside her like a hot spring, taking away her aches and hurts and worries. For the first time in days she was purely happy.

The troopers waged a good defense, but the Concordians were too much for them. After attempting valiantly to hold the police car, they were finally forced to withdraw. In a ragged group they retreated up the path, jogging backward, still firing snowballs into the throng. They left their prisoners behind.

Hastily forming up again, the Minutemen swept forward to engulf Captain MacPherson and Beaky Tate. The townspeople scattered to the sides of the path and became spectators once more, for the most part, though some stayed with the soldiers. A large group of boys—junior and senior high school age—were so carried away by the spirit of the day they splintered from the group and continued their own war in the field beside the Old Manse.

The Color Guard lifted its flags to the morning sun, Eliot called up his band and, flushed with success, the whole company marched out to "Yankee Doodle." Between the Fife and Drum Corps and the main body of Minutemen marched Captains Sutton and MacPherson and Commodore Shattuck, with the British soldiers, Andy, Kath, Dan, Oliver, and Charlotte at their heels. Captain MacPherson positively strutted, head up, back straight as a flagstaff, with the Commodore stately beside him.

Charlotte found herself sandwiched between Fred and Andy. One of the British soldiers was calling step in an aggrieved voice and she tried very hard to follow him until she noticed that Fred was on his left foot when Andy was on his right, and Dan was half-skipping ahead of her, so she gave it up altogether and concentrated on enjoying herself. No one questioned the fact that they were there, right in the middle

239

of the whole thing, acting as if they were a legitimate part of the parade. She could scarcely believe their luck. Andy evidently felt it too; he gave her a little poke with his elbow.

"Pretty neat, hunh?" he said, grinning.

She grinned back and nodded. People all along the path cheered them as they passed; every now and then someone chucked a last snowball into their midst, but without malice, and no one minded.

"Cor!" said Fred when they reached Monument Street and found a company of Minutemen from the neighboring town of Carlisle waiting to join them. "We'd've never got out with our skins 'ole with that lot ready to do us as well! Wait'll I tell me mum all about it!"

"D'you honestly think she'll believe you, old man?" asked the Redcoat in front, turning round. It was Nicholas Boutwell-Scott, jaunty and sharp, looking none the worse for the recent battle. "It would be asking a lot of anyone's mum to believe this lark."

"It'll make a smashing story, no matter," replied Fred with satisfaction.

The Carlisle Militia in their uniforms, with sprigs of white pine stuck in their hats, stood between the state police and their police cars. After one look at this new company of potential enemies, the troopers chose to head for the center of Concord on foot where they might find the rest of the town police.

So the odd-looking procession marched on Concord along a road wet and steaming in the new April sun. The townspeople kept pace on the sidewalks, conversing with the Minutemen as they went, giving encouragement to the troopers, unwilling to be left behind. Every now and then another volley of snowballs was fired between the groups, just to show that neither side had surrendered, though one was in retreat. But the snow had served its purpose and was now getting slushy. It was melting down the storm drains and making mud of the roadsides as the sun gained strength. Clots fell wetly out of the trees and slid off roofs and the clouds broke apart and scattered across the vaulting sky.

Eliot and his fifers played every tune they knew until their cheeks ached, then they began and played them all over again. Fifes and drums took the marchers every step of the way into town, challenging the birds singing in the tops of the green-and red-budding trees.

By the time they turned into Monument Square, everyone was intoxicated with air and exertion. Charlotte felt positively giddy. The doors to Monument Hall stood open and members of the Concord Lions Club waited on the steps wearing aprons and looking puzzled and interested. Normally there was no parade after the dawn exercises—simply a massive, disorganized rush toward the pancake breakfast. The Lions were not expecting orderly ranks to come marching down upon them.

In the middle of the road opposite the Hall, everyone halted, as if not sure what to do next. It didn't seem right to let things trail away without an official conclusion. The troopers and the newspeople clustered in a wary group near the War Memorial and eyed the Minutemen. Captain Sutton, Captain MacPherson, and Commodore Shattuck conferred while the fifers sucked their cheeks and felt them tenderly, and the drummers indulged in a little fancy rhythm work. Dan jiggled up and down and Kath gave him a sisterly clout. "You can't go to the bathroom until we're through," she said in a fierce whisper. "Stand *still*."

"That makes it worse," protested Dan.

Charlotte knew what he meant. She would have liked to jiggle herself, but with a great effort refrained. She didn't want to appear childish in this present company.

"What's 'appenin,' mate?" complained Fred. "I can feel me backbone through me belly, I'm that famished! We didn't 'ave time for grub this mornin'—too busy with them bleedin' wheels, we was."

"Stow it, Fred," said Nicholas sternly. "Be glad you can feel your backbone at all, old chum."

The three men finished their conference. Captain Sutton went to speak briefly to Eliot, who nodded and signaled his men. "Not again!" someone moaned audibly from their ranks. Eliot silenced him with a look. The Color Guard and the three officers mounted the steps to stand in front of the Lions:

the town flag, the American flag, the Company flag, and the Union Jack were raised together and the band played "God Save the Queen." The British soldiers stood stiffly to attention with their heads bared. Then the band played "The Star-Spangled Banner." Charlotte's eyes swam and her throat tightened. Even the troopers took off their hats for the national anthem. Then everyone cheered. Captain Sutton held up his hands for silence and gradually the crowd subsided.

"I think it's safe to say," he began, "that these have been unique ceremonies this morning. For the first time in several centuries our company of American Minutemen encountered British—ah—troops at the Old North Bridge and were forced to do battle. Although it can't really be considered a reenactment of the Battle of 1775 when men were actually killed and a Revolution begun, I think today's—ah—*event* has a special significance."

He glanced around at the mass of expectant faces. He seemed a little uncertain about how he should proceed; he knew there was a significance, but he wasn't quite sure how to put it into words.

Commodore Shattuck stepped into the breech. "The significance," he continued for the Captain, in his gravelly, carrying voice, "is that the battle is over and we are all here now, standing together in this Square. There's no hostility among us now, am I right?"

Heads nodded in agreement; people shouted, "Right."

"There is no longer war between our countries—there hasn't been for many years. We are, in fact, staunch allies, are we not, Captain MacPherson?"

"Aye!" exclaimed the Scot. "But if it hadna been for yer damned interferin' bobbies we'd've given—"

Whether deliberately or by accident, the Commodore stepped backward and trod heavily on MacPherson's left foot.

"I beg your pardon, Jimmy, I'm so sorry!" he said in a polite undertone, then to the assembled group, "I suggest we cement our friendship by breaking bread together—or more accurately, buttering pancakes. That's what you wished to say, isn't it, Captain Sutton?"

"Yes, of course. Exactly. Thank you, sir!"

The Minutemen began to shift toward the hall.

"And," the Commodore raised his voice, "to show we've no hard feelings this fine morning, we invite the members of the state and town police to share breakfast with us!"

He, the two other men and the Color Guard stepped smartly into the building, beating the stampede that followed. Once again Charlotte found herself caught up in the group and swept with it into the high, echoing hall. She realized that a good part of her dizziness was caused by hunger; she could smell pancakes cooking and her mouth watered. But first things first. She grabbed Dan, and they managed to extricate themselves inside the front door and escape to the rest rooms before it occurred to others to do the same. They got there first, much to Charlotte's relief.

When she came out, Dan had disappeared. He hadn't waited for her, which was annoying, after she'd guided him to the right spot. She edged into the barnlike room with its rows of dusty windows set high in the walls. It was lined with long tables and benches; there were even tables on the stage at the far end. Charlotte stood still in the doorway and made herself small while she tried to sort through the confusion of sound and bodies within. A long line of Minutemen, British, relatives of Minutemen, Battery men, police wound back and forth on itself like a serpent before disappearing through a door into the kitchen. People carrying coffee cups and plates heaped with steaming pancakes emerged with astonishing speed through another door. As she watched, a helpless feeling closed over her. Everyone seemed to know where to go, where there were friends saving seats for them. She saw faces she recognized, but no one she knew well; the Schuylers, the Shattucks, even Skip and Eliot were nowhere in sight. She'd been forgotten by everyone, she realized bleakly.

"Ere!" said a familiar voice in her ear, making her jump. "You'd better 'op in along of me, mate, or you'll get left out."

Overcome with gratitude, Charlotte allowed Fred Cheavy to pull her into the pancake line ahead of him. Her "Thank you" was heartfelt.

Fred grinned. "Wait'll we get through this bleedin' queue before you thanks me. We could still die a starvation, me old bucket!"

She no longer felt conspicuous; she was no longer by herself; she was one of the crowd, doing what everyone else was doing. The panic drained from her, leaving her calm and tired. She shuffled along as the line snaked forward. It moved steadily and quickly considering the number of hungry people in it. Charlotte lost touch with time; around her voices rose and fell, laughter burst over her head. The steamy, smoky hall was full of noise.

The Lions in the kitchen operated an assembly line with the skill of long practice. Half a dozen Lions and their sons were busy over huge griddles, flipping and turning pancakes, while others went from griddle to griddle with great pitchers of batter, pouring wherever there was a gap. Still another .w wove in and out with platters and plates collecting the finished cakes, which were then doled out by more men in striped denim aprons. The kitchen hummed with activity.

Charlotte took the paper plate that was thrust into her hands. Behind her, Fred negotiated successfully for a double helping. At the far door she picked up a plastic bottle of orange juice and a carton of milk. She wandered into the hall again and stopped to search for Eliot. The tables had filled rapidly—there were still empty seats, but most of them surrounded by people she didn't know. She glanced back for Fred and discovered to her dismay that he'd disappeared just as Dan had. So she had breakfast, but nowhere to go to eat it.

Still looking, she walked between the tables, trying to seem as if she was heading somewhere specific. She didn't want anyone to think she was lost or left out, but she was sure people must know it by looking at her.

She had about given up hope and decided to pick the least conspicuous gap, when Andy popped up at a table to her right and waved. "Hey, Charlie! Over here!"

She swallowed hard, shook back her hair, and forced a
 ·   hat would look casual. "I couldn't find you," she reproached him. "You raced ahead."

"I thought you were with us. We've saved a place for

244

you." His face was open and friendly. He was genuinely pleased that she'd found them. "I was getting worried."

"Were you?" He caught her off guard, but she covered the quick jolt of pleasure his words gave her. "Well, you could have waited."

"No, we couldn't!" declared Dan. "I was *starving*. I might have fainted if we'd waited any longer."

Charlotte slid into the empty seat next to Oliver.

"Where'd you get to?" he asked, as he lined his pancakes up precisely one over the other.

"I wondered the same about *you*."

"We knew where we were," Dan said. He mopped up a puddle of syrup on his plate with his last forkful of pancake.

"These pancakes aren't bad," said Kath judiciously.

"You should know." Oliver eyed her across the table. "You've eaten six big ones."

"I want to know how you got six at once," Andy put in. "They'd only give me three."

"I have my methods." Kath looked smug.

Charlotte busied herself applying butter to her three pancakes: two thick layers between them and another on top.

"There you are, Charlie." It was Eliot behind her. "I've been hunting for you. Where'd you get to?"

She turned around. "I had to stop on my way in."

He and Skip stood with their empty plates in their hands, clogging the aisle between tables. "We're sitting up at the end with the other guys from the band and some riffraff from the Battery if you want to come and sit with us. I saved you a seat."

She hoped Andy, Kath, and Oliver were listening. So Eliot had remembered her after all and thought to keep her a place with the Minutemen. She could show off her connections now in front of people she knew. The temptation was strong. She saw herself picking up her plate and milk carton and going to sit with the band in a place of honor, among her brother's friends. The vision wavered.

"No thanks," she said indistinctly, then cleared her throat and looked up at her brother. "I'll stay here—with my friends."

Eliot shrugged. "Okay, kid. I know when I'm being stood

up!" His eyes were serious. She imagined she saw in them a reflection of the regret and affection in her own. "Hey," he said to Oliver, "that was a great idea of yours, throwing snowballs! What a brainstorm!"

"You bet," agreed Skip. "It saved the day."

Charlotte watched fascinated as Oliver the Untouchable blushed beet red, all the way up his neck, over his face, to the roots of his hair. He dropped his eyes and stared hard at his plate.

"I thought somebody was going to get hurt," said Dan. "You know, it was pretty hairy standing there on the Bridge watching all of you come marching up."

"You turkey," said Kath. "It's a good thing Ma couldn't see you standing there with that baseball bat. She'd have been furious."

"It all worked out fine, though," pointed out Andy comfortably.

"And *you* saved the Captain and Beaky from getting arrested," Charlotte told Eliot. She made an effort and included Skip. "Both of you."

"We only copied Oliver," said Skip with a smile.

"Aha. Found you!" Nicholas Boutwell-Scott breezed up to the group, focusing on Charlotte. "Your smashing sister isn't anywhere about by any chance?"

"Who's he?" asked Eliot. "Who're you?"

"Nicholas Boutwell-Scott. Who're you?" Nicholas took Eliot's hand and gave it a brisk shake.

"Eliot Paige."

"Delighted to meet you, old son! Any brother of hers, and all that. You *are* a brother, I assume?"

"Yes, but—"

"Charlotte, I wondered if you'd do me a bit of a favor. I haven't been able to find Deborah this morning . . ."

"She isn't here," said Charlotte, forcing her way into the conversation.

"As I feared. I've a note for her—would you be kind enough to deliver it?"

"A note?" repeated Eliot.

"That's what he said," confirmed Skip. "A note."

"How very quick of you!" remarked Nicholas innocently. "Tell her it demands an answer, will you? *Demands* one."

"But how can she answer you?" asked Charlotte. "Aren't you going back to England?"

"Not immediately. I know a chap at Harvard who's promised me the grand tour first. It's all in the note—she'll understand."

"She was furious with you."

Nicholas flashed a broad grin. "Wasn't she though! Thanks awfully. Cheerio!" With a wave of his hand he left them.

"Well," said Eliot. "Well, well, well!" He chuckled and Skip gave him a dig in the ribs.

"We're on our way for seconds," announced Skip. "We've got to hurry—the parade assembles at eight."

"I don't suppose we'll get to march again," said Dan wistfully.

Eliot shook his head. "You don't, but Commodore Shattuck and all the British have been invited to. They've been given a place of honor in the First Division. What do you think of that? And we've made our peace with the state police."

"It wasn't easy to convince them that they really didn't have to arrest anyone," added Skip. "It's been a slow month at the barracks."

"Where is the Commodore?" asked Andy.

"Up on the stage arguing with Captain MacPherson about what would have happened if the police hadn't come."

"We expect you lot to station yourselves strategically along the parade route and cheer like sixty for us when we march past. Agreed?" said Eliot.

"Agreed," Dan said. "I'm going to get more pancakes, too. I could eat a hundred."

"You shouldn't go until everyone's had some," remonstrated Kath, "but if you're going now, get me a couple more, will you?"

"Maybe yes, maybe no," said Dan.

"You'd better, Daniel Schuyler, after the way I've stuck up for you with Ma this weekend!"

Dan frowned, momentarily serious. "Who won today anyway?" he asked.

"I don't think anyone did," answered Skip.

"But nobody lost either," said Oliver.

"True." Eliot nodded. "And that's the most important thing when you come right down to it."

Charlotte watched Eliot, Skip, and Dan weave their way expertly through the maze toward the kitchen. She felt a pang as Eliot went. It hurt, but she was beginning to think she might be able to live with it. She realized no matter where he went he would not forget about her, her mother was right. And he wasn't leaving her alone; she had friends. They were a strange assortment, these friends, and she wasn't yet really sure of them, but she had to admit she liked them. She was at ease sitting here in the seat Andy had saved for her.

But she was too hungry to meditate on the complexities of life just now, and Kath was eyeing her full plate covetously from the other side of the table.

"Pass me the syrup," Charlotte called to her. Kath slid it deftly over. "Thanks."

She drowned the pancakes in thick, amber liquid, opened her milk, and began her breakfast.